T0065639

Ogopogo
and Friends

A Nonsense Novel

Joe Remesz

iUniverse LLC
Bloomington

Ogopogo and Friends
A Nonsense Novel

iUniverse books may be ordered through booksellers or by contacting:

iUniverse LLC
1663 Liberty Drive
Bloomington, IN 47403
www.iuniverse.com
1-800-Authors (1-800-288-4677)

ISBN: 978-1-4759-9702-6 (sc)
ISBN: 978-1-4759-9703-3 (ebk)

Library of Congress Control Number: 2013911740

Printed in the United States of America

iUniverse rev. date: 07/10/2013

Contents

The Twins—
Ham And Sam Bobek

Not long ago an unusual event took place in Kelowna, British Columbia when twin boys were born to Carolina and Jan Bobek and talked while still inside Carolina's tummy.

"I want to play hockey! I want to play hockey!" the first infant said while Dr. Paul Bond, examined the expectant mother with an ultrasound.

"I want to play baseball! I want to play baseball!" the second child insisted just as loudly.

A week after Carolina was examined; the infants made their appearance on Planet Earth and international media wrote more headlines about the happy event, than when the Ukraine, part of the Soviet Union, had a catastrophic nuclear accident in the town of Chernobyl. A disaster that included an explosion and fire that released large

quantities of radioactive particles over much of Europe and
the North Pole or that the Americans were testing nuclear
rockets over Canadian soil from the Arctic Ocean towards
the Cold Lake Military base in northern Alberta.

Several days later, while Carolina was changing diapers,
she sneezed. The sneeze was so explosive that with the
help of a strong wind, the twins were blown into nearby
Okanagan Lake which is eighty miles long, three miles
wide and in places a thousand feet deep. The lake is also
the home of the elusive serpentine-like, Ogopogo who
it is said before the Whiteman came to the Okanagan
Valley, was well known to the Indians and they could
never paddle a canoe or a raft near his dwelling place
at Squally Point near Rattle Snake Island. If they did, a
sudden storm would erupt and from the water Ogopogo
would appear and claim another life.
Today, however, despite earlier ridicule by legions of non-
believers, Ogopogo who is twenty feet in length/height
with two humps, the head of a horse and a tail of a fish,
four legs and green in color, has been tamed and trained
to co-live peacefully with homosapiens. This gigantic
fete was achieved by herbalist Lo Wong who lives in a
lakeside cave.

Ogopogo is often photographed during the tourist
season but gets upset if his photo is used for commercial
purposes, like an advertising agency having him endorse
a certain product. Several years ago Japanese and Arab
entrepreneurs spent millions of dollars trying to capture
Ogopogo for that purpose but their efforts failed.

As soon as the twins landed in the water, the good natured Ogopogo swiftly rescued the infants, and delivered them to their parents. While making the delivery Ogopogo noticed the twin boys already had teeth and a huge appetite.

The parents, Jan and Carolina Bobek, thanked Ogopogo for the delivery, and as he was about to return to his home, Jan, turned to Canada's famous water creature and said, "Thank you, Ogopogo. When the twins grow up I hope they will become athletes, provide for our old age security and carry on with the family name of Bobek."

In a conversation that followed, Ogopogo discovered that the Bobek's immigrated to Canada from Poland, Ogopogo also discovered that Mr. and Mrs. Bobek were relatively poor, deeply religious and their home was filled with Chopin's music.

As Ogopogo was returning to the lake, Jan said to his wife, "I like the names Ham and Sam."

"Perfect. Congratulations, so do I," Carolina replied, and a week later, Father Joseph Kubek of the Holy Spirit parish, baptized the boys, while at the same time, Jan and Carolina promised they would provide their sons a formal education, which they themselves never had. The education would include piano lessons and the study of the scriptures in the *Bible*.

As soon as Ham and Sam could eat and drink. Their favorite food was pizza. Their favorite drink was chocolate milk. Their favorite desert was ice cream. So vast was their appetite that eventually it became necessary for the parents to use their credit card in order to provide the pizza, chocolate milk and ice cream.

Both parents worked at menial jobs day and night in order to provide their sons with nourishment and apparel.

From birth until ten years of age, Ham and Sam were brought up in the discipline of their mother who read them the *Bible* daily and taught them how to play the piano and to sing *O Canada*, Canada's national anthem.

"It's surprising how few people know the words of our national anthem," Carolina constantly reminded the twins.

Depending on the season, each time Ham took piano lessons Saturday evening, and his mother slipped out the room to answer a phone call, he switched on the radio and instead of concentrating on his lesson, listened to a National Hockey League broadcast on the radio.

When it was Sam's turn and again depending on the season, he would listen to a broadcast of a Major League baseball game.

After ten years of discipline by their mother, the father took over, whom along with the sons, spent a lot of their free time watching television, particularly during weekends. Each twin also did what other boys their age do: hate music lessons; forget to change their under shorts and brush their teeth. They also did a number of other uncomplimentary things, which would not be polite to mention.

At age fifteen, Ham and Sam were attending High School and grew almost as fast as their appetite.

On a cold wintery Saturday evening while watching a hockey game on television between the Toronto Maple Leafs and Montreal Canadiens, Ham suddenly jumped up into the air and repeated over and over, pleading with his parents, "I want to be a goaltender for the Toronto Maple Leafs!

I want to be a goaltender for the Toronto Maple Leafs! I want to quit taking music lessons! Mom and Dad, please get me a set of goalie pads, a puck and a goalie stick for Christmas!"

After hearing his brother, Sam sprang up and down too as he kicked and screamed, hoping his parents would fulfill his passionate dream and said, "Ham is right. I don't want to continue with music lessons either. I want to play baseball for the Toronto Blue Jays. For Christmas I would like a bat, a glove and a baseball."

When Carolina heard their requests she was ready to fling her sons out the door. She did not enjoy either hockey or baseball. "Listen boys!" she said. "You are too young to be running wild. What nonsense." Carolina then turned to Ham and continued, "Son, when you grow up I want you to either be a salesman or a concert pianist like Frederic Chopin."

Next, she turned to Sam and pointing a finger at him said, "And you young man. I want you to a have a meaningful career and spread the word of God and become an evangelist."

"Me, Sam Bobek, an evangelist? No such luck," Sam replied. "There are enough evangelists on TV already. When I grow up I want to be a member of the Toronto Blue Jays."

Despite portraits of the *Flying Fathers*, a hockey team made up of priests, the Toronto *Maple Leafs* and the *Blue Jays* hanging on the kitchen wall next to the *Last Supper,* Carolina insisted the twins continue with their piano lessons. A year later, however, after a round of arguments, which Jan participated in, she appeared downcast.

"What's the matter?" Jan asked as he tried to comfort his wife.

"It's terrible. It's terrible," Caroline said between sobs.

"What is the matter? Maybe I can help? "Jan asked.

"Mr. Glendon at the Seven-Eleven corner store has cut our line of credit, and the use of our credit card has reached its limit. Our predicament has reached a point where we have no money left, and our sons should be made wards of the government because we no longer can provide for them proper food, clothing and shelter."

The boys had already weighed more than two hundred pounds and were seven feet tall.

Jan threw himself into a chair and protested with all explanations that Ham and Sam as adults could become superstars and eventually get the Bobek family out of debt.

"Ham could possibly become as famous as Georges Vezina who played for the Montreal Canadiens, and Sam, could possibly break Babe Ruth's home-run record when he played for the New York Yankees."

As soon as Jan said those words, Ham did cartwheels and cried out, "Don't mention the Montreal Canadiens again. I want to play for the Toronto Maple Leafs!"

Sam sprang to his feet too. "And please don't mention the New York Yankees or even the Mets because I want to play for the Toronto Blue Jays!"

A month later, since the Bobek's had no money left, Carolina look at the sky, began to cry and after she wiped a tear from her eye, insisted that Jan speak to a social worker and apply for welfare. And when he did, the social worker, pretty Agnes Swanson, said to him, "I don't know how you managed so far with all the food your sons eat and clothes they wear out."

Ms. Swanson suggested that Sam and Ham temporarily live with a fifty year old wealthy widow who owned a vineyard and had stocks in a gold mine near Yellowknife, Northwest Territories, and above all, enjoyed attending hockey and baseball games.

Ms. Swanson suggested, "At the moment Mrs. Nichol is sad and lonely. I'm certain the twins in her custody will bring happiness into her life because her husband died recently as a result of injuries in a mining accident in."

This may be a coincidence, but Carolina and Jan were surprised that the wealthy widow Ms. Swanson referred to, was the diminutive, gentle and compassionate Alice Nichol for whom Carolina worked as a house cleaner when she first came to Canada.

Aside from having a vineyard, Mrs. Nichol was an anti-nuclear activist. Carolina and Jan felt Mrs. Nichol was of good character and lived in a home with a high ceiling. It was agreed that Alice would support Ham and Sam while the boys lived with her and continue taking piano lessons.

The twin boys understood the situation the family was in and did not object to the decision.

The first thing, Mrs. Nichol did was to outfit Ham and Sam into appropriate hockey and baseball gear and when summer came, enrolled the boys in the Okanagan Summer Hockey and Baseball School where they were taught the finer points in their chosen sport.

One day after a coaching lesson and a scrimmage game at the Kelowna Hockey School, Ham and the students watched reruns of previous Stanley Cup finals. This was followed by a hockey quiz as the instructor asked the first question that was, "Which team did King Clancy play for?"

Ham was the first to raise his hand and said, "Toronto Maple Leafs."

"And what is the Lady Byng trophy?" was the second.

A student by the name of Metro Kowalchuk replied that Mr. Byng developed the Bing cherry but Ham corrected him and said, "The answer is wrong, sir.

It's a trophy awarded to the most sportsman-like National Hockey League player. Baron Byng of Vimy was Canada's governor general at the time and the trophy is named after his wife."

Meanwhile, at the Kelowna Baseball School, Sam was taught the finer points in pitching, fielding, batting and stealing bases. At times Sam was confused, however, when on a base, he received signals from the coach with regard to the next play.

After having coached a week of lessons, the students had a practice, watched previous games of the past World Series followed by a baseball quiz.

Sam had no difficulty with the first question when the instructor asked, "Which team did Joe Carter play for?"

"Toronto Blue Jays," Sam quickly replied. Carter hit a walk-off home run to win the 1993 World Series against Philadelphia for the Toronto Blue Jays."

Sam's second question was, "Name the first Black player to break into the Major League?"

Without hesitation Sam answered, "Jackie Robinson."

As soon as the Summer Hockey and Baseball School ended, Mrs. Nichol put the two boys to work. She was impressed with their knowledge about sports but with their strength and gargantuan size even more.

"Will you please fertilize the vineyard so that I can vint the best tasting wine people in Kelowna ever sampled? My wine will be called *Friend of the Okanagan*. And come in a distinctive bottle," she said.

"Nothing can penetrate our strength and speed," Ham said after the vineyard was fertilized with *Elephant Brand* fertilizer logo on each bag. Now Mrs. Nichol owned one of the finest vineyards in all of the Okanagan Valley.

The following week, Mrs. Nichol asked the young men to lead a construction crew to dig a channel in the vineyard so that it was irrigated with plenty of water.

"There is no challenge for us," Sam said and along with his brother, agreed to do whatever Mrs. Nichol wanted them to do, which would improve Planet Earth a safety and a better place to live. While digging a with a spade, Ham and Sam worked relentlessly while nearby animals and birds, mostly ducks, marmots, Canada geese and mountain goats watched a change in their environment.

In the end, the boys helped complete an engineering feat that politicians only dreamed about, and received a letter from the Prime Minster of Canada, thanking them for their work done on the *Okanagan Vineyard Irrigation Project* which was subsidized by a government a grant, and now could rival vineyards in California.

The President of the United States also sent a congratulatory note and wondered if Ham and Sam could do something about the California earth quakes and shortage of water, In part the note read: "Why don't you like so many Canadian engineers, doctors, actors and newsmen are doing and move to America?"

Sam wrote back: "Dear Mr. President: If you get rid of those damn New York Yankees I may consider your invitation, but until then my dream is to play baseball for the Toronto Blue Jays. And as for my brother, Ham, his passionate dream is play hockey for the Toronto Maple Leafs."

A day later, the gigantic twins, wondered what project Mrs. Nichol would have for them.

They found out the following day when she said, "Ham and Sam. Please, I want you to help prevent the Americans from testing nuclear cruise missiles from the Arctic Ocean to the Cold Lake Military Weapons Range in Alberta."

"We'll give it our best shot." Ham said and when the appropriate time came, he and Sam traveled to the Cold

Lake Military base where they leaped towards the sky and diverted three missiles being tested from the Arctic Ocean, into the nearby province of Saskatchewan whose name they could not pronounce.

Ham and Sam's reward for these accomplishments was to study at Okanagan College where Ham's favorite number was number 21and Sam's 9, which some of the other students thought was there I. Q. Although prodigious and having the human frailty of not enjoying piano lessons, the twins had a sense of humor.

When his piano teacher asked Ham if he enjoyed ham and eggs, he replied only if the tune is played by Mantovani."

When his math teacher, asked Sam what is four plus five he replied, "The number of players a team has on a baseball diamond."

During the second year at college, Ham and Sam, who now were more than seven feet tall and could be basketball stars but no way, they did not hesitate to say their careers would be in hockey and baseball, although there were times when they missed classes and by their unjustified absence, played hooky.

When they tried to explain to Mrs. Nichol why they were absent, and couldn't, she threatened to punish them. Ham and Sam by now had become teenagers and thought they knew everything there is to know, even how to operate the internet on a computer.

The twins became belligerent and each time they talked to their parents or Mrs. Nichol, used phrases like: "You are old fashioned," "Freaked out," "Cool," "Diddly Dumb," and "Rock n Roll."

The difference in their ages, temperament and social status, led Ham and Sam to argue frequently with Mrs. Nichol who preferred to be called simply, 'Alice.' The identical twins called the difference a, "Generation Gap."

The twins became rebellious and at one point Ham said to Alice, "You, madam, are an antique full of prunes and that is why you spend so much time in the bathroom."

The uncomplimentary remark shocked Alice, so she quickly wrote a letter to the social worker requesting her to find Ham and Sam a different home. Hours, days, passed but the social worker couldn't find the twins another home, because there weren't many homes in Kelowna at the time that had ten-foot ceilings.

Ham and Sam by now reached the stage of their life where each also had a girlfriend. Ham courted seventeen year-old, pretty, Brenda McCain, who attended the same college and whose father was a building contractor with Brenda, the only child, and owned a mansion with a high ceiling.

Sam's girlfriend was eighteen-year-old, also pretty, Marie Greene, a farmer's daughter who as a hobby, enjoyed collecting *Air Miles*, entering radio contests, filling out newspaper and magazine coupons and entering them in various contests.

One day after a class, Ham and Sam met Brenda and Marie for a milkshake at McDonald's restaurant. On that particular day, the vibes were great and Holy, holy holy, ring-a-ring-rosy, Ham and Sam became nosy and were shocked to learn that their possible mates were fans of the Montreal Canadiens and New York Yankees.

Disappointed, Sam said to Marie, "I'd rather drown myself than live in New York City."

"And I can't wait until I wear a Toronto Maple Leaf uniform and meet the Montreal Canadiens in a Stanley Cup final," is what Ham said to Brenda.

In the end, it was decided that a relationship between the two couples would continue on a trial basis. The way Miss McCain phrased it was, "We need space to determine if our relationship should continue."

By now the twins were stressed out, and after meeting Brenda and Marie, stopped at Ms. Swanson's office to seek counseling. Taking Ham by the arm the first thing Ms. Swanson said was, "You have just gone through a major disappointment which can be dangerous, and so crushing that both of you now need psychological and spiritual guidance and should take a test."

Curious to know, Sam asked, "What kind of a test?"

"One given by the wisest psychiatrist in town, Dr. John Trenton,", whose office was in the same building and his most outstanding physical characteristics were that he was a World War 11 veteran, drove a Mercedes and wore a Rolex, and rather short and skinny with a thin mustache and yet thinner hair on his head. Since his vision wasn't perfect he wore small round glasses that were frameless, and spoke with a soft subtle tenor voice.

As he placed a test paper in front of each twin, they were nervous until Dr. Trenton said, "Boys, relax. Just answer true or false to the questions."

Some of the questions were:

Maurice Richard played for the Boston Bruins

Nancy Greene won a gold medal in Olympic skiing

Montreal is the capital of the province of Quebec

Live spelled backwards is Evil?

Moose Jaw is larger than Medicine Hat?

When a plane crashes they bury the survivors?

Apple juice has more vitamin C than milk?

Ravens steal golf balls in Yellowknife?

A Canadian, I, G. A. Creighton, invented the game of ice hockey

Americans encourage being mistaken for Canadians when abroad

Canadians should get rid of Royalty, King and Queen

A Canadian, James Naismith, invented the game of basketball?

A spaghetti tree is taller than a Christmas tree

As soon as Ham and Sam were through answering the questions, Dr. Trenton analyzed the results and first sat next to Ham and said, "Ham, they don't teach salesmanship in college. The test shows that you should be a salesman, an entrepreneur."

Next, Dr. Trenton sat next to Sam he said, "Sam, your mother is right. You should be an evangelist."

"But I don't want to be an evangelist. I want to play baseball for the Toronto Blue Jays," Sam protested vehemently.

"That's what they all say. Most boys your age want to be either hockey or baseball players. If you want to have baseball as your career, give it a try. We all have goals and dreams, many of which never get fulfilled, yours may."

As soon as Ham and Sam were through speaking with the psychologist, Ms. Swanson took the boys for a walk along the Okanagan Lake. While walking lazily along the lakefront, they came to a park and watched Canada geese pecking grass and waves hit the shore.

While explaining to the boys the test results in more detail, the trio came upon Ogopogo sunbathing and the foursome chatted. Hearing the predicament Ham and Sam were in, Ogopogo said, to them, "Maybe I can help you. Why don't you come and live with Lo Wong and me in a cave next to Okanagan Lake?"

"Who is Lo Wong?" Ham asked.

"Aside from inventing fruit leather which can do magical things, Mr. Wong drives an antique sports car that is the envy of all of Kelowna. Aside from inventing fruit leather Mr. Wong is knowledgeable in coaching the games of hockey, baseball and football."

Surprised, Sam said, "He is? That's interesting. And fruit leather, what are the ingredients?"

"It's a blend of magical dried fruit purees, which is a nourishing meal replacement that comes in six different flavors: apple, peach, apricot, pear, grape and cherry.

A strip of Wong's fruit leather, among other things, is a food supplement, can curb one's appetite or increase his or her energy and in my case, shrink me to at least one-half my normal size."

Secretly Ms. Swanson hoped Ogopogo would swallow the twins as a human sacrifice but when she told the friendly serpentine-like creature that this was a desperate situation, he recalled the time he delivered the twins to his parents. Instead of roaring like a lion or have his tail smoke like a chimney, Ogopogo invited twins to climb on his back and together they swam across the lake to a cave where they could possibly live with him and herbalist Mr. Wong.

When the ride ended, Ham, Sam, Ogopogo and Wong were inside a cave that had tunnels connecting it. The mud lay deep and only a narrow track of firm ground was above the quagmire where Mr. Wong had his laboratory and making fruit leather. In the short time that Ham and Sam were inside the cave, they had eaten a strip of apple flavored fruit leather, which curbed their appetite significantly.

"This is our home. You may live with us," Ogopogo said as soon as the twins were introduced to Mr. Wong, and had already eaten their fruit leather strip.

Ham surveyed the cave from one end to the other and then looking towards Sam said, "Well, what do you think?"

"The cave and the furniture look alright but one thing bothers me."

Wong, who to this point was busy making fruit leather, said, "What is it? Maybe I can help."

"Besides being a bit dark inside, where can we practice baseball and hockey around here?"

Mr. Wong's eyes sparkled. "No problem. For hockey we can clear the ice as soon as Okanagan Lake freezes over. And for baseball, there's a vacant field nearby."

"Excellent, we'll stay," Ham said and Sam agreed.

As soon as the winter season arrived, on the smooth and glittering ice surface of Okanagan Lake, sparked here and there with snow, Wong and Sam set up a net and took turns at shooting a puck at Ham each day. By mid-February Wong was so impressed with Ham's acrobatics that he phoned the Toronto Maple Leafs in Toronto.

"Really? Is Ham that good?" the Maple Leaf manager said suspiciously after Wong had described the teenager's talent.

In reply Wong said, "I do recognize talent. In my candid opinion Ham Bobek is a premier goaltender and will make the National Hockey League Hall Of Fame in his rookie year."

"Unbelievable! I'll be on the first flight available for Kelowna to see the kid for myself," the Maple Leaf manager said, and when he arrived, took Ham to the hockey arena where Ham's reflexes were tested, and watched him kick out pucks, especially the slap shots.

At the end, the manager was so impressed not only with Ham's talent but also his physical strength and gargantuan size, that he signed the eighteen-year-old to a lucrative contract as a free agent before the trading of players' deadline expired.

"What talent? What size? What a find? Just the goalie we need in order to win the Stanley Cup," the Maple Leaf manager excitedly said.

Actually Ham did not wear a Maple Leaf uniform until the National Hockey League semi-finals were underway and the Edmonton Oilers were leading the Maple Leafs 3–0 in the best of seven semi-final series. In that particular game Ham stopped three breakaways by Wayne Gretzky and the Leafs went on to win 5-0.

Ham's reputation soon began to spread far beyond Canada because he had stopped ninety two shots. In the end the Maple Leafs, who to this point were ridiculed by some of their fans and called "Maple Laughs" and defeating the Oilers in the remaining games and 4-3 in the series.

Media called Ham "A trick of Nature" and the Maple Leaf management proudly said, "It's a good thing Ham Bobek is playing for our team instead of the Montreal Canadiens whom we now play for the Stanley Cup."

By the time the Montreal-Toronto series began it was the month of May.

Ham was awed that he was playing in the same Montreal Forum and Maple Leaf Gardens where great superstars played before him: Georges Vezina, Lionel Conacher, Howie Morenz, Cyclone Taylor, Rocket Richard, Gordie Howe, Bobby Orr and Bobby Hull to name several.

The first game was played in Montreal and the Maple Leafs went on to defeat the Canadiens 1-0. Even Larry Robinson couldn't score on Moli Goalie when he was awarded a penalty shot.

The score in the second game was 3-0 in Toronto's favor and when the series switched to Toronto it was the same story—the Maple Leafs won 2-0 and 3-0, thus sweeping the series and winning the Stanley Cup in four straight games.

There was pandemonium on the ice as soon as the Stanley Cup was presented to the Maple Leafs captain who then led his team around the rink in victory as the Stanley Cup was passed on to each player.

Once the players were in their dressing room, champagne bottles seemed never to cease popping, and outside, fans went wild by lighting a bon fire on Yonge Street, climbing up telephone poles and congregating in night clubs celebrating the historic occasion. The name Ham Bobek seemed to be on everyone's lips.

A day after the Maple Leafs won the Stanley Cup the city of Toronto held a parade and a banquet honoring the team.

It was at City Hall that the Mayor congratulated each player and singled out Ham Bobek as the best "goalie" ever wearing a Maple Leaf uniform. "Even better than Turk Broda," the Mayor said.

During the time that followed, Ham was interviewed by every major radio and television network in Canada and United States. Ham also received invitations to speak at high schools and colleges on the subject why he kept away from drugs and alcohol. Ham also appeared on *Front Page Challenge, Bob Hope Christmas Special, Wayne and Shuster Show* and *Dallas.*

And made the front cover page of *Hockey News, Time, McLean's, Sports Illustrated* and even *Pravda* in the Soviet Union ran an article about him.

Ham also signed advertising contracts endorsing various products that included a car, which needed less maintenance than an old ostrich, a chain of restaurants what featured ostrich meat during the weekends and a cereal that promised to give one, arm muscles the size of a baseball. The name Ham Bobek was either seen or heard in newspapers, magazines, radio, television and billboards. Ham Bobek was so popular that the superstar was presented to the Queen of England when she visited Canada and the Progressive Conservative Party sought him him to seek election and become Canada's non-bilingual member of parliament.

Even an author began writing an unauthorized version of the *Ham Bobeck Story*, hoping this fine book would become a bestseller and then a min-series on television.

Ham took his sudden success in stride despite his tender age, and still madly in love with Brenda McCain, remained in Toronto financially secure but eventually disillusioned. Many of the hockey players he had met in the National Hockey League, their career lasted an average of four years and those that remained longer, often had no career after hockey.

Some of the players were using steroids and excessive alcohol.

This led Ham, a teetotaler, to wearing blue tailor-made suits and spending a great deal of his free time observing activities at the Toronto Stock Exchange and reading books at the Public Library.

One day, Ham recalled the test psychologist Dr. Trenton gave him and at the time said, "Ham, you don't need a university degree. You should be a salesman, an entrepreneur."

Instead of reading books on improving hockey skills, Ham read about entrepreneurs who became both, wealthy or famous.

He studied the biographies of Richard Sear, who was a mail order salesman, John Diefenbaker, who sold Bibles and later became Canada's prime minister. Ham read about Sam Bronfman who sold booze during Prohibition and his family ended up with Seagram's and dozens of other companies.

The book that interested Ham most, however, was a biography of Jim Penny who was ill and seven-million dollars in debt at age 56 but when he died at age ninety had two-thousand J. C. Penny stores. And of course he read about Sam Walton who was an active student of discount retailing at Wal-Mart's.

Ed also read the biographies of Canada's wealthy, which at the time included:

David Thompson, Galen Weston, Jim Pattison, Paul Demarais, Ted Rogers and Frank Stronach, among others.

While at the Toronto library Ham also read about merchandising and why multi-level selling and franchising were becoming popular. He recalled the years when he was under his mother's discipline and she wanted him to continue with piano lessons.

"Winning, never losing, the thrill of victory and no defeat, an empty life, traveling from city to city, no home-cooked meals and lonely," Ham suddenly said to the Maple Leafs manager, picked up his belongings and returned to Kelowna to live in the cave with Sam, Ogopogo and Mr. Wong.

While in Kelowna, sometimes referred to as Ogopogo Town, Ham's stress increased and so did his visits to Brenda's home. The couple took time out, however, to watch Mr. Wong mix herbs and spices into fruit leather and then, taste the substance for nutritional and magical value.

Then one day following a baseball practice with his brother, Ham took Ogopogo and Wong aside and said, "I'm quitting playing hockey for good. That's it."

"Sad, but why should you retire so soon?" Wong asked, disappointed.

"Because my mother, the psychologist and now even Brenda, suggest that I should be an entrepreneur instead of a hockey player."

"Since you don't want to play hockey any longer, what is it that you plan to do as a career?" Ogopogo asked in a concerned manner.

"I have an idea."

"What kind of an idea?" Wong asked

"Why don't we manufacture fruit leather on a large scale and distribute it across Canada and United States and make a profit?"

Wong burst out with a roar of laughter.

"Don't laugh," Ham said. "There are big rewards for entrepreneurs who take risks."

Wong's next question was, "Are we going to franchise the fruit leather or are we going to distribute through multi-level selling?"

As soon as Ham answered, "Through multi-level selling" Wong glanced towards Ogopogo who nodded his head signifying it was an excellent idea.

Under the premise that if one is nifty one could also become thrifty, Wong continued, "Hey, let's give it our best shot. What have we got to lose? You work out a business plan. Ogopogo, you answer the telephone and take care of the billing department as needed. We can start manufacturing fruit leather and marketing the product soon.

In the meantime, however, Sam and I will concentrate on carving out a career for him in the game of baseball."

And away Wong and Sam went to a vacant field, where Wong coached his protégé the proper way to pitch and hit the ball.

Wong was so impressed with Sam's batting and pitching that when the month of September arrived, he phoned the Blue Jays in Toronto.

"Can Sam Bobek really pitch that well?" the Blue Jays manager asked.

"Have you heard of Mark Konig, Bob Feller or Nolan Ryan?"

"Can he pitch like them?"

And I haven't told you the best part."

"And that is?"

"Listen, Sam Bobek is an extraordinary talent, he's incredibly strong and has developed an unorthodox wicked curve when he pitches, and when it comes to batting, and he may hit more home runs than Babe Ruth for the New York Yankees."

"You say that Sam Bobek can do both, pitch and hit?"

"You haven't seen anything like it. I assure you that if you sign Sam to a contract, the Blue Jays won't need a designated hitter."

"I'll stop chewing bubble gum if what you say is true," the Blue Jays manager said and continued, "I'll be on the first plane available to Kelowna and see Sam Bobek for myself."

On the day the Blue Jays manager arrived in Kelowna, he took Sam to a baseball diamond and first played catch with him. The manager then watched Sam pitch, steal bases and hit the ball and was so impressed with Sam's talent and gargantuan size which led him to say to Wong, "Just the pitcher we need to beat those damn New York Yankees in the Eastern section of the American League."

The manager immediately phoned Blue Jays owners in Toronto and they gave him permission to sign Sam to a two-year contract. Next day, Sam was in a Blue Jays uniform during a crucial game against the New York Yankees who were leading the best-of seven series three games to none.

In winning game four, Sam fanned twenty one batters that set a Major League record and hit four home runs, three of which were grand slams. The final score was Yankees 0 and Jays 21. Sam Bobek had pitched his first Major Baseball League no-hitter game.

Because of his fruit leather diet, Sam pitched the remaining three games for the Blue Jays as well without any rest, and each time at bat, hit a home run or was intentionally walked. In the end the Blue Jays pulled off one of the greatest upsets in the history of baseball by defeating the Yankees in four of the four remaining games.

Next, the Blue Jays took on the Montreal Expos of the National League in an all-Canadian World Series.

Again Sam pitched all the games and when it was his turn to bat he was either intentionally walked or else the ball would land in either the St. Lawrence River or Lake Ontario.

After the Blue Jays won the World Series by defeating the Montreal Expos in four straight games the city of Toronto held a parade and a banquet for the team.

While at City Hall the Mayor congratulated each player and signaled out Sam Bobek as the super-star of the series and presented him with a 'key' to the city which meant, among other things, he had a line of credit at Dunkin Joe's Donuts, which was a popular place to meet and exchange baseball stories.

Following the World Series, every major radio and TV network in Canada and United States interviewed Sam and he had invitations to appear on the *Johnny Carson Show, Front Page Challenge, and Morningside with Peter Gzowski* and to act a role in the daytime soap opera *The Young and Restless*.

Advertising agencies clamored for Sam endorsements, which among those he accepted were for a pair of suspenders that could be used as a tummy tuck and when pulled from the rear would go 'zing" and guarantee the owner a minute of flying time through space.

Sam also endorsed a brand of boxer shorts, which assured men over sixty five, that they could become a Dad again, and a bank that promised to get rid of petty service charges.

Newspapers and magazines wrote articles about Sam Bobek whose picture made the front cover of *Sports Illustrated, Baseball News, Saturday Night and Wall Street Journal.* Evan baseball fans in Japan heard about Sam Bobek.

When hockey training camp opened in September, Ham did not report to the Maple Leafs. At first the manager thought Ham was absent because he wanted his contract renegotiated.

"That is not so," Ham said to the manager when he arrived in Kelowna to discuss the absence. "It's that suddenly I have lost interest in hockey and am in an entrepreneurial spirit, marketing Famous Okanagan Fruit Leather. In my spare time I play the piano and sing *O Canada* in the Convention Centre, the Capri Hotel and the Kelowna Arena."

"Look. The Maple Leafs and you have a binding contract," The manager reminded Ham. "It's imperative that if the Maple Leafs are to win another Stanley Cup, you must report to the training camp."

"I know who can get us out of this difficulty," Ham said.

"Who?"

"Mr. Wong, who is responsible for drawing up the contract."

Ham, Wong and the Maple Leafs manager met in Wong's cave and there was no doubt about the contract wording.

"Look," Wong said placing a copy of the contract in front of the manager.

"I realize it was dark when the contract was negotiated but see, on page 3 section 2, subsection 5, paragraph 9, clause 11 marked B, it states that Ham Bobek is to play for the Maple Leafs."

The Maple Leaf manager was ecstatic. "There, even you agreed Ham must play for the Maple Leafs."

"That's right. Ham must play for the Maple Leafs but not necessarily play hockey."

The manager was shocked. His heart began to beat with uneasiness. "What do you mean?"

"The word *play* means Ham Bobek can play the piano before and during Maple Leaf games.

"I beg your pardon?" the Maple Leaf manager cried out, and after examining the document, particularly the fine print, conceded the wording was ambiguous. "A technical error. The lawyer, Thomas Huff, must have been under the influence of an abuse substance when he examined the contract," the Maple Leaf representative admitted.

At this point in time, the popularity of Famous Okanagan Fruit Leather was growing so rapidly that health authorities said the product was ahead of its time as a meal replacement. Although five centuries elapsed since Christopher Columbus discovered America, then like the present, everyone was interested in improving his or her health.

In this optimistic perspective, an Ottawa bureaucrat said publicly, "Famous Okanagan Fruit Leather is the greatest breakthrough of the twentieth century.

Astronauts are using it and so are franchised fast food restaurants selling it. Although smoking tobacco and marijuana is gaining popularity many residents use fruit leather instead."

Sales of Famous Okanagan Fruit Leather exploded throughout North America.

Ogopogo, Wong and Ham functioned as entrepreneurs, but aside from marketing a new product, created opportunities for people. The trio created something the public wanted but to this point in time had not existed.

Olympic athletes were quitting using steroids and switching to the product. It was also rumored that Mr. Wong was about to receive an honorary doctorate degree from the University of British Columbia because of the fruit leather.

Newspaper editorials and Open Line radio and TV shows also spread its popularity as distributorships opened throughout the world at a relentless pace. Faster than McDonald's opened restaurants or Coca Cola established bottling plants. Ham kept traveling and focusing to European, South American and Asian cities and always seeming to see ahead and say to the distributors, "Let me teach you how to sell. Success depends on the individual's willingness to work and learn."

The Famous Okanagan Fruit Leather story was such a success that Ham Bobek, Ogopogo and Lo Wong soon became exceptionally wealthy.

So wealthy that they almost instantly had built a factory in Kelowna featuring the latest technology: computers, robots, lasers, sensors, webcams, satellites and the latest state of the art equipment. Next to the factory on the twenty acre property near the edge of Okanagan Lake they also built a store and an apartment high-rise tower.

The complex was named Okanagan Tower and had a sign that lit up at night that read: *Headquarters Of Famous Okanagan Fruit Leather International Corp.* The huge sign was in multi neon colors.

Most of Kelowna was delighted that the city had a new non-polluting industry; vineyards and orchard owners could market their fruit locally and a change in its skyline. Mind you there were several concerns initially expressed that the tower would dwarf all the buildings in the neighborhood.

Several residents said the city might have improperly allowed the Ogopogo, Wong and Ham Bobek triumvirate to build a high tower. One resident even said, "If anything deserves attention is to renovate the parliament buildings in Ottawa."

Concerns about health matters were withdrawn after the local health officer assured those complaining that, "The tower will not interfere with the ozone cloud or aircraft landing at the Kelowna airport."

The Mayor too boasted about the tower and Famous Okanagan Fruit Leather at each convention he attended. For example, when the Mayor spoke to the Free Enterprise Club in New York he said to the members, "Famous Okanagan Fruit Leather is the ultimate meal replacement in the world."

And when he spoke at the Empire Club in Toronto, he said, quote: "Mark my word. Fifty percent of Planet Earth will be enjoying fruit leather by the year 2010 when the Winter Olympics will be held in Vancouver."

As soon as the tower, factory and store were completed, Ham, Ogopogo and Wong left the cave and moved into individual suites in Okanagan Tower that was connected to the factory with tunnels, some with water and some without. Moli chose to live in a penthouse on the 24th floor, Wong a unit on the 7th and Ogopogo decided to live on the ground floor that was easily accessible to Okanagan Lake and a sandy beach.

For their parents Ham and Sam purchased a thirty unit motel on Lakeshore Drive, a GMC pickup truck, and got them out of debt.

It was February, while Sam was still in Toronto and Ham relaxing in his penthouse in Kelowna, that he received a long distance phone call from the Soviet Union. Ham picked up the receiver and after the first ring said, "Hello."

"Mr. Bobek, please. Long distance is calling," a voice of a telephone operator said. There was noise on the line.

"Speaking," Ham replied thinking it was an important call about a distributorship being planned for Moscow. After several seconds another voice came on the line. "Mr. Bobek?"

For the second time Ham said, "Speaking."

It was the voice of the manager of the Canadian World Hockey team that was participating in the Planet Earth Hockey Championship in Moscow.

"An emergency!" the World team manager exclaimed. "Ham, we want you in Moscow as quickly as possible."

"What on earth for? Is there a problem?"

"Problem? Our hockey team is in trouble, that's the problem."

"Tell me about it."

The World Team manager continued, "Our first string goaltender has been injured and the backup has the flue."

Being a patriotic type and playing for Canada instead of a professional team, Ham finally said, "Okay. I'll come but on one condition."

"What's the condition?.

"That I bring along several cartons of Famous Okanagan Fruit Leather for our players."

"That's not a condition but a blessing."

Ham took the first available flight out of Kelowna and when he arrived in Moscow, the Canadian players were already putting their gear on as Ham gave each player a strip of fruit leather to enjoy and then said, "Let the game begin."

As soon as Ham led his team onto the ice there was instant booing by the partial Soviet crowd that had never seen such a gargantuan goaltender and players chewing fruit leather during warm up. As soon as the referee blew the whistle for the game to begin, there were various comments from fans that had a program of the two lineups.

One Soviet fan was heard to say, "Ham Bobek is larger than a Siberian bear."

And another fan, "And his reflexes are those of an Indian tiger."

Ham was both. His gargantuan size covered the entire net behind him and when the puck did come his way he flipped it towards centre ice where a Canadian player would usually wait, get a breakaway and score. In the end the Canadian National team defeated the Soviet Union 5-0 and Ham's goaltending record was still intact as he hadn't been scored on in professional or amateur games that were important.

Organizers of the tournament were so certain of a Soviet victory that they forgot to have a recording of Canada's national anthem on hand.

It was another moment Ham cherished as he skated to the microphone and sang *O Canada* in English and colloquial French, live instead.

"My mother warned me there would be moments like this," Ham said to reporters who gathered near the dressing room following the game.

When questioned about his goaltending Ham said that he was out of shape and why the Canadian team won was because of the Famous Okanagan Fruit Leather.

On the day that Ham returned to Kelowna from Moscow, he received a long distance phone call from Sam who was living in Toronto. "Congratulations on winning the World Hockey Championship in Moscow," Sam said, but Ham detected sadness in his brother's demeanor.

"Thank you," Ham said and asked Sam about the Blue Jays spring training camp that was about to open in Dunedin, Florida.

"I feel awful," Sam said.

"Is something the matter?"

"There is."

Ham wanted to know and said, "Well, what is it?"

"It seems the culture shock of living in a large city along with the euphoria of winning the World Series has finally got to me psychologically."

"And you are lonely?"

"That too."

"And you miss Mom and Dad?"

"And my honey, Marie Greene."

"What does Marie say?"

"That I should return to Kelowna if our relationship is to continue."

The following week, Sam unexpectedly showed up in Kelowna and took up residence in an Okanagan Tower unit, next to Ogopogo.

While in Kelowna, Sam and Marie spent a lot of time together watching television and studying the *Bible*. Sam enjoyed both because of the murder mysteries laced with violence, horror and sex each part of the Bible had. As an athlete, Sam specially enjoyed reading about David slaying Goliath with a slingshot. He could not understand the Trinity. And when it came to the part where Jonah was swallowed by a whale, Sam jumped into the air, his eyes popped as he hugged Marie and said to her, "That's it, Mother, was right. The psychologist was right. I should have been an evangelist instead of a professional baseball player!"

While in Kelowna, Sam and Marie participated in contests by filling out coupons in shopping malls, newspapers and magazines, and those conducted by radio and television stations. It was a worthwhile hobby. Although Sam's and Marie's lips were sore from licking envelopes, they won all sorts of prizes.

In a short while, Sam and Marie won a car after purchasing a ticket in a raffle. Then they won a trip to Disneyland after filling out a coupon at a drugstore.

They also won, among other things, a Barbie doll, a fainting goat and a shopping spree at the IGA Store. And then when a Kelowna radio station had a food contest to boost its listenership, there were ten draws a day.

The contest allowed multiple entries and over the next week Sam and Marie wrote as many as 1,000 entries for the contest and their winnings began to pile up in Marie's apartment: cans of veggies, meat and juices. There was also pasta, cheese and dried fruit.

"What are we going to do with all this food?" Marie said to Sam. "We are running short of storage space. There is hardly any empty space to breathe."

At that precise moment, Sam had difficulty concentrating. Ham didn't know what he knew and the more he mixed up his thoughts, the more he became mixed up. Finally he said, "Let's have Mr. Wong compact the food into pill form."

"Hey, that's an excellent idea, let's," Marie said an hour later packages and cans were delivered to Wong's laboratory, where Wong wasted no time and said, "It makes me sad to see all this fine food wasted. Having it concentrated into pill form is an excellent idea."

That night, Marie and Sam helped Wong place the food into a meat grinder, and then through a food processor. Next, Wong laid out the concoction on a table and with a rolling pin, rolled out the ingredients thin like one, rolls dough while making cookies.

A cookie cutter was used to have the concentrated food into pill form and placed in the laboratory oven to dehydrate. Once out of the oven, each pill, the size of a Canadian dollar coin, and containing nourishment for an entire day, was placed in a refrigerator.

Finally, Wong said, "There, no more food wasted. It's in pill form which diluted with water, is all that is necessary to sustain life."

Sam looked forward to marketing the pill as a new concept in the fast food industry but it had its drawbacks compared to fruit leather, pizza and even the Big Mac.

The following morning while enjoying the *new* discovery for breakfast, Marie was impressed with the pill's small size, containing a pound of concentrated nourishment, but the pill she was eating soon got lodged in her throat causing her to cough and choke.

Sam kept slapping Marie across the back, but this had little effect. Seeing a glass of water he had Marie swallow a mouthful but this was fatal. The water caused the pill to expand and minutes later Marie had a huge tummy and it got larger and larger every minute. This was followed by a terrific explosion.

It was so huge that a fragment of Marie's body was found as far away as Alice Nichol's vineyard. In no time, the grape vines around the fragment turned a luscious green in color.

It is sad to think that Marie Greene, this pretty, vivacious, young woman, instead of marrying Sam Bobek became a piece of fertilizer.

Seeing the tragedy that befell Marie, Sam could not sleep at night, he tossed and turned, and even after the funeral, slept badly, sitting upon a bed, thinking about the tragedy.

It was during the following week, that Sam said to Ogopogo and Wong, "I have definitely made up my mind. I'm going to become an evangelist like my Mom, the psychologist and Marie suggested, and walked into a drugstore where he purchased the latest edition of a weekly tabloid that is published in Los Angeles.

Sam flipped through the pages until he came to an advertisement that read. "Living in a religious vacuum?" and that one could become a minister of the No Name Universal Church by sending a $100 cheque, and a certificate would be sent in the mail to that effect.

Instead of sending a cheque, Sam used the all–expense paid trip; he and Marie had won to Disneyland. While in Los Angeles Sam made contact with the No Name Universal Church, paid his $100 fee, and was given a certificate saying he was a minister of that particular faith.

Fortunately for Sam, this religious group did not believe it was necessary for its clergy to attend a theological school of some kind or else Sam, being a Catholic, had been hard pressed to define his new philosophical and religious beliefs.

At any rate, Sam found his God near Sunset and Vine while in Los Angeles, made a leap and then a plunge, and converted to the No Name Universal Church faith. This of course upset his parents but both said simultaneously, "So whatt?"

And when Ed returned to Kelowna, residents were surprised to see this young giant and famous baseball player, standing at the intersection of the Okanagan Highway and Bernard Avenue, preaching to anyone who cared to listen. Residents were even more surprised the following week, when Pastor Sam Bobek had his own television program answering questions about the *Bible*.

Pastor Bobek's first caller on the talk-show program came from the nearby town of Osoyoos who said, "Reverend Bobek. I'm calling about hunting. From the standpoint of the *Bible* is hunting animals and birds a sin?"

"Good question," Pastor Bobek replied choosing his words carefully. "God gave man domain over fish and land."

If you need food, hunting is fine but if it's merely a sport involving a high-powered rifle for the sake of a trophy, hunting animals and birds is wrong."

Another call came from the city of Penticton and the caller wanted to know what Pastor Sam Bobek thought of Halloween.

"I don't think it's wrong to go around Halloween night provided we don't vandalize," Pastor Bobek replied. "Halloween gets borderline, however, when we get into demons, spooks, witches and other images. Some even go to the extent of putting razor blades inside apples. God doesn't like that."

Another caller phoned from the city of Vernon and said, "Reverend Bobek. My doggie has just died. Will he get to Heaven?"

"As I see it, dogs have a soul but not a spirit to know God," Sam answered.

"But I love my doggie that acted almost like a human being."

"I'm sure dogs even pit bulls, are intelligent but their soul and spirit will not be connected again, like man, by resurrection. At the risk of offending dog lovers I don't think there is a doggie Heaven."

Changing the subject, the same viewer asked, "How do you think the New York Yankees will make out this season?"

Pastor Bobek was blunt, "This isn't a sports show so I rather not comment on the Yankee's or the Mets."

But when pressed on, Pastor Bobek admitted that he loved the game, which was first mentioned in the *Bible* in *Genesis,* when one opened the book and on the first page were the words, "In the big inning, the first double play occurred when Eve was on the way to first base and Adam stole for second and both because of the double—play were thrown out."

Alice Nichol called next and was concerned about the role of preachers preaching on television and pocketing money.

"I consider my job as a calling from God," Pastor Bobek replied but Alice complained that to a previous caller

Sam had said that people in India treated cows better than humans.

Pastor Bobek followed the tradition of outspoken talk-show hosts to be candid, forthright and to the point.

During the conversation, Mrs. Nichol said that he had a tendency to blow things out of proportion. "That would be dangerous," Mrs. Nichol protested but the Reverend thought it would be more dangerous to his audience ratings if he stopped being opinionated.

The next caller was from Peachland and said that she had just purchased a *Ford Tempo* and would the Pastor bless the vehicle.

"Listen. There's a limit as to what I will bless," Pastor Bobek answered. "I will bless all Ford products but not a Tempo."

After several months on local television, Sam felt he could serve God better on an international level traveling around the world, doing missionary work.

First he traveled to the Middle East where he helped find a home for the Palestinians and had Israelis and Arabs sign a peace treaty. Later he flew to the Soviet Union and freed those who were jailed in Siberia and introduced fruit leather to the poor in Africa and later still, tried to negotiate a compromise when the female angels in Heaven were on strike and wanted more free time so that they could practice playing their harps, but Pastor Sam failed in his attempt to negotiate a deal.

Sam's plan made a hopeful beginning but because he challenged God, betrayed the Almighty and returned to

Kelowna to seek forgiveness. The following day, with a pack sack on his back Sam set out for the Monashee Mountains for a retreat, got caught in a severe snow storm, got lost, and seemingly doomed to die.

For sparing his life, Sam gave a commitment to God that for the rest of his life he would help the homeless and the poor living and struggling on streets.

By now, the baseball season was about to begin and some thought that Sam had perished during a blizzard because he stayed away from public view.

The Blue Jays manager thought differently, however, and took a flight to Kelowna where a search for Sam was organized. During the search, Sam was found in one of the dark tunnels connecting the Famous Okanagan Fruit Leather factory with Okanagan Tower. There, the Blue Jays manager urged Sam to come out of retirement.

In reply Sam said, "At the moment I'm in conscious crises. Do you mind if I step outside where I can be alone and say a prayer to the Lord above? I will give you my decision at three".

"That's three in the afternoon?"

"Three in the morning."

"Do that," the Blue Jays manager said. "I will wait for you inside the tunnel."

This time Sam said, "Do that."

On his way out, Pastor Sam Bobek got lost, but after twenty minutes was successful. To prevent anyone else getting lost in the tunnel, searchers boarded the entrance with heavy timber.

Sam did not know this until an hour later, and then told the searchers the Blue Jays manager was still inside. The search party immediately ran back to the tunnel but unfortunately found the manager dead behind the blocked entrance due to lack of oxygen.

The following day, the body of the Blue Jays manager was flown to Toronto and Pastor Sam Bobek accompanied it for a funeral.

As soon as the funeral was over, Blue Jays owners took a Sam, the preacher and baseball man, aside, and pleaded that he should forget about his ministry and help the club win another pennant and said, "Listen our friend, you had a successful year last season and now without you, we will miss you."

"And I will miss you too."

And without you, the Blue Jays will be dead and so will you."

The Blue Jays owners used every conceivable method possible for Sam to sign a long term contract. They even promised to double his salary and a supply him with fruit leather and a cellular phone in the event of a players' strike.

Sam however, could not commit himself to the offer without first consulting God. And when he did, the Almighty granted Sam permission to play another season provided his salary was equal to that of Wayne Gretzky, an exceptional athlete in his own right, and that the salary be used to fill food banks in Toronto. To this the Blue Jays owners agreed.

As the baseball season progressed, Reverend Sam Bodek, the baseball player, was under constant pressure to perform like he did the previous season, but it was not so.

To overcome a sophomore slump and nagging injuries, Sam went for walks and one day seemed to be covered with tainted substance, but later it was discovered not blood, but acid rain from the smoke-stacked industries surrounding the Great Lakes.

Next, Sam began to itch and had trouble seeing things so he was referred by the Blue Jays to three medical specialists but they were as confused as Sam was.

The first, diagnosed Sam's illness as diabetes, the second that he ate too many donuts at Dunkin Joe's, while the third, thought Sam behaved the way he did, was because he had not eaten enough fruit leather or perhaps, had used steroids that were prevalent among baseball players in those days.

Sam began missing games, and when he did show up, didn't pitch well. This eventually disappointed Blue Jays management, and without warning, traded him to the New York Yankees for a third round draft choice.

Sam was greatly disappointed that he had been traded to the Yankees and with events that led to the trade. The following day there was a tragic ending in Toronto.

Following a severe electric storm with high winds, Ed's body was found in Lake Ontario.

Naturally as parents, they grieved and were disappointed what had happened to their son. But the disappointment did not last long because due to his baseball accomplishments with the Blue Jays, Sam was instantly inducted into the Baseball Hall Of Fame and a week later, because of his charitable work on Planet Earth, Sam Bobek was canonized a saint.

While in Heaven, God handed Saint Sam Bobek a cell phone and power to communicate with his parents, brother, Ham and fruit leather inventor, Mr. Lo Wong for free.

Meanwhile, Ham didn't get overly excited about his twin brother becoming an instant Baseball Hall famer or even a saint, as he was madly in love with Brenda McCain, who agreed to marry him.

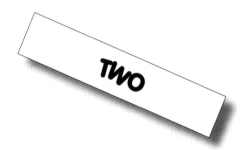

Ham and Brenda's Wedding

At first the weather, like their romance, was stormy but by the afternoon it turned to sunshine and Ham Bodek and Brenda McCain were married during the month of February, a time the city of Kelowna became alive with parades, dances, snow golf, skiing and hockey events, sharing the spotlight with zanier activities like taking a dip in a chilly ice crusted Okanagan Lake.

The marriage ceremony at the Holy Spirit Church concluded at 4:00 p. m. There was a crowd of people in the street watching as the bride and groom left the church, taken to a portrait studio, and then to the reception at the Capri Hotel ballroom.

For better or worse Brenda's wedding dress was perfect for the bride. The ruffled voile dress came with an oversize stole that duplicated the ruffles of the skirt. The headpiece was French lace and flower confections wrapped with open Swiss veiling, an original design by Francesca of New York. Brenda also had three stems of red roses to complete her attire. The gloves and shoes matched her wedding dress and veil each with sprigs of fern attached to them.

As for Ham, he wore a white tuxedo with a burgundy colored counterbun. He also wore a red rose in his lapel.

The number of guests attending the reception, which included Lo Wong acting as master of ceremonies, and Alice Nichol who contributed gratis her *Friend of the Okanagan* wine.

The ceremony was small compared to the wealth Ham Bobek had accumulated.as he was chairman of the board of Famous Okanagan Fruit Leather International Corp. that had distributors throughout the world and about to be listed in *Fortune* Magazine.

Brenda and Ham's parents were there. One set of parents was of Polish heritage and the second, Scottish, and from the time the bride and groom entered the reception suite to the last dance, a day later, Polish and Scottish traditions were observed.

First, the parents went to the centre of the floor in front of the head table where on a second small table there was a tray containing a small dish of salt, two slices of rye bread and a glass of wine. As the parents were waiting to greet the Bride and Groom the bandleader announced their coming. A Polish wedding march was played as the bridal party each had a shot of whiskey, and then placed themselves in front of the head table. There were cigars for the gentlemen.

With the bread, the parents hoped their children would never hunger or be in need. With the salt, they were reminding the couple that their life may be difficult at times, and they must learn to cope with life's struggles.

With the wine, the parents were hoping the bride and groom would never thirst and wished they have a life of good health; good cheer and share the company of many friends. The parents then kissed the newly married couple as a sign of welcome, unity and love.

After the sharing of bread, salt and wine, the bride's veil was removed and replaced with a small lace *czypek*. A string of tiny dolls tied with pink and blue ribbons were placed around the bride and groom's neck and a bright 'funny' hat placed on the groom's head. This custom signified the bride's shedding of her maidenhood as she assumed the responsibility of a marriage.

The dolls were a wish that the couple have many happy, healthy children and the hat was a wish that their marriage be filled with much happiness and laughter. As soon as this ceremony was concluded, both sets of parents sat close to each other at the head table where Carolina Bobek said to Brenda's father, Gavin McCain, "No other nation can dance like the Poles."

Brenda's father disagreed and casually replied, "Tonight we'll prove that the Scots are better dancers than the Poles."

"Provided you remain sober," Mrs. McCain interrupted her husband.

"I've been drunk only twice in my entire life"

"And when was that?" Carolina asked.

"The first time when I drank a bottle of Alice Nichol's *Friend of the Okanagan* wine. The side effect was that I had a headache."

"And the second?"

"When Brenda told me that although she was a Montreal Canadiens and a New York Yankee fan, but she loved Ham more and that she was going to marry him."

As the dinner was about to begin, which consisted of roast beef as the main dish along with pierogi and holubtsi, Lo Wong asked Father Kubek to say grace.

And he did by saying, "Since this a Polish-Scottish wedding, it is appropriate that we pray this way. Let us bow our heads. Some have meat but cannot eat. Some would like to eat but lack food. But this evening at Ham's and Brenda's wedding, we have meat and we can eat. We thank the Lord. Amen."

While facing the bride and groom, Father Kubek then said in Polish, "Die Sdrovie. Sto lat," which translated into English means, "May you have good health, for one hundred years."

The wedding cake, which was placed in the centre of the table was three-feet tall and made by a baker at the local Safeway store. It was the second tallest cake the baker had ever made. The first was when the Mayor's daughter Jane, who was married a year earlier.

Before the cake was cut into pieces and distributed, the master ceremonies, Lo Wong, went through the congratulatory messages wishing Brenda and Ham happiness. They heard from relatives and friends. The Toronto Maple Leafs didn't forget Ham or hundreds of Famous Okanagan Fruit Leather distributors.

One of the telegrams came from Prime Minister of Canada and read: "Weather in Ottawa is kind of stormy especially during Question Period. Congratulations, Brenda and Ham. Hope you have a little son."

Halfway through the banquet, Wong asked Father Kubek to say a few words, so the pastor genuflected, stood up amid a chattering and said, "Two bright, intelligent people bonded by holy matrimony. I know I speak for everyone here this evening when I say God has chosen you Brenda and Ham as a perfect couple. Please don't let Him down. And remember to keep the commandments of the Lord your God, and walk in His way."

Then the saintly-looking priest quoted the *Bible* and talked about King Saul's jealousy because David killed more Philistines that he did.

And how, Saul tricked David, to be his son-in-law, only privately wanting to kill him with a javelin. Having said this, Father Kubek continued, "It happened during the time of the *Bible* but I feel things haven't changed twenty-one centuries later."

Father Kubek urged Brenda, petite and pretty, and Ham muscular and almost twice her height, to share as husband and wife and to communicate their feelings to each other. The Reverend also urged the couple to take care of their parents when they got old and decrepit. Next, Father Kubek asked those present to stand and join him in proposing a toast to the bride and groom.

As the guests stood, Father Kubek picked up a glass filled with *Friend of the Okanagan* wine and said, "To Brenda and Ham. May God bless you with a long loving life."

As soon as Father Kubek said those words, guests applauded and banged their plates with forks and knives until Brenda and Ham stood up and they kissed each other again.

Following the meal, the bar was opened, the tables cleared, and dancing began as a five-piece band played waltzes, mazurkas, polonaises and polkas.

First, the father of the bride danced with his daughter while the mother held on to an apron attached the bride's gown.

Money was thrown into the apron by all of the friends and relatives who wished to dance with the bride. At the end, the groom threw his wallet into the apron and carried his bride off to another room.

As soon as the bride and groom returned they danced to the *Wedding Waltz*. Upon completion of this slow tempo tune, other couples took to the dance floor and the fun began.

As the evening progressed, hilarity increased, and then after consuming several glasses of wine, Mr. Wong sang a Chinese folk song while Ogopogo attempted to sing one in Polish, but had difficulty pronouncing the words. Realizing this, Ogopogo joined Wong and together sang Scottish tunes.

Hearing this, Brenda's father pulled out a bagpipe, joined in, and the threesome sang *Harry Lauder* songs.

Next, Brenda flung her bouquet at a group of prospective brides and then Ham, her garter, at grooms in waiting, dancing began again.

It was here that the bride and groom slipped away to their penthouse in Okanagan Tower and changed their wedding attire into casual clothing.

Before departing for their honeymoon, Ham and Brenda admired the wedding gifts they had received, and these included: a set of sterling war. a vacuum cleaner, a place setting of china along with pots and pans, linin and towels, electrical appliances and an Alice Nichol an all-expense paid flight to participate in the Yellowknife Midnight Sun golf tournament held in June.

As soon as they returned to the banquet room, some thought the bride and groom were about to take a flight to Switzerland for their honeymoon, but it was not so—with empty beer and cola cans dragging behind their Mercedes Benz, they drove to the nearby Big White Ski Resort, where there was an extraordinary amount of snow on the ground, making it ideal for night skiing.

It was past midnight by the time Ham and Brenda unpacked, went to bed and had a wonderful time in a cabin that had a fireplace, animal skins as rugs and an elk's head with the giant rack mounted above the mantel. They slept until noon.

The following evening, Brenda and Ham, put on their skiing gear and headed for the mountain slopes. Brenda was an experienced skier, but that was not so with Ham, who had only several lessons in his entire life. The bride and groom first rode the T-bar and then the poma lift. Ham mustered enough courage to say to his bride, "Let's try the chairlift and ski down the summit."

"An excellent idea," Brenda said and while riding the chairlift went on, "Let's pretend that I'm Nancy Greene and you, Jean Claude Killy."

Greene and Killy were two exceptional skiers who had won Olympic gold medals for Canada and France.

This time, Ham said, "An excellent idea."

Once they reached the summit, Brenda got off the chairlift, but the inexperienced Ham, stumbled and fell, and the couple behind, fell on top of him.

As soon as Ham untangled himself and on his feet, he noticed arrows nailed to a post pointing to different ski runs. A yellow colored arrow meant easy, red intermediate and black for the experienced.

Ham scanned the view below, which was breathtaking and thought the black run didn't appear difficult and a shorter distance to the lodge that was flooded with lights.

While on the mountain top, Brenda suggested a race to the lodge below. Ham experienced in taking risks, accepted. The winner wouldn't have to do the dishes for a week.

The couple would also have an après drink at the lodge with friends they had met. On the word, "Go," Brenda took the easiest run while Ham the one that had a black sign and appeared to be the shortest.

At first, Ham's run appeared easy, believing he was winning the race that is until he took a sharp turn to the left and found himself near a sign that read *SKI AT YOUR OWN RISK*. There was solitude and only the sound of Ham carving a path through virgin snow echoing during the moonlight night. The temperature was—15 Fahrenheit degrees.

To begin skiing at his age took courage, but Ham felt the risk was worth it, for what he learned he would pass on to his children. Suddenly, Ham found himself on a bumpy path with fir, hemlock and cedar trees on both sides.

For a moment, Ham thought he could ski as well as Killy, and would win the race, that is until he came through a clearing and then a sudden vertical drop.

Ham was going so fast at the time that if he were going any faster, one would have to need an airbag to make him stop. Eventually Ham lost his balance, stumbled and fell, with his right ski a short distance in front of him. Ham sidestepped the slope until he found the stray ski, and as he was putting it back on, a member of the Ski Patrol skied by and shouted, "Hey there! Are you all right?"

"I'm okay, thank you," Ham replied.

As the ski patrol moved on, Ham began to ski down slowly. The lower he came, the larger the moguls got. Then Ham fell again but this time he wasn't so lucky, both skis came off and by the time he could claim them, they were shooting down the mountain towards the lodge like cruise missiles racing between the Arctic Ocean and the Cold Lake Military Weapons Range in Alberta.

It took ten minutes for Ham to compose himself following the spill, and as, he was sitting on the snow alone and thinking about what to do, another Ski Patrol member shot by, not noticing that Ham was in pain. Ham, frustrated, frightened, recalled how his parents prayed to Saint Sam Bobek in Heaven, and wondered if he should do the same.

"Help!" Ham shouted but no one heard him. He was still near the steepest part of the mountain and thought "What do I do now?"

Ham realized he had lost both skis and the race with Brenda. He then debated with himself if he should climb up or downhill. He finally decided to walk down but the snow was to his waist and his ski boots felt as if they were made out of lead.

The ski patrol that saw Ham earlier, skied down the run again and when he saw the predicament Moli was in, stopped suddenly, took off his skis and placed them upright next to him. "Here, let me help you, sir," the ski patrol said, but as soon as Ham complained about pain to his right side, the patrol laid him down in the snow, comforted him and by two-way radio ordered a toboggan. While waiting for another ski patrol, Ham began to breathe heavily and the breath he exhaled froze around his mouth, nose and eyes.

"Don't worry," the patrol said. "I'll make certain you don't get frost bitten and get you safely down the hill as soon as possible."

Once the toboggan arrived, Moli was tucked into blankets and then the toboggan that was pulled down the hill with one patrol pulling in front and the second holding on to the rope at the back so it wouldn't go downhill too fast.

By the time they reached the lodge it was 9:00 p. m. and Brenda walked out and greeted her husband by saying, "See. Honey, I won the race. You'll have to do the dishes next week."

Ham was going to say, "Brenda, drop dead," but instead used good judgment and said, "Congratulations, Brenda, dear, Okay, I'll do the dishes. You have won the race."

While helping the two patrol remembers transfer Ham from the toboggan to a stretcher, and then into an ambulance., Brenda remained cheerful until a skier came swiftly down the hill, going out of control, crashing into Brenda and breaking her leg.

An ambulance was called and Ham and Brenda were taken to the Kelowna General Hospital where in Emergency, Dr. Paul Bond diagnosed Brenda's injury as a broken fibula and put her leg in a cast. The doctor wasn't certain, however, when he diagnosed Ham's pain in his side as an acute attack of appendicitis. Ham lay on top of a table as Dr. Bond felt Ham's stomach and asked him to raise his feet into the air and back again.

"It must be appendicitis," Dr. Bond said, and after several feet up's and down's he asked the nurse to book the operating room for an emergency surgery.

Still uncertain of the diagnosis, however, Dr. Bond said to the nurse, "In my opinion, I'm not certain my diagnosis is the correct one," and called on Dr. Bob April who was in Emergency also, for a second opinion.

After making Ham raise his feet up and down and punching his stomach like baker punches bread dough, Dr. April said to Dr. Bond, "It isn't appendicitis but a pulled muscle in Mr. Bobeck's stomach. It happens often when the skier isn't experienced and there is a lot of snow on the ground. Give Ham a strip of *Famous Okanagan* peach flavored fruit leather and the pain will eventually go away."

Dr. April then turned to the bride and groom and said, "Congratulations on your marriage Mr. and Mrs. Bobeck. Enjoy your honeymoon."

A Weekend at the Alice Nichol Vineyard

As soon as Ham and Brenda recovered from their skiing accident and the month of April arrived. They, along with Ogopogo and Wong, were invited to spend a weekend at the Alice Nichol Vineyard, where the weather was in a holiday mood and flowers, especially roses, bloomed everywhere. The dainty five-petalled pink faces smiled from every bush and grove while clematis climbed like a growing child, and all the marigolds were on fire.

The guests had never spent time at a vineyard before where grapes grew to the size of an apricot and some of the things they experienced, they found extremely interesting. For instance, on the first morning everyone was up at sunrise awakened by roosters greeting them with a, "Cock-a-doodle-doo," song. As the sun rose a plethora of birds took part in the back yard 'Bird Concert', fluttering, chirping and frolicking from tree to tree. The Concert was led by several robins with their, "Tweedle-dee, tweedledum. Tweedle-dee tweedledum," rhymes.

Several oriels also took part in the concert with: "Tiweet, tweet, it's time to eat," song and a, "Pip, pip, pip, I'm a bird that's hip."

A flock of sparrows then landed at birdbath made from a section of a pine tree and sang, "You are not, you are not, you are cheap, cheap, cheap."

Six pigeons then joined in the chorus with a, "Hi sweetie. Hi sweetie. Come and meet me."

Then several seagulls flew overhead, towards Okanagan Lake and they too stopped and contributed the Backyard Concert with a, "Squawk, squawk, and squawk."

The seagulls were followed by crows sitting on a branch of a spruce tree cawing away with, "Caw, caw, and caw."

While having breakfast, Alice pointed to four baby swallows about to vacate their nest, a shell cup made of mud, plastered with feathers and grass, underneath a metal awning shading the kitchen window. It was an ideal nesting place with an abundance of insects on the bench land that had a panoramic view of Okanagan Lake where with a set of binoculars, one could see loons, pelicans, swans and many species of ducks.

"A barn swallow one would think would build a nest near a barn instead of a house," Ogopogo who had bird watched before, said, "The nest seems to be well protected by the awning and permits a direct flight for adult swallows when it's feeding time."

Packed tightly together in their nest, the four baby swallows presented the guests a front seat view and an irresistible attraction.

"Any moment now, the baby swallows will fly away to be on their own," Alice said as she edged closer to the window for a better view.

Alice made the comment because she noticed tiny single feather antennas above the baby swallow's eyes had disappeared and the birds weren't as glossy looking compared to the adult swallows.

Alice also observed that the baby swallows had forked tails with reddish-orange colored under parts and, that they were doing a wing flapping exercise.

The nest appeared to be the focal point for adult swallows each searching for insects, and when they found them, they would drop the insects into each baby beak that seemed to be always open.

All of a sudden, while Brenda was trying to get a better view, there was confusion near the nest and scores of adult swallows flying back and forth with excitement. The first offspring had left the nest landing on a handrail leading to the back door of the house. Following this initial procedure, a parent swallow swooped down and while fluttering its wing nudged the baby swallow sitting on the handrail on the rear end, urging it to continue flying, which it did, coming to rest on a nearby power pole. In the meantime all eyes were focused on the nest, as the second baby swallow was about to make its maiden flight. As birdwatchers the guests were not disappointed. The second baby swallow placed its rump outside the nest, went to the bathroom and then clung to the side of the nest with its talons while its wings were fluttering. A minute later it let the nest go and flew directly to the near power pole where now adult and young barn swallows mingled.

The gathering, amid the chattering reminded Brenda of a press conference announcing another achievement for bird—kind.

As soon as the four baby swallows had flown away, a skunk was seen strutting across the yard, unafraid of humans. In order to get a better view of the rodent, Alice's miniature collie dog, named Huckleberry, slipped out of the door and began chasing the animal.

"No! Huckleberry! Come back! The skunk may be rabid!" Alice yelled but the warning came too late and the inevitable happened—poor Huckleberry got sprayed as the skunk discharged a bad smelling fluid to defend itself.

"Pew," Ogopogo said, holding his nose tightly. "What an awful smell."

After everyone agreed the pungent odor was intolerable, Alice suggested the dog needed a bath immediately.

"I'll give it a bath if you show me how," Ogopogo said.

Alice's reply was, "First we need some tomato juice."

Surprised, Ogopogo said, "What on earth for?"

"If we have no tomato juice on hand we can use my new *Friend of the Okanagan* wine.

Curious Ogopogo said, "Tomato juice or wine, to get rid of the skunk's odor?"

"You can use either, but make certain the dog doesn't come inside the house until the skunk odor is gone."

"Okay, I'll use wine," Ogopogo said and went on, "But pray, tell me, how will the wine get rid of the odor?"

"Not only will it get rid of the odor but also fleas," Alice said when she was interrupted by Wong, "What do you mean?"

Wong said that in making fruit leather he had experimented with herbs but never tomato juice or wine.

"Well, you see," Alice continued, "The fleas will get drunk on the wine they drink and start throwing rocks at each other. There will be so much commotion that the odor will disappear and the fleas will kill themselves."

In the end, it involved wrestling with Huckleberry in a back yard tub, shampoo and water. The one-hour ordeal could have been better spent listening to the birds singing in the back yard than putting an arm lock on a wet dog. But this wasn't the first time Huckleberry had got into trouble. Two weeks earlier while walking with Alice at the Bear Creek Park the dog stumbled upon a porcupine in a den and Huckleberry, had his nose filled with quills. It took Alice an hour to pull the quills out with a set of pliers.

The following hour, Alice and her guests sat in the deck in the back yard where four American gold finches sat on a nearby lilac tree. The skunk's odor must have reached the birds because they gave a short musical concert uttering a distinctive four syllable, "Pir-chick-o-pee, pir-chick-o-pee and then flew away.

The Bird Concert continued, however, as several blackbirds perched themselves on a fence and despite the varied arrangement of musical notes there was a quality about their singing that was attractive. Unfortunately the blackbirds were suddenly crowded out by a dozen magpies that Brenda felt were: screechy, insolent, bold and brash.

Next, a wren provided an aria. This was a special treat because a wren as a rule isn't a member of a backyard choir. Another addition to the concert was the staccato tap-tap—tapping of a woodpecker as the robins continued to regale with their warbling notes of "Tweedle-dee-tweedledum. Tweedle-dee-tweedledum."

Creatures, other than birds, contributed to the concert also. There was a squirrel nearby scolding another and the "Click, clicking" of the dragonfly, the "Hum," of a bumblebee and roar of an airplane flying above. A short distance away a neighbor was cutting his lawn, another practicing on his bagpipe, and a third, sawing and hammering while renovating a home.

Bird watching was the very best kind of fun, easy, inexpensive, healthful and satisfying.

Taking a page from Henry David Thoreau, "We consider any day wasted that we didn't go for a walk and enjoy nature," Ogopogo said, and with Wong, took a stroll along the vineyard where they spotted a red-tail hawk soaring in the sky. The hawk, at times flying aloft, without a stroke from his wings, sized up its potential meal that could be a mouse, a chipmunk and even a rabbit.

As soon as the hawk was directly above Ogopogo, it dropped a poop on his shoulder which led Ogopogo to say in jest, "I'm glad cows can't fly, aren't you?"

Wong nodded his head signifying that Ogopogo was correct with that assessment and went on to say that bird droppings are very acidic and can carry disease, "So as soon as we return to the house you better put on a mask and give your jacket a cold-water rinse as Soon as possible.

Then Wong, as he gazed at the splendid cloudless sky, went on to say that the hawk was a beautiful bird fitted into the role of nature. "As for myself, I would like to be like that hawk someday, flying in an air balloon across Canada, scanning the scenery below."

As soon as Ogopogo and Wong returned to the house, Ogopogo water—rinsed himself and then with Wong, watched a magpie attempting to take a small piece of a meat, or was it a peanut, away from Huckleberry who had been bathed and shampooed earlier. For most of the year magpies are wonderful neighbors, chortling in our gardens in the morning. They eat vast quantities of insects and bugs. Magpies are members of the crow family, which also includes ravens and jays and have evolved the highest degree of intelligence among birds. Members of this family have learned to count, can solve puzzles, and can quickly learn to associate certain noises and symbols with food.

Ogopogo and Wong sat down on the lawn without disturbing either the dog or the extremely gregarious birds.

At first, the magpie sat on a fence and then landed near the dog, teasing it. Eventually, the magpie soft-talked Huckleberry to give up, whatever it was, with its constant, "Yak, yak, yak."

Huckleberry moved only slightly and after several minutes of grandstanding, the magpie pecked the dog on the tail. Huckleberry let out a bark and while turning around the magpie picked up the tiny piece and flew away.

By mid-morning, Ogopogo and Wong were dirt motorbike riding in the back yard, and with Alice's encouragement, agreed to have a friendly race. They laid out a track that went around the barn up a small hill where dandelions were in bloom, between several marmot holes, over a manure pile that provided a jump and then several S turns and ending in a straightway for acceleration.

It was agreed the race would be a ten lap best-of-three series and the loser would clean the fish for a fish fry that was planned for the evening. Since the motorbike that Wong was riding, he gave his competitor a lap handicap. Before racing they checked out the motorbikes for loose screws, fuel and lubricants and then put on long sleeved jerseys, gloves and helmets. It was going to be a friendly race.

"It certainly isn't going to be anything like the 500 World Championships or the Grand Prix of France," Ogopogo said as the racers revved up their motorbike engines and on a "Go," signal given by Alice, they took off.

Wong won the first race but just. Following a short rest Ogopogo won the second race by one-hundred feet. After the third race, which Wong had won, Alice said, "Fellas, do you want to race on a real dirt track located on the outskirts of Kelowna?"

"Why not?" Ogopogo replied. "Even at my age, motorbike racing can be fun."

The motorbikes were placed into the back of a pickup truck and once everyone arrived at the track that was designed by professionals, Ogopogo let out a scream, "Whoopi! A real dirt racetrack! I can't believe that I should be fooling around with a dirt motorbike instead of swimming in Okanagan Lake."

At first, the course appeared to be dangerous for the uninitiated so Ogopogo, Wong, Brenda, Ham walked it to familiarize themselves with the topography and the twists and turns. The track was over a mile in length with steep climbs, sharp curves, sand hills and a vast array of rocks, ruts and jumps. The penultimate corner, a sharp right-hand turn, featured a puddle of water and seemed specially challenging with its obstruction.

As soon as the motorbikes were unloaded Wong started his and went down the hill with extreme caution.

"I'm not certain I'll be able to make those steep hills," Ogopogo said and followed Wong according the track respect reserved for experienced motorbike racers.

At the same time, Ham, Brenda and Alice Nichol climbed onto the announcer's booth adjacent to the bleachers for a better view.

It took five minutes before the first lap was completed and although Ogopogo and Wong weren't racing they were wet and covered with mud.

"Dirt motorbike riding is a travesty to the nature of the sport of dirt riding," Alice said to Ham and Brenda and then asked Ogopogo if bike riding was fun.

"It's fun but a bit scary. And you should see the sand hill. My back wheel kept sliding dangerously as I came down."

Ogopogo didn't scare easily, but one could tell by his voice that the size of the slope worried him.

"Later, you can reverse your motorbikes and go around the track clockwise," Alice said. "Then instead of going uphill you will be coming down."

Ham's fear that Ogopogo and Wong could get hurt was overcome by his philosophizing, "Dirt is dirt. When I was a child I use to roll in it. Pigs bath in dirt. Indians use dirt for medicinal purposes. And soap commercials on radio and television tell us how easily dirt disappears."

During the second lap, minor tragedy struck when Ogopogo had a spill and was more embarrassed than uncomfortable. Near the crest of the hill his motorbike lost power, stalled, collapsing to one side. Ham witnessed what had happened so he, Brenda and Alice rushed to the scene where Ogopogo's skin had changed from green to orange in color and his tail was making smoke rings.

"I needed more power to make it uphill," Ogopogo said when he returned to his normal color. "As I was coming down the crest of the hill I delayed gearing down and the motorbike stalled."

As soon as Ogopogo recovered, he and Wong rode their motorbikes for another hour. After each lap they stopped and talked with Ham, Brenda and Alice about their experience. Later, Ogopogo and Wong rode the coarse in reverse direction gaining sufficient confidence to the point where Ogopogo was doing nine-foot jumps, three feet off the ground, twist his motorbike and land on the ground like a cat.

For a change Ogopogo and Wong then rode the sand adjacent to the racetrack and a garbage dump where sea gulls congregated. The riders charged the gulls and when the birds landed in another area, they were charged again.

The sport of chasing seagulls on a motorbike lasted ten minutes and on return to where Ham, Brenda and Alice were waiting, the riders discovered that their helmets were covered with bird droppings. Seeing this Wong simply said, "Yuck."

When everyone returned to the vineyard, there was bench racing. Ogopogo and Wong were exchanging their experiences and what seemed serious earlier in the day, now was amusing—even the seagull droppings on the helmets.

After enjoying dinner, everyone went outside and sat on the lawn watching ducks, Canada geese, swans, killdeers, pelicans and loons swimming in Okanagan Lake.

"I wish there was a bird sanctuary near Kelowna," Alice sighed as she spotted two loons landing on the lake. Alice said she had written to the Kelowna City Council and the Provincial Government that a bird sanctuary should be considered for the area but she had not received a reply from either.

Brenda said she had read that on a stormy night loons occasional became confused while landing.

"That's true," Alice said and went on, "Occasionally loons face certain death because they take wing only from water and even after a long puttering take-off, like a jet at an airport."

Brenda thought the two loons were quite vocal with their weird haunting calls echoing across the sliver-blue tranquil Okanagan Lake, but Ogopogo, who spent a great deal of his time either in or near the lake, disagreed. "They are crazy like a loon. They are lunatics," he said.

Never before had Ham, Brenda, Ogopogo and Wong been exposed to so many birds, animals, insects and nature in one day. Honeybees, hummingbirds, dragonflies and butterflies that came to the multi colored flowers that surrounded the ranch style house, white in color with blue shutters.

As darkness approached, a light breeze began to blow and the leaves continued their circuitous movement.

Soon, a nighthawk began patrolling the sky and often came down with a dive and swooping up again. Later as it got darker still, a bat flew out an abandoned shed signaling that nocturnal life had indeed taken over.

Ogopogo said he wasn't afraid of bats although he wasn't certain about skunks. "I'm afraid of skunks, especially at night time," he said.

As it got darker still, a spider raced across a cobweb in fright and landed on Brenda's shoulder. The spider startled Brenda who felt relieved when she gave the insect a flick with her finger and said, "Get out of here, little critter." The spider landed on the ground and scampered away taking shelter near a barbed wire fence protecting the vineyard.

As the night progressed, everyone watched a full moon and fireflies sparkle in front of them, and at the same time listened to the eerie sound of coyotes howling in the distance. Later an owl, in the distance also, made a, "who, who, who," sound.

As soon as the owl appeared, Alice suggested that everyone go to sleep because it was past midnight. Turning to Ogopogo and Wong she said, "Best of luck on your fishing trip in the afternoon. Till then have a good rest."

And when afternoon arrived, Ogopogo asked Wong if he could drive Wong's antique sports car. Wong said he didn't mind because the fishing hole that Alice suggested wasn't far from where she lived.

"Okay, let's go!" Ogopogo said after swallowing a strip of cherry flavored Famous Okanagan Fruit Leather that made the creature shrink to one-third his normal size, so he could climb into the car. With the fishing gear in place, Ogopogo sat behind the steering wheel and drove.

As soon as they reached the Highway 97, Ogopogo said to his fishing partner, "From experience I know that fish in Okanagan Lake are intelligent. As a matter of fact they are so smart that they travel in universities instead of schools."

Wong who did not fish often, said, "And I assume you know every fish species by name?"

"I do," Ogopogo said and went down the list, "I know Mrs. Salmon, Mr. Jack, Mrs. Pike, Mr. Trout, Mrs. Sturgeon, Mr. Bass, but I know Dolly Varden best of all."

"And who is Dolly Varden?"

Dolly is the fish that is the most serious of all Okanagan Lake fish and communicates regularly with the Mayor of Kelowna, the police and even Santa Claus."

By the time Ogopogo and Wong arrived at a fishing hole where Okanagan Lake and Trout Creek converge, they had already wagered a dollar as to who would catch the first, the largest and most fish. With the second cast Ogopogo caught a trout and minutes later a second and then a third.

At this point, Wong was frustrated and changing his hook to different bait, but when Ogopogo caught his limit within a space of an hour, it led Wong to say, "Enough of this fishing, I can't stand you catching all the trout and me none. Let's pack up our gear and head back to Alice Nichol's vineyard."

While returning, Ogopogo and Wong were looking forward to a fish fry that Alice had promised, but as they kept driving, a dramatic thing happened—they met a police car with lights flashing and an officer besides it, flagging the driver to stop. The policeman identified himself as Corporal Ron Pickens and seeing fishing gear tucked in the rear of the car he asked, "Catch any fish?" Ogopogo showed the policeman a bucketful.

"May I see you fishing license?" Pickens continued.

Wong reached for his wallet and showed his, but Ogopogo said he didn't need a license because he wasn't a homosapient and had certain privileges.

Looking directly at Wong, after checking the car registration, Corporal Pickens went on, "Mr. Wong, should Ogopogo be involved in a traffic accident, I trust you realize, you wouldn't be covered by insurance."

"I realize that, sir," Wong said. "Sorry."

Turning towards Ogopogo the officer with a notebook and a pencil in hand, continued, "What's your occupation?"

"I'm the maintenance supervisor at Famous Okanagan Fruit Leather International Corp. and aside from that I'm a scavenger at Okanagan Lake."

"Well, let this be a warning for not having a driver's license, you may proceed."

Ogopogo and Wong changed places and the two fishermen proceeded to the Alice Nichol vineyard. Ogopogo was silent for several miles but later said with a smile, "See, I told you fish in Okanagan Lake are the smartest in the world."

"How did you reach that conclusion?"

"Who do you think tipped Corporal Pickens that I didn't have a driver's license?"

"Got you. It was Dolly Varden. Wasn't it?"

"It must have been."

By the time Ogopogo and Wong returned to the vineyard, Alice, Brenda and Ham had a fire going in the courtyard. After Wong cleaned and cut the fish into pieces. Alice congratulated Ogopogo for catching so many and sweetened the pie by saying that she would like to go fishing with him some day.

After the fish were fried and eaten, it began to get dark and the lights of Kelowna shone in the distance. It was at this point that Brenda asked Ogopogo, since he lived in Okanagan Lake, if he knew a fish story.

'Believe it or not I do," Ogopogo replied and said that it dealt with the Okanogan First Nations Indian Band in Vernon, Chief Cardinal and his teenage daughter, Rita. Ogopogo told the story this way:

"Chief Cardinal became a friend of mine long time ago and he taught me how to appreciate the wonders of nature. The Chief didn't drive a car or concern himself with a driver's license.

"He showed me the right from the wrong, beautiful from ugly, to respect the environment and people, no matter what race, color or faith and to be respected by them. Chief "Cardinal has a wonderful daughter with the name Rita and I haven't told anyone, so I'm going to tell you now, how she caught her fish.

"People along Okanagan Lake began to wonder if the Great Spirit was helping Rita or if she was lucky because she was about to get married, or if she was communicating with Saint Sam Bobek in Heaven.

"The curiosity became so intense that some of the residents on the banks of Okanagan Lake would do almost anything to find out what Rita was using for bait. They were thinking of sending a diver to the bottom of the lake to examine the hook and bait. Some even used powerful binoculars and spotting scopes to see what they could discover.

"Well, I pledged in the name of Rita's ancestors that I would never divulge the secret and why she fished away from other anglers, unless it was with someone I truly loved.

"Since I love all of you and I know the secret, here it is: Rita always attached a piece of Famous Okanagan fruit leather to her hook. As soon as the fruit leather took on moisture it began to unroll. Seeing this, fish got excited and scooped up the fruit leather as bait."

Before retiring for the night, Ham said that he was looking forward to the upcoming Midnight Sun Golf Tournament in Yellowknife. Ogopogo and Wong agreed to join him, but Brenda declined for reasons known only to her.

The Midnight Sun Golf Tournament

It was time to put Alice Nichol's wedding present to use, so when the month of June arrived, Ham. Wong and Ogopogo traveled to Yellowknife, Northwest Territories to take part in a nine-hole Midnight Sun Golf Tournament.

On the first day of arrival in the self-proclaimed *aurora borealis* capital of the world, the Kelowna threesome discovered the midnight sun had no intention of setting and were surprised at the large number of honeymoon couples from Japan who had visited the area before them, that winter. The couples at the time were equipped with bright thermal overalls and mukluk snow boots, and came to Yellowknife, hoping their marriages would be blessed under the celestial light of the sky. The Northern

Lights season had come to an end thus ending the annual pilgrimage of thousands of Japanese and the beginning of another, to the Midnight Sun Golf Tournament.

"Why were there so many Japanese couples in Yellowknife during the winter season?" Ham asked Yurina Yakomoto who flew in from Osaka to take part in the tournament and was paired with the Kelowna threesome.

"Because the aurora borealis has a symbolic significance in Japan, we often see newlywed break into tears when they first see the phenomenon," Yurina said and continued to say that a Japanese tradition says a child conceived under the aurora borealis glow will be blessed with good fortune. "Over the past half century the Magnetic North Pole has moved north winds and the lights are no longer seen in Japan. This means Japanese newlyweds wishing to continue the tradition, now have to come to Canada."

Yurina said she traveled from Japan to Yellowknife in February to see the northern lights, not to conceive under them, and after two nights of searching the sky in vain, the swirling green clouds above them overwhelmed her and the newlyweds. According to Yurina, the lights twirled in the night sky for two hours beginning as a faint glowing band of green light, growing to cover over three-quarters of the sky, at times billowing back and forth like curtains in a breeze. At the climax, the multi colored light stretched overhead, from east to west horizon, racing, surging, and twisting.

"I'm very happy to have seen the aurora borealis," Yurina said. "I always wanted to see them since my parents told me of the aurora they had seen over their home before I was born. I'm also happy to take part in the Midnight Sun golf tournament. Seeing the aurora borealis may help me with the game of golf but I notice one thing."

"And what is that?" Ogopogo said.

"There are no golf carts here."

A staunch proponent of walking instead of riding, Ham said, "One of the reasons why, is that if golfers were meant to ride around a golf course, they'd have been born polo players and the second, here in Yellowknife since many of the miners are on strike for better wages, they can't afford golf carts."

The following day, at precisely midnight, golfers from through the world teed off and fought their way through swarms of black flies and mosquitoes. It didn't take long for Ogopogo to say, "Now I know why Brenda didn't want to come. The only winners in this tournament are insects that turn the game of golf into a feast. With fewer bites I could probably play better."

Wong's regret at the moment was that he had not invented fruit leather that could curb mosquitoes and flies from attacking golfers. "I didn't realize the bugs stayed up all night and bite in Yellowknife."

"Like the newlywed Japanese, we should be wearing overalls and snow boots," Yurina said as golfers swatted, stamped their feet and scratched.

"The mosquitoes are driving me crazy. We should have stayed in Kelowna, or at least brought along a shotgun to get rid of the pests," Ogopogo said.

"Be patient. They aren't that bad. You Canadians, like the Americans, seem to have a knack for exaggerating," Yurina said.

When the foursome finished playing hole number 1, Ham was surprised that although the Yellowknife golf course was the crown jewel of the Northwest Territories, its fairway was no Glen Abby or Pebble Beach. The greens were made out of sand and oil, and a straw matt was used to cover the footprints.

On hole number 2, Wong said it wasn't unusual in smaller northern Canadian communities to have golf greens made of sand a light coating of oil. "Golfers in this part of Canada do not have the luxuries of people living in the southern part."

The second hole was a difficult par 4 with a water trap just after a tree. Cam proceeded to hit the ball, which landed on the fairway. So did Wong's. Ogopogo was next, but he hit the ball into a body of water. To retrieve it he simply approached the water and extended his golf club. Yurina too hit the ball directly into the water where it began to sink. As the ball was sinking, a fish grabbed the ball into its mouth. At that very moment a raven plucked the fish out of water and began carrying it aloft. As the raven soared higher and higher, a bolt of lightning startled the bird, which dropped the fish onto a boulder and after several bounces rolled right into the hole.

"Congratulations," Wong said. "Seeing the aurora borealis must have helped you to get a hole in one."

On hole number3, Ham, Wong, Ogopogo and Yurina caught up to another foursome that included Alice Nichol and her companion, but initially they weren't recognized because of the screen meshes covering their heads. When they did recognize each other, Alice introduced her companion, who appeared to be considerably younger than her, as, "Jeffery Hunter."

Jeffery spoke with a southern drawl and like Alice, said he lived in Kelowna although originally came from Atlanta, Georgia and also that he was a Vietnam draft dodger.

"That's okay. We are against the war too," Ham said.

Following a brief conversation Jeffery said, "I heard about the Midnight Sun Golf Tournament and the aurora borealis from my fiancée, Jane, before she died from injuries received in a car accident. That's when Mrs. Nichol asked if I wished to live at her home, and I accepted."

As Alice and Jeffery were applying insect repellent to their arms and legs, the announcer on the radio, which Alice carried with her said, "The battle of the itch continues in Yellowknife and sales of repellents are booming. Calcimine lotions are in heavy demand and even the hospital emergency ward is treating victims. Welcome golfers from throughout the world to the Yellowknife Midnight Sun Golf Tournament on this 21st day of June. Now the sports scores . . ."

Alice gave the Ham foursome some of her insect repellent. "You may even pass us if you wish, while our foursome will rest," she said.

"Thank you," Ham graciously replied, and when his foursome was about to tee off on hole number 4, they came upon another foursome that included Yellowknife druggist, Sam Spade, who after introducing himself and his partners, said to Ham, "Mosquitoes are good business in this part of Canada. We have done 25% more sales this year compared to last year. I have seen young men, about your age, so badly bitten that they could hardly open their eyes."

Ham agreed that some people are more attracted to mosquitoes than others, and that was the reason he scratched less than his partners. "It's not because of the Seven-Year-Itch that they are scratching so often."

Yurina said that she didn't bother with that entire New Age airy-fairy hide-your toenail stuff.

"I've read self-help books which are no use whatsoever, apart from saying that when the mosquitoes bite you, they are balancing their diet."

On hole number 5. Ogopogo placed the ball on the tee and gave it a blast. The hole was a par 3, but the ball landed in a sand trap. Moli teed-off next and had a poor shot. So did Yurina, and both blamed the mosquitoes. Ogopogo teed off last. He walked up to the tee, pulled back his club, closed his eyes and swung with all his might. The ball hooked to the side, ricocheted off several rocks and took a fantastic bounce onto the green and into the cup for a hole in one

"So, you have been practicing," Yurina said. "We now each have a hole in one. Let's try for another."

What Wong said, was that he would wager Ogopogo a Whooping Crane feather that Ogopogo could not repeat shooting another hole in one even with his eyes open.

"I accept the challenge," Ogopogo replied and on hole #6. Alice Nichol's foursome caught up to Ham's. After congratulating Ogopogo on a wonderful shot, Alice asked Ham about his personal strength in golf to which he replied, "My greatest strength is probably irons 6 and 7."

"Why so?" Jeffery asked.

"A lot of it has to do because of my gargantuan size, so I welded on a piece to make them longer. The other reason is that I enjoy eating Famous Okanagan fruit leather as part of my diet. If the exact amount is eaten in the precise manner, anything can happen."

Ham then gave the opposite foursome each a packet to enjoy.

Next, Alice asked Ogopogo about his game.

"Flashes of brilliance in my short experience are only a hint of what is to come. I wagered Wong a whooping crane feather that I would get another hole in one in this tournament," Ogopogo replied and continued, "Just watch me. When the story of my life is written in *Sports Illustrated*, and not only will the article deal with mosquitoes and flies in Yellowknife, but that I was the first golfer ever to get two holes in one during the same tournament."

Jeffery noticed Ogopogo's unusual stance so he said, "Please explain your stance to me."

Ogopogo scratched and swatted while moving towards the tee.

"Well, I first stand behind the ball and line up my target, picking the spot I want the ball to land and imagine its trajectory. Next, I move opposite the ball with my hind feet together, take a practice swing and next give the ball a whack."

Ogopogo did give a whack, but it missed the ball, and like golfers the world over, although Ogopogo had a hole in one he desperately was trying to get another. But Ogopogo also had problems with the game of golf, so Ham took him aside and said to him, "Let me give you a brief lesson in playing golf." Ham said and showed the proper grip and went on, "We start with the grip, then the takeaway. Combine that with a steady position and you are all set."

When Ogopogo teed off the second time, the lesson Ham gave him, paid off because the ball soared into the air where a raven caught it while flying in space in the direction of the green. The ball, however, slipped out of the raven's beak and dropped it into the pouch of a squirrel. Believing the ball was an oversized nut, the squirrel ran to the flag and popped the ball into the hole without ever touching the ground since Ogopogo took his shot.

"I did it! I did it!" Ogopogo exclaimed. "Two holes-in-one in the tournament, on the same course, I can't believe it!"

Both holes-in-one were witnessed by tournament officials, who after searching in the latest edition of a *Golf Fact Book*, one said, "The approximate chance of someone shooting two holes-in-one on the same golf course like Ogopogo did, is 727-million and occur once in 20,741 years."

Wong conceded that he had lost a wager to Ogopogo, and reminded him of the tradition of buying those in the clubhouse a round of drinks. "One round for each hole-in-one," Wong said.

On hole number 7, Ham was the last to tee off. He pulled out a ball from his bag, walked slowly towards the tee placing the ball on a rubber matt and then picking up the driver from his bag. "Just watch the ball sail as soon as I hit it," Ham said while taking a practice swing and at the same time attacked by a swarm of mosquitoes for the umpteenth time.

Ham scratched, swatted and did a little dance, which made those in the gallery burst out with laughter. When Ham finally addressed the ball, it landed in the middle of the fairway.

"That was an exceptionally long shot," Ogopogo complimented Ham.

"It certainly was. A little further and the ball would have landed on the moon."

"Arnold Palmer couldn't have done better," Ham returned the compliment as he watched Yurina, Ogopogo and Wong tee off.

On hole number 8, the foursome teed off again, and then took their second and third strokes leaving no doubt that was the better golfer. Ham's and Yurina's ball went straight down the fairway. Ogopogo sliced.

Wong hooked. With their fourth stroke the balls landed on the green and this is where another dramatic thing happened—four ravens appeared to think he game of golf was for the birds, swooped down, picked up the balls and flew away to their nests. Well, you should have seen Ogopogo burst out with laughter. "I bet the ravens will take the balls to their nests and try hatching them."

What Wong said was that ravens were not only wise birds but like Ogopogo, scavengers, and wondered if he was going to be penalized a stroke.

"Haven't you read the rules," Ham said while looking at his scorecard. "Rules prevail on this golf course that no penalty is assessed when the ball is carried away by a raven."

On hole number 9, Ham had to sink a twenty-foot put in order to win the tournament but the ball rolled and stopped on the lip of the cup. Ham resigned himself for a playoff with an Australian, when suddenly there was a mild earthquake in Northern Canada, and the ball slipped into the cup.

Golf officials searched the rulebook but there was no mention about a ball slipping into a hole on account of an earthquake and thus Ham was declared the winner of the Yellowknife Midnight Sun Golf Tournament.

When the tournament was over, golfers came to the clubhouse that was a ramshackle structure. Wooden boards hung loose and the odd sheet of corrugated iron flapped on the roof.

A telephone wire stretched out to a pole, appearing to hold up the building. It was inside this clubhouse that some of the golfers were suffering from *Post Tournament Depression,* and as they chatted, Ogopogo bought each two-round of drinks.

It was while the golfers were enjoying themselves that Ogopogo said to Alice, who sat at the same table, "I haven't seen a golf course like the one in Yellowknife.

"The sun never sets during the month of June, northern lights come to an end and mosquitoes and flies are the size of vultures."

"And don't forget the raven's," Alice said.

Pointing to a sign on the clubhouse wall that identified golfers who got a hole in one or were victims of a raven, Alice congratulated Ham on winning the tournament.

"Now, that you name is inscribed on the Stanley and World Hockey cups, and soon the Midnight Sun Tournament scoreboard, what next as an athletic achievement?"

Ham replied, "To win the Okanagan Lake Fishing Derby."

The conversation was interrupted, however, when the bartender hollered, "Hey, Mr. Bobeck. You are wanted on the phone!"

The long distance call originated from Kelowna where an operator said, "Mr. Ham Bobek, please. Long distance is calling."

"Speaking."

When Ham was connected, Brenda his wife, on the other end said, "Honey, dear. Guess what?"

"I'm guessing that the golf balls the ravens picked up during the tournament will be hatched soon."

"No, guess again."

"The two holes-in-one that Ogopogo made will make him into an instant golf celebrity."

"No, no."

"What is it then?"

"I have been seen to Dr. Bond, and we are going to have a baby."

"Wonderful!" Ham said excitedly. "Have you picked a name?"

If it's a girl we'll name her Alice, after Alice Nichol."

"And if it's a boy?"

"I like the name, Eddy."

"Congratulations Brenda, so do I," Ham continued. "And don't forget to meet us at the airport at twelve-noon tomorrow."

"I'll be there, waiting."

Ham and Brenda Visit The City of Vernon

even years had passed since Eddy was born, and now like then, fruit trees were bursting with blossoms in the Okanagan valley. Orchardists too, were waiting for their crop of cherries to ripen so they could market the berries at the Famous Okanagan Fruit Leather Corp. factory. This particular weekend, was beautiful, as Ham, Brenda and Eddy were relaxing in the Okanagan Tower penthouse that had a commanding view of Okanagan Lake and the mountains behind it. As the threesome looked out the window they saw sailboats on the lake and people driving along roadsides appreciating the flowers and fruit tree blossoms. It was at this point that Brenda reminded Ham that Eddy had a 7:00 p. m. soccer game in Vernon, a city fifty miles north of Kelowna. The time was 1:30 p.m.

"Let's go early and along the way, see the anti-nuclear demonstration taking place there. According to the radio, a group of people are protesting about Americans testing the Cruise missile from the Arctic Ocean to the Cold Lake Military Weapons Range in Alberta," Brenda said.

"An excellent idea and at the same time we can enjoy the orchards and vineyards in bloom along Highway 97."

An hour later, after helping Eddy pack his gear, the Bobek family climbed into their Mercedes Benz and headed towards Highway 97, and then to the city of Vernon itself.

Traffic was heavy, as the tourist season in the Okanagan had begun. There were recreation vehicles, automobiles, pickup trucks and motorcycles parked on both sides of Shoreline Drive. Ham had to stop to let pedestrians through a crosswalk that included teenage girls wearing bikinis, a man riding a unicycle, an obese woman enjoying an ice cream cone, an elderly man using a walker, two young men waving their arms and singing *The Maple Leaf For Ever*. But the most attention was focused on a man who looked like Mahatma Gandhi as he walked barefoot. He was rather frail in appearance.

At the northerly outskirts of Kelowna, Ham was stopped by a traffic jam—a wedding. The bride, Rita Cardinal, was from Vernon and the groom, Charles Smith Jr. from Kelowna.

"We can't have this," Ham said to Brenda, seeing the wedding couple stranded so he got out of the car and began conducting traffic. "Let's break this up! Where are the cops? What are we paying taxes for? Okay, you to the right, and you, blowing your horn, to the left! Hold it a minute! Where do you think you're going? Let's try this again!" Ham said, and as soon as the traffic was cleared, he climbed back into the car and drove again.

After crossing the largest floating bridge in Canada, they passed by the Orchard Shopping Centre where a sign read Kelowna Regatta 'July20-July 22—No Rioting This Time.' Then another water slide, Flintstone's Bed Rock City, an estate winery, an airport and eventually, drove past Woods Lake and Ogi's Adventure Land, where next to it, Ham passed by a house that had clotheslines nearby. On each line was a family wash with jeans, skirts, T-shirts and undershoots, many shapes, colors and sizes. At the front of the house a collie dog stood watching crows sitting on a fence. Beside the fence was a garden plot.
As Ham was passing by the house, there was an old church next tot to it with a sign painted in bold black letters that read: *JESUS SAVES* and underneath in slightly smaller letters the words *REFUSE THE CRUISE.*

As Ham drove through the scenic Okanagan Valley, cradled between two mountain ranges, the traffic got heavy with long lineups going in each direction, north and south. Why was the traffic so busy aside from orchards blooming? What makes the Okanagan Valley so great? There many reasons besides Alice Nichol owning a vineyard or that the Famous Okanagan Fruit Leather International Corp. factory is in Kelowna.

First, there's the sunshine and there is plenty of it. Next, a chain of lakes stringing along the valley, each seems lovelier than the last.

The terrain is interesting throughout the eighty-mile stretch and varied with desert slopes, forests and mountains, orchards and vineyards, fruit stands, campgrounds and cattle grazing on grass. No matter what the season, the Okanagan valley is Canada's year round paradise.

As Ham drove further still, he approached a country setting where orchards backdropped snowcapped mountains.

"Isn't this pretty? The scenery is like on a post card," Brenda said.

"It certainly is pretty," Ham replied, and several miles further, as he negotiated a sharp curve with a steep embankment to the left and a cliff to the right, he pointed below. "Look, that's Kalamalka Lake. Today one can see the lake in every shade of blue and green imaginable."

Ham parked at the Viewpoint, and everyone admired the lake below and the distant splendor of the Coldstream Valley branching off to the right where the snow-capped Monashee Mountain range could be seen.

On entering Vernon City outskirts, Ham came to the Vernon Military Camp, where soldiers had trained for both World Wars.

It was here that the demonstrators, including Alice Nichol and her co-vivant, Jeffery Hunter, had gathered, and were waving placards and shouting anti-Cruise missile slogans. Ham parked his vehicle and spoke with Alice for several minutes, who at the time said, "We'll do our best to stop America and the Soviet Union deploying nuclear weapons."

What Jeffery said was something similar.

Next to the military Camp, was a multi-colored sign that greeted visitors and read: *WELCOME TO VERNON— THE LAND OF EVERYTHING.*

It was near the sign, that Ham switched on the radio and a talk-show host spoke about Father Charles Pandosy, an Oblate missionary, who spread the word of faith in the Okanagan Valley in the early days, and dabbled in the magic of horticulture.

The talk-show host said that in 1862, Father Pandosy planted apple trees at his mission what is now Kelowna, and proved to the world that this was a fine area for growing fruit. His work, though well known, was similar in many ways to the work of Jonathan Chapman, otherwise known as Johnny Appleseed. When Father Pandosy came to the Okanagan Valley, he brought with him seedlings prorogated from trees grown at Mission in the Fraser Valley. The tree was considerably larger than the apple trees grown today.

The tree planted by Father Pandosy survived at the mission location until the devastatingly cold winter of 1949. The winter also killed many cherry and apple trees in the Okanagan.

Fortunately, an offspring of this tree is still growing at the Canadian Department of Agriculture Research Station in Summerland. It took decades from the time Pandosy planted his tree for awareness to build among settlers that the Okanagan was the perfect place for fruit tree growing.

It wasn't until 1890 that the first planting of apples at the Ellis Ranch near Penticton took place. The Ellis orchard set in motion additional plantings that have resulted in the finest orchards in the world.

As Ham left Highway 97 and turned on a side road, Brenda asked, "Do you think we'll find a decent place to eat?"

The road led to a crest of a hill where Ham, Brenda and Eddy caught a glimpse of Okanagan Lake again, and then a marina, a park and a small hotel came into view.

"Let's eat at this hotel," Ham said pointing to a rustic building whose parking lot was filled with cars, trucks and motorcycles.

"It will be more private than downtown," Ham admitted.

Brenda and Eddy agreed and when the car was parked, the trio came inside and sat down in a restaurant that had a commanding view of Okanagan Lake. A waitress stepped up and handed each a menu. When the waitress returned, she asked Ham politely, "What will you have, sir?"

"What do you suggest?" Ham asked,

"Our special today is roast beef with apple pie for dessert."

"Fine, I'll have the special."

"An excellent choice, I'll have the same," Brenda continued

Eddy had an order of fish and chips, just to be different.

Scanning the dining room, Ham said, "Looks, like a very busy day."

"It is," the waitress said. "We have a wedding downstairs and many anti-cruise missile protesters staying here."

The Bobek's were enjoying their meal and at the same time, watching sailboats on the lake, when a stranger wearing blue jeans and a red jacket, approached Ham and said, "Excuse me, sir, but do I know you from somewhere."

Ham thought that he had recognized the stranger also.

"Aren't you Ham Bobek who use to play for the Toronto Maple Leafs?" the stranger continued.

"I'm him."

"Jan's and Carolina's son?"

"That's right. You have a good memory."

"I can't believe it. Ham Bobek. Do you remember me?"

"Your face is familiar. You wouldn't be Metro Kowalchuk?"

"That's me, but since that time, I have changed my name from Metro Kowachuk to Metro Baker."

"What on earth for?"

"Because of my Ukrainian heritage, people use to make jokes about me. Some of the jokes weren't exactly nice, if you know what I mean."

"I understand," Ham said. "You were also the brunt of ethnic ridicule at the Okanagan Summer Hockey and Baseball School.

Ham and Metro "Baker" first met while attending the Okanagan Summer Hockey and Baseball School. As soon as they identified each other, they shook hands and Metro said, "I remember the time when we were attending the Okanagan Summer Hockey and Baseball School and the instructor asked me what the Lady Byng Trophy was and I answered that Mr. Byng developed the Bing cherry. Do you remember that?"

"I do."

Following further conversation, Baker asked, "So what are you doing now that you stopped playing with the Leafs?"

"I'm sort off retired and one of the owners of Famous Okanagan Fruit Leather International Corp. How about yourself?"

"I quit playing hockey also, and presently with the Royal Canadian Mounted Police stationed in Vernon. Since I have several days off, I decided to invite a friend of mine, Kato Ukom, to come along and do some fishing in Okanagan Lake. Why don't you and Brenda join us?"

"It would be a pleasure, but we want to watch Eddy play soccer."

"What time is the game?"

"Seven o'clock."

"What team does Eddy play for?

"Kelowna Sun"

"And his team is playing the Vernon Lumberjacks, right?"

Ham nodded his head signifying, "Yes."

"And how are your parents?"

In reply, Ham said, "My father is suffering from cancer and an Alzheimer's disorder. Mom, she's in a nursing home with osteoporosis. How about your family?"

"I'm married," Baker said and went on, "My Mom died three years ago and Dad owns a twenty two-unit apartment block in Kelowna. My brother Tony, became a doctor, had a fling in federal politics and now is practicing medicine in Victoria."

Ham and Metro chatted for ten minutes when the policeman in casual clothing, said, "Excuse me, Ham and Brenda, I must go but once the soccer game is over we can have a beer or two in the tavern and reminisce?"

"A splendid idea, say at 9:00 o'clock."

As soon as Baker made his exit, Ham and Brenda made theirs, to the soccer game, to watch Eddy where players from both teams raced up the dirt field in cleats, kicking dust in their opponent's eyes as they demonstrated their prowess through a series of scissor kicks, punts and dives. Leaping up and around fallen players in shorts and knee socks-clad seven-year-old boys raced after a black and white ball, determined to be noticed as the quickest, most agile and highest-scoring on the field.

When the game was over, the Kelowna Peaches defeated the Vernon Lumberjacks 3-2, and Moli and Brenda were proud parents, because Eddy was one of the players who scored.

"Soccer gives Eddy a competitive arena in which to excel," Brenda said after the game was over. "It gives him a good attitude about winning."

"And Eddy hates losing, but I still maintain that the game of hockey is more interesting," Ham said.

Next, Ham and Brenda treated the team at MacDonald's. While the players were enjoying themselves, Eddy took his parents aside and asked if he could return home and stay overnight with the coach's son, John.

"Provided you behave," Brenda said.

Once permission was granted, Ham and Brenda returned to the hotel and sat in the tavern enjoying themselves while waiting for Metro Baker to return. They sat near a corner chatting, when within the crowd they spotted, racist, Charles Smith Sr. talking with the bride's father, Chief Harry Cardinal.

Ham and Brenda did not begin a conversation with Smith because of his known reputation of hating Jews, Chinese, Sikhs, and native Indians, but not necessarily in that order.

The barmaid brought Ham and Brenda each a beer, and said she was born in Vernon, and that one of her high school projects had been to uncover the history of the hotel they were in. She said the research showed that the hotel was built in 1886, the same year that St. Anne's church was built at the nearby O'Keefe Ranch, now declared a historical site.

As the barmaid was speaking to Moli and Brenda, Smith Sr. hollered across the room, "Hey, barmaid! How about another, round here?"

The barmaid served Smith's Sr. table and when she returned to Ham's, continued, "Today the hotel is still busy but the clients have changed. It's filled with loggers, ranchers, farmers, anti-Cruise missile protesters and wedding guests."

"Speaking of guests," Brenda said. "Look. Metro Baker and Kato Ukom have returned."

"Welcome back," Ham greeted the two anglers as the barmaid excused herself.

"Did you catch any fish?" Brenda, asked Metro

"We caught several rainbow trout," Metro replied and then asked, "Did the Kelowna boys win the soccer game?"

"They did, but I still maintain boys of their age should concentrate on playing hockey instead of soccer. One will never make money playing soccer in Canada.

Immediately after Baker and Ukom joined the table, Brenda asked Ukom the inevitable. "What do you do for a living?"

"I'm a man Friday who can't say no," Ukom replied.

"So what does that mean?"

"Aside from murder, I do everything, provided the price is right."

"What do you mean?" Brenda said again.

"I'm a Japanese benringa."

"Benringa? What is that?"

"I'm a convenience man."

Baker then said that Ukom's talents varied from the mundane to the absurd at which point Ukom broke in, "In addition to unplugging sinks, I paint walls, rescue cats, play catch with kids, and accompany elderly people on trips to their ancestral graves."

"So you are a Jack of all trades?"

"Something like that, I'm probably the only professional handyman in Vernon whose ancestors came from Japan."

Ukom next told his story how his community got wiped our near Vancouver during World War 11 when he was a child.

"I was born in the fishing village of Stevenson, at the mouth of the Fraser River in British Columbia when Pearl Harbor was attacked; I was one of the 22,000 Japanese Canadians who were forced into internment camps.

The Canadian government moved us into the interior of British Columbia, fearing since we know the inlets, we would help Japan plan an invasion of Canada."

When Brenda said she had heard another angle to the story, and that Japan indeed had threatened British Columbia forests on fire by sending balloons across the Pacific Ocean. Ukum burst out with laughter.

"The government didn't subject the Germans and Italians to the same measures. Did it? Our homes, our cars, our belongings were seized and sold at bargain prices," Okum said.

Following another swallow of beer Ukum continued, "At any rate my parents were moved to the mining town named New Denver in the West Kootenay.

The able-bodied men were put on road construction crews, families were kept under guard. The families were ripped apart. They had the option of moving to the sugar beet farms in Southern, Alberta or Manitoba. Later, when the war was over and restrictions were lifted because we weren't a threat to national security, I worked in many places and ended up in Vernon driving a taxi."

Ukom thought for several seconds, and continued, "Canada takes pride in is inhuman rights but it was not always the case, so I became a benringa."

During the course of beer-drinking, eating pretzels and chatting 'Ukom told of his tasks that included walking dogs, watering plants for people on trips, helping with tax forms, standing in for people in traffic court and helping the Japanese government fill out forms when they exported automobiles, computers, stereo sets and cameras into Canada.

"During the 1985 World University Games in Edmonton' I helped the Japanese team find accommodation. And when the Japanese and Arabs were searching Okanagan Lake, but found only raw sewage, I interpreted the results for them."

It was at this point that Ham interrupted Ukom and said, "I think you are full of baloney," but it was Baker, who took over, and looking at Ukom said, "You want to know something?"

"What?"

"I have a similar story, only it took place during World War 1 and it involved my grandparents who once lived in the Austro-Hungarian Empire district of Galicia before immigrating to Canada."

This time Ukom's curiosity was aroused. "What happened?"

"When World War 1 broke out and the British Empire attacked Germany, my grandparents and thousands of Ukrainians met hostility by Anglo Saxon Canadians. They were regarded as enemies of Canada and repressive measures followed, because through no fault of their own, they entered Canada as Austrians and not as Ukrainians."

"And what kind of repressive measures were taken?"

Baker's reply was, "Their naturalization papers were suspended and they lost the right to vote. Many were dismissed from their jobs and over eight thousand were rounded up by police into twenty four concentration camps across Canada. One of these camps was right here in Vernon."

"Why your grandparents were met with hostility was because Canada was at war with Germany and at one time lived in Galicia which was part of the Austro Hungarian Empire," Ham said. "And that their relatives fought for Canada by joining the armed forces, didn't matter."

As they were talking about the Canadian injustices during the two wars, a war of words erupted between Smith Sr. and Chief Harry Cardinal sitting at the nearby table.

"You guys figure you can fall back on welfare," Smith was overheard saying and the Chief Cardinal replying, "All through school I was taught the White missionary saved my soul by preaching the *Bible*."

"And what's wrong with that?" Smith said while downing another beer.

Cardinal almost laughed, "Indian has the *Bible*, the Devil has his soul and Whiteman ends up with Indian land. That is the problem."

The almost laugh turned into anger, as Cardinal banged his fist on the table and beer spilled over. Despite this, Cardinal continued, "I even thought it was a blessing to look like a Whiteman."

"You Indians are all the same, sitting in the beer parlor most of the day or drinking in the park, while I'm out there working my butt off," Smith complained. "I don't like it when Indians sit back and sap off the Canadian government."

"Nonsense!" Cardinal yelled. "You think Indian lazy. Whiteman stole our land and said he will take care of us by placing Indian on a reservation. Then Whiteman say to Indian, "We will give you money just don't bother Whiteman. Later Whiteman speaks of mineral and oil rights, but doesn't want to talk about aboriginal rights. He tells Indian how to worship and where to hunt and fish. Whiteman drives an expensive car, smokes fancy cigar, and you think Indian stupid? No sir, it's the Whiteman who lives off our poverty that is no accident."

For the next while, there was hollering and screaming, and while this was happening, Smith Sr. slipped outside and in another bar, said "This Paki." about an individual who wore a turban and asked the bartender:

"Why are we letting Sikhs into our country when there is so much unemployment? We can't solve their problem with birth control. What they do in India. I'm sure they'll eventually do in Canada."

It was near midnight, when Ham appeared tired and casually said to Brenda, "It's time we better return to Kelowna."

Brenda noticed that Ham was slurring his words, and appeared intoxicated. The drinks he had, combined with the heat and smoke and the war of words between Smith Sr. and Chief Cardinal, got to Ham, and made him drowsy.

"Drinking and driving don't mix," Brenda said to her husband.

With a Mountie in civilian clothing sitting next to him, Ham had no alternative but to get a hotel room and spend the night in Vernon.

"You are right," Ham said, and once Baker left, he staggered through the lobby with Brenda by his side. Seeing the night clerk at the registration desk, he said, "Pardon me, sir, but have you any vacant rooms?"

"Just two, Number ten and eleven," the clerk replied.

"And what have they got?"

The night clerk looked at the list again. "Room ten has a double bed but no television."

"How about room eleven?"

"Eleven has a phone but no television or bathroom. A public loo, for you should you take the room."

"We'll take number ten," Ham said and handed the clerk two-twenty-dollar bills that covered the cost of the room.

"And sir, don't expect tranquility," The night clerk said, while putting the bills into a cash register.

"Why is that?" Brenda said apprehensively.

"Because there's a country wedding in the main room downstairs," the night clerk said and went on to say the wedding had gone well earlier in the day but in the evening, had turned into a shambles because of a snide remark one family member made to another.

"So what happened to the bride?"

'She picked up a gunny sack, grabbed the wedding presents and disappeared."

As Ham and Brenda were walking up a flight of stairs to their room, it was dark along the corridor, and a bumpy sack was noticed by the door of one of the rooms. Suddenly the sack began to move. Whatever was inside appeared to be fighting for survival.

Brenda became paralyzed by a fear as the sack started to jump. Her imagination ran wild and a horror movie she had seen the night before raced through her mind.

"No doubt this sack contains the remains of a chainsaw massacre," she said to Ham as legs, arms and other parts of a body flashed through her mind. Brenda began chocking with fright and finally, although Ham was by her side, screamed as loud as she could, "Help!"

Ham grabbed Brenda by the arm and both ran downstairs, two steps at a time, and asked the night clerk to call police. The clerk as soon as he heard the complaint, dashed upstairs, knocked on the door of room number eight.

"Who is it?" a female voice asked.

"Open the door. It's the night clerk."

"Just a minute, while I get dressed."

A short time later, the bride, Rita Cardinal, appeared at the door.

"What's in the gunny sack?" the night clerk asked.

"Oh, that? There are three chickens inside which a farmer gave us as a wedding present. They are very special chickens, and my husband and I didn't want them left in our car outside for fear someone would steal them."

When the groom Cardinal poked his head through the door, Brenda was relieved and the search for Mrs. Smith Jr. discontinued.

As Ham and Brenda were going to bed, Ham placed a kiss on Brenda's lips and softly said, "What a day this has been. I didn't realize there was so much prejudice on Planet Earth."

"Neither did I," Brenda sighed, while pushing on the switch, which made the lights go out. "Thank goodness, because of apartheid, we aren't Blacks living in South Africa."

The Time Ogopogo
Helped Santa Claus

Six months after Ham and Brenda visited the city of Vernon, the Okanagan Valley experienced an unusual winter when an elderly, plump, white-bearded man in tattered clothing, walked into the Famous Okanagan Fruit Leather International Corp. store in Kelowna and seemed confused.

"There's something familiar about the old man," eight year-old Eddy Bobek, dressed in an elf's costume, said to himself but didn't know what.

As the Christmas carol *Joy to the World* played in the background, customers in the store saw the old man as a threat, a derelict, dangerous, neglected by everyone except Eddy.

When the old man mumbled something about the *North Pole* a security guard stepped up to him and said, "Get out of here, old man. Beat it."

Eddy didn't like the way the security guard treated the old man, so he walked up to him and said, "Come with me, sir. I want you to meet Mom and Dad who are in the office next door."

Eddy didn't care being a helper to a young make believe Santa his father had hired several weeks earlier, because it seems, the hired Santa smooth-talked to every woman who came into the store.

"The old man is probably the real Santa," Eddy said to his parents when he brought the old man into the office. "Why don't you hire him instead of the other Santa?'

After taking a cursory look at the old disheveled man Eddy's father said, "Come again."

"Why don't you hire him?" Eddy protested pointing to the old man.

"Can't you see, son, he's nothing but a tramp," Brenda said.

"Just smell him. He's a wino," Ham agreed.

When Eddy did smell the old man he replied, "That's not the smell of a man drinking wine."

"What is it then?" Brenda asked.

"That's sweat of a hard working man," Eddy replied. "Please hire him. I think he's the *real* Santa Claus."

"Besides sweat, what else makes you believe the old man is the real Santa? "Ham continued to cross-examine his son.

"It's the sparkle in his eyes," Eddy replied and began to cry.

"And son, you better not get too friendly with the old guy," the protective Brenda warned.

Hearing about an escape from the local jail the night before, Ham said, "You may be right. I better call the police."

And when Ham placed the call, Corporal Ron Pickens arrived at the store, and said, "Oh, him. He's not dangerous. I often see the old man at the men's hostel and the food bank. He's been in Kelowna since the nuclear explosion in Chernobyl in the Soviet Union."

To Eddy, the old man was a gentle soul and in need of a friend, so to his parents he pleaded again, "Please Mom and Dad, won't you hire him?"

As Corporal Pickens, Eddy and his parents were in conversation, the telephone rang. Ham picked up the receiver after the third ring and said, "Merry Christmas. Famous Okanagan Fruit Leather Store. How can I help you?"

It was the young Santa Ham had hired. "I won't be in this afternoon. I have the flu," the new Santa apologized.

"You have what?" Ham said, not expecting the young man to take a day off in the middle of the week.

"I won't be in this afternoon because I have the bug," the young Santa repeated.

"Oh, dear, what will we do?" Brenda said after her husband hung up the receiver and told her, that the young Santa wasn't coming to work.

"Hire the old man," Eddy said, and then taking him by the arm went on, "Come on Santa I'll find you a suit. Famous Okanagan Fruit Leather International Corp. needs you."

"We might as well give the old man a chance," Ham said to Brenda, but she wasn't that certain, "Not before he has a bath first."

When the old man had a shower and got dressed in the storage room, and began work by talking to children, he ran into his first encounter with Brenda. It seems that one of the customers found an empty wine bottle in front of the store and brought it inside placing it near the chair where the old man sat.

Seeing the bottle, Brenda nearly had a bird, admonished the old man, and then pointing her finger at Eddy said, "See, I told you the old man is a bum. Look. He drank an entire bottle of Mrs. Nichol's Friend of the Okanagan wine and has been at work only an hour."

The old man refused to be subjected to further embarrassment, so he took off his Santa suite, thanked Eddy for his interest in him and left through the side door.

"Santa, come back! Santa, come back!" Eddy hollered but it was too late, the old man had disappeared.

"What are we going to do for a Santa now?" Ham said. "The only way we'll attract customers is if we have a Santa in the store."

Seeing the predicament the store was in, Brenda said, "Well, I'll play the role of Santa myself until we find another."

Brenda quickly put on the Santa suit the old man had worn, and went up and down the store ringing a bell, but Eddy looked at her suspiciously and said, "Mom, since when does Santa have a woman's voice?"

Brenda was so embarrassed that she decided her career as Santa Claus was over, but it was just the beginning, as Mrs. Santa Claus. She had a Mrs. Santa Claus costume made that day.

The following day, after a considerable amount of publicity on the radio, Brenda arrived at the store wearing a Mrs. Santa Claus costume made of red and white satin.

She became an instant hit and hundreds of children lined up for a chance to chat with Mrs. Santa Clause. One girl, about seven, and wearing a snowsuit, even refused to go home when it was time to close the store.

"What is your name?" Brenda still wearing her Mrs. Claus costume, asked the little girl but she refused to give it.

"Then have you got a phone number so I can call your mother?" Brenda asked, but the little girl shook her head.

"Will you come to my home and have a piece of Christmas cake with us?" the little girl asked.

"Has your Mom got company?" Brenda continued to question the child.

"It doesn't matter. Mrs. Claus comes first," the little girl replied and asked, "Are you coming to my house on Christmas Eve?"

"If I don't, Santa will."

"I'll light a candle in my bedroom window so you know exactly where I live."

"Fine," Brenda said, but at that precise moment, Eddy came to her side, and seeing the girl on his mother's lap said, "Kim Jones. What are you doing here at this hour?"

Surprised Brenda said, "Eddy, do you know Kim?"

"We are in the same class at Belgo Elementary School. Do you want me to show you where she lives?"

"It would help," Brenda said, picked the little girl up and with Eddy by her side, drove to Adventure Road and the home where Kim lived.

Mrs. Jones lived in a modest apartment in a walkup and said she had bought her daughter an inexpensive snowsuit, warm shirts, shoes, socks, mitts and underwear at the end of last month and that was the reason her kitchen cupboards were empty.

"And my welfare cheque isn't due until after Christmas," Kim's mother said.

A bag of frozen vegetables, some hamburger, a jar of peanut butter, a litre of milk and a package of pasta were all Kim and her mother had left to eat. As for conversation, Kim's mother said, "It's hard, really hard to be on welfare. A lot of the time I would have gone for extra help but I didn't because I didn't think I would get it."

Kim's mother said she felt trapped by the welfare system because she was healthy and willing to work. "But you know, one can't apply for jobs in jeans I'm wearing." There was a rip on the knee. "There's so much one can't do when one is on welfare. You are trapped and it takes a long, long time, if ever, to get off."

"How long have you been on welfare?" Brenda asked.

"Six months."

"And you would like to work?"

"I would."

"Good. I have a job for you."

"Doing what?"

"Playing the role of Mrs. Santa Claus at the Famous Okanagan Fruit Leather store and functions. After that as a clerk. The pay is good and the rewards are many."

Kim's mother agreed to play the role of Mrs. Santa Claus and while on her way back to the store, Brenda and Eddy drove past St. Anne's church where there was a light in the basement window.

"Let's stop here for a while," Eddy said to his mother. "I think this is the church where the old man stops to pray."

"Let's do that," Brenda said and parked the car in a way that had an excellent view of a partially opened window. As it turned out the old man was inside but he wasn't praying. He was at a Food Bank in search of food.

"Number 92," Sister Rose was heard saying and the old man approached her desk for a hamper he had been waiting for—slightly bruised grapes, bananas beginning to blacken, tin cans of pork and beans, soup, fish cakes and a sack of skimpy hamburger meat.

Brenda and Eddy waited patiently until the old man picked up his hamper and when he stepped outside the church, Eddy hollered, "Santa! Santa! It's me, Eddy!"

The old man recognized the voice and came to the car. To Brenda he didn't appear dangerous or a derelict. As a matter of fact, he looked quite respectable despite the tattered clothing he wore, long hair and white beard.

"Why are you doing at the Food Bank?" Eddy asked to the old man. "I thought Santa took care of everything."

The old man smiled and replied, "I was at the Food Bank because like so many people in Kelowna, I'm unemployed. Once you reach my age no one wants to hire you."

"I have a job for you," Brenda said.

"What would you want me to do?" the old man asked. "I worked for you previously but you fired me."

Brenda felt embarrassed. "I'll give you another chance. How about being a Santa again?"

"What happened to the Santa that's there already?"

"He's still not feeling well."

"Okay," the old man said. "That's kind of you but, I'll work only until he recovers."

"That may be a long, long time," Eddy said.

"I'll work only until Christmas Eve," the old man continued.

"And then what?" Brenda probed.

"I should have enough money saved by then, which will enable me to get to the North Pole."

"To the North Pole?" Brenda said as a feeling came over her that the old man was confused.

"See, I told you he's the real Santa," Eddy said which led the old man to smile again, but not say another word.

"You may start tomorrow but not before you agree to a personal favor," Brenda continued.

"What kind of a favor?"

"I'll do that if you agree in doing me a favor in return."

This time it was Brenda's turn to say, ""What kind of a favor?"

"That after we surprise the pupils at Belgo Elementary School, you and your husband join Mrs. Jones and me in entertaining the patients in the psychiatric ward of the Kelowna General Hospital."

Brenda thought for a moment.

"The old man must be a mental case," she said to herself but to the old man, "It's a deal."

The following day, during the lunch recess, the old man and Kim's mother, in their proper costumes, the pupils of Belgo School had an early Christmas, thanks, to the donation from Famous Okanagan Fruit Leather. The jolly Santa and vivacious Mrs. Clause, delivered candy canes, fruit leather and gifts of books. In return they accepted big smiles, crushing hugs and requests to visit the girls and boys on Christmas Eve. Two pupils even slipped a note into Santa's packet. The first read:

Dear Santa,

I am seven years old, but don't expect a happy Christmas because my parents are separated. Mom is presently on welfare and doesn't get much money. Last month she bought me a snowsuit and other clothing. For this Christmas would you please bring me a toboggan, so I can slide down the hills like girls and boys are doing?

"I love seeing you in shopping malls because you give the kids candy canes. You'll know the apartment I live in, because I'll have a candle burning in my bedroom window.

And Santa, see if you can find my Mom a job, and when you come to visit me on Christmas Eve please don't catch a cold.
Signed,
Kim Jones

The second note read:
Dear Santa,
I'm eight years old. There aren't many things I want for Christmas this year including your good health. I know things have been rough for you since the nuclear explosion in Chernobyl and your reindeer got sick. I understand the elves and Mrs. Clause aren't feeling well also. If you feel the reindeer are unable to pull your sleigh this Christmas Eve, I know someone who will.
Signed,
Eddy Bobek

At the psychiatric ward at the Kelowna Regional Hospital that evening, there were smiles on the faces of patients as Santa, Mrs. Jones, Brenda and Moli helped the patients open their gifts.

As soon as the electronic door closed behind them, Ham and Brenda realized they were in an institution. To have Christmas on the psychiatric ward is all about the patients could hope for.
For some long-time residents it meant the holiday season was a time that could be sad and often lonely, particularly for those without a family or friends. That was why every year, staff at the hospital arranged to bring the spirit

of Christmas to the patients by holding a party with a Christmas meal, entertainment and of course Santa.

"Patients who do not have relatives are not left out," the ward supervisor, Olive Branch, said to Ham and Brenda who were sitting at the same table and enjoying their meal. "We make certain that a patient doesn't go away without receiving a gift."

After the table was cleared and Santa distributed the gifts, the ward supervisor said to Santa, "Why don't you lead them in singing of carols?" And he did, with Mrs. Santa at the piano everyone, including patients and staff, sang Christmas carols for the next hour beginning with *Silent Night* and ending with *Joy to the World*.

"It makes me feel happy; the patients are so unhibited, they are not afraid to show joy and surprise," Brenda said as she, Ham, Santa and Mrs. Santa were about to leave for home.

"It really makes one feel good inside when someone makes the patients happy," Santa agreed and then as a side remark went on, "That is why I must be at the North Pole Christmas Eve."

The following afternoon, Ed met with the old man in the storage room, as the old man was preparing himself for the next shift. The room overlooked Okanagan Lake and the mountains behind it. Twice the old man tried to speak and twice he failed.

"Is something the matter?" Eddy asked the old man, slumped into a chair. The old man's head began to spin so he closed his eyes and finally said, "Eddy, I have read the note you have written to me and . . ."

"And, what?"

The old man was desperately forcing himself to speak. His voice was cracking and sounded strange to Eddy's ears. The old man took a deep breath, Eddy by the hand, and finally said, "Eddy, you are right. I am the real Santa Claus."

A sigh of relief came over Eddy as he exclaimed, "I knew it! I knew it! I must tell my Mom and Dad!"

As Eddy was walking towards the door, the old man stuck out his arm. "Don't. It could be a traumatic experience. It could be unpleasant for all of us. I don't want any publicity, just one thing."

"What?"

"Your note."

"What about the note?"

There was a pain coming back to the old man's voice and while taking a step towards the window said, "Eddy, my reindeer are unable to deliver the toys to the girls and boys this Christmas because they are still not feeling well due to what happened in Chernobyl."

"Tell me more."

"The nuclear fallout has reached the North Pole causing the reindeer to, how shall I put it, not feel good. Rudolph's nose doesn't glow as brightly as it did last Christmas and Donner, Comet and the rest of the reindeer are sidelined with cramps."

"And?"

"And I'm worried that within me, something snapped, so I spent a short while in the Kelowna hospital but now I feel fine."

"So you need help to deliver the toys on Christmas Eve to the girls and boys?"

Santa buried his face in his hands. "Maybe it's improper for me to ask but you are right. I need all the help I can get."

"I always said the world needs Santa." Eddy said.

Taking note that Christmas Eve was rapidly approaching, Santa said to Eddy, "Do you think, if I speak to your parents, that they will help me by using the Famous Okanagan Fruit Leather executive jet, Apple 1, to distribute the toys?"

"There are no airports large enough for the jet to land near the North Pole," Eddy said. "But relax, Santa I know someone who is a solution to the problem."

"Are you suggesting Sister Rose at the Food Bank?"

"Sister Rose enjoys helping people in Kelowna is a known fact, but this is someone else who may help."

"A friend of yours?"

"Not only a friend of mine, but like Sister Rose, a friend of everyone in Kelowna. His name is Ogopogo."

"Ogopogo? I have heard of him. Ogopogo who lives in, or near Okanagan Lake?"

"And the Okanagan Tower. You see Santa, Ogopogo is a director of maintenance at our store."

"I didn't know that."

"There are a lot of things people don't know about Ogopogo. I'll introduce him as soon as you are finished with your shift."

As soon as Santa was finished working his shift, he summoned Eddy and together they went to the apartment where Ogopogo lived in Okanagan Tower, but he was nowhere in sight. Fortunately they met Wong in a common area, as he was on his way to the laboratory and said, "Ogopogo is taking part in a Christmas carol concert at the Penticton Game Farm."

When Eddy and Santa told Wong the dilemma Santa was in, and the reason they wished to speak to Ogopogo, Wong said to them," I'm certain Ogopogo will help.but there is a problem."
"What kind of a problem?"
"We'll have to make Ogopogo fly like a bird so he can pull the sleigh like the reindeer did last Christmas Eve."

"I never thought of that," Santa said and was delighted when Wong went on, "You and Eddy go and speak to Ogopogo. By tomorrow I'll invent a fruit leather that will make Ogopogo soar like an eagle."
And Wong did. The fruit lather was apricot flavored.
When Eddy and Santa, without his Santa suit, arrived at the Penticton Game Farm they were greeted by the owner, Dr. Bond. The farm was decorated with wreaths, holly, mistletoe and candles everywhere, a sign that Christmas Eve was just around the corner.

There were Christmas decorations symbolizing belief in an everlasting life, but the decoration that caught Santa's and Eddy's attention the most, was the nativity scene of figures of Mary, Joseph, baby Jesus, the wise men, angels, shepherds, and live animals around it, singing *Come All Yee Faithful*. There were exotic species from India, Africa, China, Tibet and Mongolia. There were also animals from other parts of the world including Australia and South America.

As soon as the caroling ended, Eddy spotted Ogopogo standing next to a camel, and said to Santa, "Look. There is Ogopogo, chatting with the camel. Let's go and speak to him."

And when they did, Ogopogo said he would be delighted to pull Santa's sleigh. "The problem exists however, how to pull the sleigh since I can't fly."

Mr. Wong is taking care of that. This very moment, he's working on a fruit leather formula which will enable you to do that," Eddy said.

"In that case we will use the company jet and as soon as we fly over the North Pole. I can parachute to Santa's toy factory."

Early next morning, Apple 1 and a pilot were already waiting for Santa and Ogopogo at the Kelowna Airport and head for the North Pole. Moli and Brenda were going to come for the ride but in the last minute decided since it was Christmas Eve, to stay in Kelowna for a shopping scrum that usually takes place at that time of the year.

As soon as the jet reached the Arctic Circle, Ogopogo said to Santa, "It's an unusually mild winter. There are no trees in this part of the world but plenty of ice and snow making it appear as if Planet Earth has been dusted with icing sugar."

And then when they reached the North Pole, the jet circled Santa's workshop and at an appropriate time the pilot said to Ogopogo, "Okay. You and Santa may parachute down. Good luck."

It was the dark season at the North Pole, but despite the lack of sunshine, Ogopogo and Santa made a perfect landing. Mrs. Clause was the first to greet Santa and Ogopogo. "Welcome back to the North Pole, Santa," she said giving the old man a huge hug. "Where have you been for the last three months?"

"All Santa would say is, "In Kelowna, British Columbia."

After formally introducing Ogopogo, Santa then congratulated the elves for making so many attractive toys during his absence.

Seeing what an isolated place the North Pole was, Ogopogo asked Mrs. Claus, "What do you do for recreation here when not working in the toy factory?"

"There are parties, of course, and plenty of music. We dance the reels and circles. There are traditional contests and games and near Christmas there's a feast for the whole community—turkey to be sure, but also caribou, seal, fish and muldtuk."

"It must be quite a time," Ogopogo said. "What else?"

"Other activities include playing checker-like games with bones of seal flippers. The most popular, however, are hunting contests where elves compete to bring back the most number of ptarmigan, as well as seals, caribou and fish in a given time. And then the elves are kept busy designing toys for the following Christmas."

Mrs. Claus looked towards Ogopogo. "Speaking of fish, would you like something to eat before you and Santa deliver the toys to the good girls and boys?"

Ogopogo felt his tummy. "I do feel hungry. I didn't realize Kelowna was so far from the North Pole."

For Ogopogo, Mrs. Claus prepared an Arctic Char salad and for her husband, a ptarmigan meal. They also had soup, cookies and cake and herbal tea to drink.

An hour later, Santa put on his new red suit, combed his hair and beard, cleaned his spectacles with tissue paper and said to Mrs. Claus, "Thank you for a fine meal, dear."

To Ogopogo, Santa said, "Time now to deliver the toys throughout the world for the girls and boys."

"I'm ready," Ogopogo said and joined Santa and Mrs. Claus by walking to the toy factory that was a short distance from Santa's house, which was made out of ice and shaped like an igloo.

Once inside the factory, Ogopogo noticed a special closeness among the elves that had the toys neatly placed on rows and rows of shelves. One of the elves, the shop foreman, walked up to Ogopogo and in a soft voice, said. "Since the reindeer aren't feeling well this Christmas Eve, who is going to pull the slight tonight? Husky dogs?"

Ogopogo surprised the elf foreman when he said, "No, that is why I am here."

Ogopogo knew what was expected of him.

At first, the elves laughed and joked and one even said louder than the rest, "Ogopogo, with your figure, how can you?"

"Just watch me," Ogopogo replied.

As soon as the elves realized Ogopogo was serious, they called more elves and brought the sleigh packed full of toys, outside. Next the elves hitched Ogopogo to the sleigh and once he popped a piece of fruit leather into his mouth, turned to his normal size and said, "Are we ready for takeoff?"

"Not before I do an inspection," Santa replied as he got his logbook and made sure all paperwork was in order. Then he slowly walked around the sleigh and checked Ogopgo's harness and the landing gear.

Santa reviewed his weight and balance calculations for the sled's enormous payload. Finally he climbed into the sleigh, fastened his seatbelt, and checked the compass and the jolly man in red said, "Okay, Ogopogo, we are on our way."

The elves and Mrs. Claus shoved the sleigh from the rear until it had the right trajectory and was off the snow and ice. Like a loon taking off from a lake Santa and Ogopogo were airborne and the elves and Mrs. Clause cheering them on until they were out of sight. So did the polar bears cheer, when they saw Ogopogo flying and Santa in a sleigh behind him hollering, "Onward Ogopogo! Onward! To the top of the clouds. We must visit all the good girls and boys on Planet Earth before midnight."

As they were southward bound, Santa laughed, whistled and sang. This was the day he was happiest of the year. As they flew further south, Santa and Ogopogo encountered their first trouble near Inuvik, North West Territories where a blizzard was in the making. Thanks to Santa's experience, however, he steered Ogopogo around the storm and by the time they reached Yellowknife, the entire sky was lit because of the aurora borealis, the northern lights.

As soon as Santa and Ogopogo were racing through Alberta, they were picked up on radar and a radio station in Edmonton described Santa's trip this way: "We interrupt this program of Christmas carols to bring you a news bulletin:

Santa has left the North Pole to visit all the girls and boys but this Christmas Eve isn't using his regular reindeer but Ogopogo to pull his sleigh. It seems that Comet, Cupid, Donner, Blitson, Rudolph and the remaining reindeer have become ill because of a nuclear explosion in Chernobyl, Soviet Union. Please stay tuned for further bulletins."

As Santa and Ogopogo kept flying southward, a dramatic thing happened—a fiery object streaked across the sky from east to west almost hitting them.

"What was that? Aliens from another planet?" Ogopogo hollered back to Santa.

"The fireball was a meteor. Not an unusual thing for Northern, Alberta," Santa hollered back.

"It happened so quickly that when I saw the fiery object I nearly . . ." Ogopogo said but did not finish the sentence.

"You nearly what?"

"I nearly lost my sense of direction."

Between the meteor incident and the next time Santa and Ogopogo spoke to each other, they were flying over the Rocky Mountains. There were no more northern lights but a bright full moon took over to guide them.

By the time they reached the Okanagan Valley in British Columbia, large snowflakes were falling. The flakes were so huge that they made it difficult for Santa and Ogopogo to land.

After circling Kelowna several times Santa spotted a light shining in a bedroom walkup apartment.

"Look! Over there! Near Belgo Elementary School," Santa said to Ogopogo and when they did land, discovered the candle belonged to Kim Jones.

Santa immediately climbed down Kim's chimney and although the hole was a tight one, Santa managed to slip Kim a toboggan.

Next, Santa climbed into the chimney where Eddy Bobek and his parents lived. Besides leaving Eddy a toy he also left him a "Thank You" note in an envelope with a copy of a letter from Santa's doctor. In part the letter read: "Santa you are now fit as a fiddle and in shape like a brand new drum. Both physically and mentally you are A-1. Merry Christmas, from the staff of the Kelowna General Hospital.

Signed,

Dr. Jack Calvert.

P. S. And Santa, despite what happened to the reindeer, because of the Chernobyl nuclear incident, they will be healthy next Christmas.

After visiting Kim's and Eddy's homes, Santa and Ogopogo visited homes of other girls and boys throughout the world, leaving each a toy and a wish for a Merry Christmas, peace throughout the world, and a prosperous New Year.

SEVEN

Turmoil in the Bobek Family

When Ham's father got to be sixty-five, he moved in with Ham, Brenda and their thirteen-year-old son Eddy. They thought the senior Bobek would live with them until he died. Each was aware that Jan Bobek had skin cancer and an Alzheimer's disorder. Ham's mother, Carolina, meanwhile, was in a nursing home and doctors had given her five months to live.

The trauma of the first step of taking care of an elderly and sick man didn't end there, it was just the beginning. Ham's father's Alzheimer's disorder progressed to the stage where caring for him led to arguments with relatives, censure of neighbors and pressure on their own relationship that ruined their marriage.

Even admitting his father into the Kelowna Extended Care Unit brought a spectre of guilt and recrimination that Ham will never forget. An editorial in the local newspaper put it this way: "The dilemma which Ham and Brenda Bobek face is experienced by thousands of people each year and many more will face in the future. Kelowna, because of its moderate climate and a retirement haven for many, will certainly have its share."

Before Jan Bobek moved in, Ham and Brenda discussed alternatives for him. Brenda was reluctant at first, but due to his persuasiveness Ham said, "Dad can live with us.

"Be placed in an institution or we can help him lead a semi-independent life using community support services."

After discussing the alternatives, they decided on the first. Moli felt it was the right decision and one of the most important he had ever made. Ham's' mother, Carolina, had already been placed in a nursing home. It was both, because of her age, that she couldn't get around suffering from osteoporosis.

Moli recalled that his father took care of his own mother before she died. He cared for her, medicated her and even carried her to the bathroom. "It was a symbol that every son should be—tolerant and kind," the senior Goalie said to Moli at the time. "I'm frustrated that it's something beyond her control that makes this necessary. I want to keep her alive as long as possible."

And when Jan's mother did die, Ha remembered his father standing by the graveside while Father Kubek at the time said, "May her soul rest in Heaven."

Then when the Reverend blessed the coffin with holy water Ham's father burst into tears. After recovering from the down feeling, he placed a hand on Ham's shoulder, and said to him, "Son, if you aren't going to take care of your parents, who are you going to take care of them? When I get old and gray I want you to treat me in the same way."

The first thing Ham and Brenda noticed was that Jan Bobek's memory was fading and his habits were appalling. Jan once recalled that he had photographed Ogopogo but wasn't certain when or where.

Later, he recalled Ham playing hockey for the Toronto Maple Leafs and Sam baseball for the Blue Jays, but couldn't recall the year. As for habits, the most prominent one was to go to the bathroom but not close the door behind him. He would also start making dinner by putting plaster fill into a dish and say, "I'm making a hamburger."

The last straw came when Brenda entered his room and there was a pungent smell. "What is this?" Brenda asked pointing to a plastic bag.

"It's filled with pucks and baseballs," the elder Bobek said.

"What kind of pucks and baseballs?"

"Pucks that were used when Ham played for the Toronto Maple Leafs and balls that were used when Sam played for the Toronto Blue Jays."

As it turned out they weren't pucks or baseballs, but laundry, and it had been in his room a long time.

As soon as Brenda's relatives found out that Jan was living with Ham and Brenda they began to react. One uncle said, "Look, they're fleecing the old man."

Another said something similar while an aunt criticized Ham and Brenda for being over protective. The accusations went on and on.

Jan Bobek would often ask about Ham's and Brenda's health and they responded "Just fine." When they asked about his, they knew his speech and memory were failing.

"It's incredible how some Alzheimer's patients can hide the disease for so long," Brenda said. "This is typical of Alzheimer's sufferers who appear outwardly healthy while the disease quietly pillages the brain."

Ham agreed with Brenda's assessment, and a day later, when he asked his father if he had brushed his teeth, he removed his false ones and handed them to Ham. And on the same day, Brenda asked Jan if he was hungry and he replied, "No, never," that something was definitely wrong.

Before Ham and Brenda realized how strange Jan had gone they traveled to Vancouver for a weekend. While away, a tenant at Okanagan Tower, Mae Hemingway, saw Jan cleaning the walls of their penthouse with strips of fruit leather.

In the morning, he locked himself out and wandered the streets of Kelowna, where RCMP Corporal Ron Pickens, brought him home and said, "Jan Bobek, everyone knows your sons were super stars playing hockey and baseball. You need care and attention and should be in an institution where there are meals on wheels and you are cared by doctors and nurses."

When Ham and Brenda returned home, Miss Hemingway, living in a condo nearby, rushed over and said, "Why are you folks leaving the old man alone? Why don't you institutionalize him?"

Another neighbor, Charlene Jovie, agreed and said, "Can't you see Karol is senile?"

A short time later, cancer treatments for Karol were every day, which took at least an hour from Ham's work.

When Brenda's aunt, Jessa, learned Jan had cancer as well as Alzheimer's, she reacted with a barrage of suggestions. "Moli, why don't you do this? Moli, why don't you do that? I knew all along living with Brenda and you wouldn't work. Has Ham's will been changed?"

When the first uncle found out, he brought along a bottle of vitamin pills. And when the same uncle said, "Brenda even isn't a member of the family" the strain on Ham and Brenda became so intense, that their marriage began to suffer. "It's difficult to get intimate. We sneak into the kitchen for a hug or a kiss and the ghost follows us," Brenda lamented.

"What you are saying is true," Ham replied, but from that day onward, one argument followed another.

One day Ham's father chased Eddy throughout the living room with a fly swatter. It isn't clear, if Ham's father thought Eddy was a fly or if Eddy did his grandfather a misdemeanor. At any rate, this enraged Brenda and she let out a scream at Ham. "You father is a dangerous man!

Who needs this? If you won't institutionalize the old man, then I will pick up my belongings and leave!"

Han replied, his voice trembling, "Then leave."

"Thanks a lot, I guess I will," Brenda said and ten minutes later was packed and out the door.

The problem of taking care of Ham's' father increased because he became incontent, couldn't recognize Ham or Eddy and frequently went to the storage room where his memorabilia was kept. To Ham, who often helped his father negotiate the stairs, Jan would often say, "Where is Carolina? Is she in Heaven yet?"

One day while climbing the same stairs, Ham's father took a tumble and broke his hip. It wasn't certain if Jan broke his hip and then fell or if he fell first and then broke the hip, but Ham did the most natural thing a son could do—he called an ambulance that took his father to the Kelowna General Hospital. After the hip surgery, Ham's father was transferred to the Extended Care unit.

"I know our limits," Ham said to Eddy. "We will leave granddad there until he recovers."

The next day, Ham met with the Extended Care social worker, Anna Brown, to determine the most appropriate form of medical and social care for his father. "Sometimes home tensions become explosive," Ms Brown said after Moli told her that Brenda had left and was planning to sue for divorce. "One man I know, at ninety-four, assumed his former authoritative role and caned his seventy-two-year-old daughter caring for him."

Ms. Brown cited other examples of children taking care of their parents who got into arguments and said, "It's an endless thing,"

But the endless care by Ham came to an end that evening when he and Eddy were sitting in the living room watching television and the telephone rang.

Hoping it was a call from Brenda; Ham sprang to his feet, picked up the receiver and after the first ring said, "Hello."

It was Dr. Bond who informed Moli that his father had died.

Following the the funeral, endless care for Ham was replaced by endless guilt.

"Under normal circumstances Mom would not want a divorce," Ham said to Eddy as they sat in the living room.

"Yes, Alzheimer's disease is a terrible thing," Eddy said as he tried to comfort his father who was sad and depressed.

"So is missing you mother," Ham said, "If only there was a way to reclaim her."

Then Eddy changed the subject and asked, "I wonder how Granny Bobek is doing at the nursing home?"

"Well, let's find out," Ham said and they did, by climbing into car and driving to the Borden Manor Nursing Home.

As soon as Han and Eddy entered the nursing home lobby, they heard a voice saying, "You are doing fine

Mrs. Bobek, Left foot up. Left foot down. Right foot up.
Right foot down."

As Ham and Eddy came within speaking range, they saw a
nurse guiding Granma Bobek with their daily exercises.

Carolina Bobek had been a patient in the nursing home
for three years. Besides his mother being seriously ill
and his father dying recently, Ham had another crisis on
hand, Brenda had indeed petitioned for a divorce and the
document was served on him.

For a while at least, Ham thought visiting his mother
was a diversion from the legal hassle that was about to
take place. The least Ham could do was to spend several
minutes with his mother whose life, like his marriage,
was coming to an end.

"Hello," a nurse greeted Ham and Eddy as she interrupted
conducting the exercises. The nurse apologized that the
receptionist had temporarily stepped outside and that
besides her own nursing duties, she also attended to
visitors and answered phone calls at the switchboard.

"Hello," Ham replied. "I'm Ham Bobek and this is my
son, Eddy. We are here to visit with Carolina Bobek."

"Are you from out of town?" the nurse, who identified
herself as Mrs. Betty Bartlett, asked,

Shaking his head Ham said, "No, you know how it is.
One thing leads to another. We are busy at the Famous
Okanagan factory and store and don't seem to find the
time to visit with Granny as often as we should."

"I understand," Mrs. Bartlett said and then hollered to
another nurse, "Linda, would you take care of Mrs. Bobek
while I bring her son to visit with his mother!"

There was a *No Smoking* sign in the lounge area and under the sign a bulletin board with the words printed with chalk, "Present Temperature 76."

Once Ham and Eddy left the lounge where men and women, all elderly, most disabled and in wheelchairs, others walking about with the use cane's and walkers, but all pioneers of Kelowna, the nurse led Ham and Eddy to an auxiliary room where Carolina was sitting, bent over and head cocked to one side. She appeared helpless, humiliated and sobbing. On the table in front of her were her dentures soaking in a glass of water.

Sitting across the table from Granny was an elderly man, and every time he took a deep breath, his mouth opened and two large protruding monster-like incisor teeth appeared. The scent of a smoked cigarette became his signature of nearness. Glancing at the elderly man, Eddy said softly to his father, "That man reminds me of Dracula."
Ham did not pay attention to what Eddy had said as he was concentrating on his mother who had failed to recognize him.
"Shall we move your mother to her room?" Mrs. Bartlett asked. "I think Eddy feels uncomfortable in this room."
"Do it," Ham said and when they reached Carolina's room #17, Mrs. Bartlett put her into a bed and comforted her by placing a pillow behind her back.
"There," Mrs. Bartlett said when she finished comforting Granny. She turned towards Ham said,, "You may now visit with your mother in privacy and tell her that you love her."

When Eddy asked how his grandmother was doing, Mrs. Bartlett's reply was, "Considering your Granny's age and what she has gone through as an immigrant, a World War, difficult economic times and raising two sons, she is doing well. Mind you she does have memory lapses, bedsores and decalcified bones."

"Is it Alzheimer's disease?" Eddy asked recalling that what his grandfather, Jan, had.

"No," Mrs. Bartlett replied shaking her head. "The disorder is known as osteoporosis."

As soon as Mrs. Bartlett left the room to see another patient across the hallway, Carolina motioned that she wanted her bedpan.

"Yoo hoo, nurse, Mrs. Bartlett!" Ham hollered. "Granny has to go to the bathroom!"

Mrs. Bartlett hollered back, "Just a second."

"But Grammy has to go now. Better hurry."

As soon as Mrs. Bartlett returned, she pulled the dividing curtain and asked Ham and Eddy to be excused. When Granny finished doing her thing, Mrs. Bartlett said, "Never fails. They all want to go to the bathroom at the same time. You may now come in."

As soon as Ham and Eddy returned to the room and were alone, Granny looked up at Ham and finally said in a soft quivering voice, "You are Ham?"

"I am," Ham replied and pointing to Eddy continued, "And this is Eddy, my son and your grandchild."

Granny Bobek smiled and minutes later, Ham presented her with a family portrait taken prior to Ham and Brenda separating.

"You have one son?" Granny said while surveying the portrait. "And where is your wonderful wife, Brenda?"

Ham was going to say, "Suing me for a divorce," but used good judgment and didn't. At Granny's age and state of her health, if the truth were known, it could be devastating. All her life Granny had been an upright Christian and did not believe in either abortion or divorce.

"Brenda is windsurfing on Okanagan Lake," Ham answered instead. He didn't lie and yet he wasn't evading the question.

When Granny said, "Brenda deserves the best and I hope she's good at it," Ham smiled, and when she said, "I'm happy Brenda became your wife even if she used to be a fan of the Montreal Canadiens and New York Yankees," he took her hand and stroked the thread of calluses that meandered down the side of her palm.

Carolina's mind seemed to wander when she continued and said, "You know, son, I pray daily to the Black Madonna of Czestochowa and Saint Sam that I may die soon."

Ham wasn't surprised. He had often heard his mother pray for a splendid life after death and had no particular stand on euthanasia, but realized his mother was in a great deal of pain and suffering,

"Old and chronic people should have the right to die," Granny said, when suddenly a nearby patient singing in the hallway interrupted her. This particular patient was singing in Polish, *Jeszce Polska Nie Zigniela*, a national song in Poland.

The patient was another Kelowna pioneer, Julia Stark, who immigrated to Canada the same year that Jan and

Carolina did, and through a radio newscast learned that there was martial law in Poland, after Lech Walesa of Solidarity had been arrested in Gdansk.

Eddy found the singing rather amusing, not realizing that elderly people cling to their heritage even though they immigrated to Canada. The singing got louder and as far as Julia Stark was concerned, Poland would never capitulate to the Soviet Union or Communism. After all, Pope John 11 was Polish, and had a hotline to Heaven. When the singing subsided, Granny motioned to Ham, "Please show me the portrait again."

After studying the faces Granny said, "Ham, do you want to know something?"

Curious Ham said, "What?"

"Brenda is a beautiful woman. You are fortunate to have her as your wife, always at your side."

Ham nodded his head but did not answer. "Oh, how I wish that was true," he thought as Granny continued, "With all the divorces these days, common law living, in bed today and wed tomorrow. Brenda must be from the old school that stresses family, children and taking care of their parents?"

Moli remained silent.

Then Granny said, "Before I die I would like to see Brenda one more time."

"Oh, mother," Ham finally broke his silence while brushing a salty tear from his eye.

Seeing the teardrops Granny said, "Ham, is something the matter?"

"It's all right Mom. It's all right," Han answered suppressing the feeling how he felt.

By now, Eddy felt restless and asked if he could excuse himself and wait in the car that was parked in the parking lot. With Eddy gone, Ham spent another fifteen minutes with his mother. He glanced at her bedside desk and the clock on it read 3:00 p. m.

Granny was experiencing difficulty in keeping her eyes open and said it was at this time of the day that she took her regular nap. Her breathing was shallower when Ham first came to see her, so he took her arthritic and callused hand and to himself softly said, "These are the hands that pointed to Brenda when Mom said she would make me the ideal wife. These are the hands that originally came from Poland and prepared thousands of meals, kneaded the bread, milked the cows, fed the hogs and chickens and taught me to read the *Bible*, to play the piano and sing *O Canada*. These are the hands that scrubbed the floors, worked the soil and cradled Holi and me when we were children. These are the hands that spanked me when I was wrong and caressed me when I deserved praise.

These are the hands of the Man from Galilee and did whatever was necessary to give our family its sense of cohesiveness in a large and lonely country."

Soon tears and fear shaped Ham's next move as his mother closed her eyes and said almost in a whisper, "Son, I'll rest now. You better go home and spend some time with Brenda."

"Okay, Mom," Ham replied in almost a whisper too, but knew he would never see his mother alive again. He pressed his lips against hers one more time and left the room closing the door behind him.

As Ham proceeded towards the exit, he felt uncomfortable as a chill ran down his spine. He had kept things from her when doctors said that she had only five months to live. It was his secret.

And then, as Ham passed through the final door, he thanked Mrs. Bartlett for allowing him and Eddy spend some time with Granny Bobek, and quickly joined Eddy, who was waiting in the car listening to the radio announcer giving the news. The announcer said that over one hundred people had already registered for an Alzheimer's ten-kilometer marathon fundraiser from Kelowna to Rutland. Eddy was one of those who had entered the race.

"I'm not going inside the Nursing Home again," Eddy protested after the announcer was through with the newscast, and seeing the Dracula man and other patients within the nursing home walls.

"Why?" Ham queried.

"Although Granny Bobek is elderly and crippled, she speaks sensibly when she can, while other patients don't. They groan, they complain and do the weirdest things hollering "Oy, Oy, Oy" or, "Pleas help me.""

Eddy did not visit Granny Bobek again. Neither did Brenda and both wished they had. Ham did not tell his mother that his wife was divorcing him and that was okay. The next day, Granny Bobek's prayers were answered, and she died peacefully in her sleep. The very instant she was gone, Ham and Eddy missed her.

A week following Granny Babek's funeral, Ham's thoughts of losing his parents and a divorcing wife, were turning to

autumn and the Famous Okanagan Fruit Leather factory
the annual Kelowna to Rutland Alzheimer's foot race.

When Alice Nichol, who started the runners, said, "We
certainly have a good turnout for the ten kilometer run,"
she fumbled on the word *kilometer*. Alice was one person
in Kelowna who did not appreciate conversion to the
metric system that was taking place in Canada at the
time.

"The changeover seems to drag on and on," she lamented,
but that same feeling wasn't shared by Eddy who claimed
the metric system presented no problem when it came to
enjoying fruit leather.

"The ounces convert automatically in my mouth and are
mill-metered by the time the fruit leather reaches my
stomach," he said to Jeffery Hunter, who also entered
the race.

"During the run, watch for traffic and keep to the left
hand side of the road. There are water stops to quench
your thirst and an ambulance will follow in the event a
runner passes out," Alice reminded the runners, using a
bullhorn.

Most of the runners were from Kelowna and came in
all sizes, shapes and ages. Most opted out for the non-
competitive side of the race but not Eddy, Lo Wong and
Jeffery Hunter.

Ogopogo said, "I entered the race for the camaraderie and
will give it my best shot. The proceeds go to a good cause.
If it was a swim race I know I could place first."

"I admit I may have made a mistake because I haven't run
in months and I'm not in shape," Corporal Pickins said.
"But until I have a strip of fruit lather in the morning

I'll do anything. That is why last week I participated in a Demolition Derby.

Wong said he was participating in the run not only to raise funds to help cure Alzheimer's, but also to research which flavored fruit leather, cherry or grape, provided more energy when it came to long distance running.

The Mayor of Kelowna said," I'm running because it's a good cause but also to see which is better fruit leather or beans, as part of my diet,"

Father Kubek who was getting on in age, said, "I'm running just for the fun of it and guess the Lord wants to see if I can reach the finish line."

As soon as Alice fired the starting gun, runners thundered up a hill, some stumbled but later settled down and caught up to the other racers. Together they ran past fruit stands, houses built on clay banks, orchards and vineyards and the Famous Okanagan Fruit Leather complex. Okanagan Lake was always in view to the left.

h and Brenda were across the street from each other when the race began. "Brenda! Why don't you join me and watch Eddy run?" Ham suggested when he saw his estranged wife standing alone and dejected.

"Okay, I'm glad you asked," Brenda acquiesced and climbed into the car with him, first exchanging glances without words. Then while Ham was driving and they were following the runners. Ham and Brenda began to speak to each other. They talked about Ham's parents who had died. Later, after Ham stopped at a viewpoint and had taken several photographs of Eddy running, they discussed their marital relationship.

"Let's start from the beginning and find out what went wrong," Ham suggested.

"You mean it?" Brenda said sympathetically.

"I do," Ham said and began driving to the next viewpoint where racers were bunched up. But when Ham stopped at the third viewpoint, the racers had separated and Jeffery Hunter was in the lead followed by Mr. Wong. As for Eddy, he was some distance back but in the lead for his age group.

It was here that Brenda said about Eddy, "He reminds me of an athlete training for the Olympics. You must have given Eddy a lot of encouragement to run, or else he must have eaten an extra amount of fruit leather."

"Both. And don't forget his soccer training. But on the other hand I can't take all the credit for his athletic ability. Eddy is our son, yours and mine. You deserve credit also."

"Only if there was a pill to free me from the hang-up of old people," Brenda said.

"There is something better than a pill."

"What is it?"

"A marriage encounter."

"A marriage encounter? That's for . . ."

"It's not," Ham interrupted, and drove to the final viewpoint that provided an excellent view of the runners. At this particular location the runners were separated by various distances. As Wong and Jeffery Hunter passed in front of Ham and Brenda, they were in the lead and Eddy wasn't far behind. Running with sweat streaming down his face Eddy, after noticing his parents, Ed hollered, "How am I doing, Mom and Dad?"

"You are doing fine. Only Wong and Jeffery Hunter are ahead of you," Ham replied.

Brenda didn't say anything, confining herself to a smile suggesting both pride and sadness.

"How far are we from the Finish Line?" Eddy then shouted again.

"There are about two kilometers remaining. Up the hill and then a sharp turn to the left and there, the Finish line and Okanagan Lake should be in sight."

And once the runners crossed the FINISH line that was next to a sandy beach, a waiting crowd greeted the runners. When the race was over Wong was declared the overall winner.

"I had all those runners breathing down my neck." Wong said to Jeffery Hunter who placed second. "When I saw you I took my final strip of fruit leather and out-ran you to the finish line in one-hour, seven minutes and twenty-seconds."

Eddy placed third but first in his age class.

There were unusual excuses from those who had not done well, which included Ogopogo. While discussing the excuses with other runners Eddy mixed with the crowd that was served fruit juices and watermelon.

While discussing the race Ham and Brenda slipped away from the crowd and strolled along the sandy shore of Okanagan Lake, and on a path, met a blind man guided by a dog. The more they watched the blind man, the more Brenda wanted to say something. When they came to a bench and sat down, Brenda said contritely, "I'm sorry for abandoning you and Eddy. I made a foolish mistake when

I said I didn't want your father living with us and I didn't love you because of that."

All right," Ham said. "I shouldn't have been so short-tempered and said 'Leave' when you said you would."
Suddenly, Brenda was in Ham's arms and tears began flowing down her cheeks. "At first there was shock, denial and now sadness," she said.
"What do you mean?"
"I was trying to remember what Dr. Bond told me when I spoke to him about our separation."
Ham and Brenda then strolled further along the beach, sat at a second bench and watched the waves crushing towards the shore. Brenda smiled, stood up and in the sand with her finger wrote the words, "Ham and Brenda" and drew a figure of a heart next to their names.
There was an expression of pain as Brenda said, "Had, dear, I don't want a divorce. How can I say I'm sorry?"
Brenda rested her head against Ham's shoulder and he stroked her hair gently as Brenda continued, "Life has strange ways. And you still love me although I have petitioned you for a divorce?"
"I do," Ham." replied and went on, "Let's forget the past and think only of our future."
As if she had doubts Brenda said, "Ham, could you really learn to love me again?"
By some invisible force Brenda and Ham were attracted to each other. It was the start of a fulfillment, reconciliation, redemption and the joy of the purest kind. Here was a couple with eyes and a heart of a man and a woman who understood life's futility and felt its pain and sorrow.

Let's make a marriage encounter," Brenda suggested and Ham agreed.

The world of living separately Brenda conjured up wasn't panning out. The following weekend, there was a close encounter of a very special kind between a wife and a husband, at a retreat in the basement of the Immaculate Conception Church where they found themselves communicating, discussing their parents and themselves

When the marriage encounter ended, Brenda said to Father Kubek who helped conduct the encounter, "There is so much to my husband, much more than I initially knew."

"I had no idea how he really felt about me though I knew he cared for his father and mother. I did not realize how big a part of my life Ham could be or that he was even proud of me."

"It was a relationship to start with and we understand one another as we had not done since our courtship," Ham said while discussing the encounter with other couples in the group.

"The marriage encounter was a beneficial and exciting experience for both of us," Brenda said and went on, "If we can't know our partner's feelings, particularly about their parents, than we really don't know our partner, that's the truth."

Brenda sidled up to Ham and as they were standing together, she shook his hand and squeezed it. Ham returned the squeeze. There seemed no obstacle to their happiness. "We came to realize that our marriage can work be rewarding and much joy found in sharing,"

Ham said facing Brenda, and then pressing his lips against hers.

Both agreed their separation was a period of loneliness and grief. "Grief is a time to reflect. It isn't a time to retreat," Brenda said.

The next several days were hectic as happiness, shock, relief, sadness and love flowed together while Brenda returned home to Okanagan Tower. The day Brenda moved in, Ham and Eddy embraced her and then pulling Eddy closer to their side, Brenda said, "And I love you too, Eddy."

When released, Eddy entered the bedroom and brought his mother a stem with three red roses, which prompted Brenda to say, "Eddy, you didn't have to do that."

"I knew you like roses after I saw Dad holding your wedding portrait," Eddy said.

"And here's a bottle of the famous *Friend of the Okanagan* wine that Alice Nichol sent us" Han said.

Eddy poured the wine into glasses and then proposed a toast. Lifting his glass upward he said, "To my parents, may they have a long, happy and healthy life."

Ham and Brenda simultaneously replied, "We'll drink to that."

The Cruise Missile Catcher

Bobek still experienced flashbacks of the separation during the time Ham's parents had died. But there were positive things happening in their personal lives also. One bright spot was their seventeen-year-old son Eddy, who was on the honor role in high school and an air cadet, who just completed a leadership course at the Cold Lake Air Force Military Base in Alberta.

"Where to, sir?" a security guard at the base entrance asked, as Ham and Brenda pulled up in their car at a STOP sign.

"To the cadet parade and graduation ceremonies," Ham replied and went on to say that he and his brother Sam had visited the base when they were teenagers.

Ham and Brenda had traveled from Kelowna to the Cold Lake Military Base, a distance of eight hundred miles.

"Proceed ahead to hanger six and follow the directional signs," the security guard said pointing in the westerly direction.

Before leaving, the security guard reminded the travelers that this was the week Americans were testing the Cruise missile from the Arctic Ocean to the Cold Lake Military Weapons Range.

By the time Ham and Brenda parked their car and entered hanger number 64, air cadets from throughout Canada were already taking part in a precision marching drill. "We are a bit late, but there's Eddy in row number 7," Brenda said to Ham as soon as she spotted their son who like all the other cadets, had shiny boots, a starched shirt collar and wore a neatly pressed uniform. Each girl and boy, from the tallest to the shortest, from the skinniest to the fattest, was marching, but by the time Ham and Brenda found a seat in the bleachers, the cadets were each standing at ease.

"Shhh, the Administration Officer is about to say something," Brenda said while glancing at a four-page program that was handed to her earlier by a cadet.

The Administration Officer stepped up to a dais and facing the parents, relatives and friends, said, "We are extremely proud of these you people. In our life they are the elite youth of Canada."

The Administration Officer spoke for three minutes ending with the closing remark, "Despite different ethnic backgrounds, the cadets have learned that cooperation and not confrontation assures success."

The Commanding Officer spoke next but instead of directing his remarks to the parents, relatives and friends, he directed them to the cadets themselves and said, "You have learned the skills necessary to cope with an ever changing society. Yours will be the future that will have a foundation in understanding multi-ethnic makeup of our great Canadian country."

The Commanding officer spoke for three minutes too and complimented the graduates by saying, "I'm extremely proud of the young men and women today and feel secure the future of Canada is in good hands."

"That's our Eddy, he's talking about," Brenda whispered into Ham's ear. At home he doesn't pick up his clothing, make the bed or turn off the stereo."

Moli smiled. "And there are other things that Eddy does but it would be impolite to mention."

"Like what?"

"Well, like I use do as a teenager, he wipes his nose on his shirt sleeve and chases girls."

After the presentation of certificates the ceremony ended and a cadet band struck up a musical march leading the remaining cadets to a vacant parking lot. There the cadets flung their caps into the air and congratulated each other by shouting, "Hooray! We have completed a grueling course in senior leadership. "Hooray!"

When the self-congratulatory ceremony was over Eddy noticed that his parents were watching him. Seeing his parents Eddy came over, shook hands and said, "Hi Mom and Dad. I'm glad you could come to Cold Lake."

"We are delighted to be here and watch you perform. Your marching was wonderful," Brenda said.

"Was the course difficult?" Ham asked.

"I passed with a mark of 82%. Considering I met a girl from Quebec that I like, I'm satisfied with the results."

"A girlfriend? From the province of Quebec?" Brenda questioned with surprise. She had never heard Eddy speak of girlfriends before.

"See, I told you Eddy chases girls," Moli said and asked Eddy, "What town is she from?"

"Rimouski and she's bilingual."

While Eddy and his parents were talking about the province of Quebec, the separate revolution that was taking place, and the course Eddy completed, their conversation was interrupted by a fly-past of four CF-104 military jets courtesy Squadron 419. As the planes gained altitude they separated from each other and disappeared into the puffy clouds.

"Still want to be a pilot?" Moli asked during the roaring noise of the aircraft.

"I do but we may traveling to the moon by the time I graduate from High School, attend college and apply to be a student in the CFB Cold Lake CF-18 pilot training program."

"And when you graduate as a pilot you'll take us for a ride in a CF-104?" Brenda said.

"No way," Eddy replied reluctantly.

"Why not?"

"Because so many CF-104 crash and I'm too young to die."

148

Eddy had a valid point. Three CF-104's had crashed with a space of a month and were replaced by the CF-18 Hornet, trusted by the Allies and feared by others.

Eddy said he was glad the CF-18 was replacing the CF-104 Starfighter because the new plane was the plane of the future with pilots trained by computers. "I hope when the time comes that I'm accepted into the pilot training program."

Like gladiators circling one another, eight of the CF-18's were already at the base playing cat and mouse in the sky. Unlike earlier dogfights, the aircraft had friends and foe on their radar screens, including realistic targets and models of Soviet surface-to-air missile columns of tanks seen crossing rivers and hiding behind hills. The CF-18's used ammunition with high explosives to attack what was supposed to resemble a Soviet invasion of Europe.

"The practice battle against the Soviets is stored on a computer tape and relayed to pilots the way a hockey or a football game is filmed for the benefit of the athlete," Eddy said.

Moli could relate to that part, because at one time he played for the Toronto Maple Leafs and the coach would often play back tapes so the team could improve for the next game.

As those present were watching the CF-104 jets in the sky Brenda brought a 'Restricted Area' sign in the distance to Eddy's attention. "It must be a top secret?"

"It could be where the Cruise missiles are temporarily stored," Eddy replied, shrugging his shoulders. "As you know Canada and United States have agreed to have the missiles cold-tested here. As a matter of fact the first missile was tested this morning, all the way from the Arctic Ocean to the Cold Lake Military Weapon's Range."

Ham nodded his head, signifying he was aware of the missiles being tested that morning.

Eddy continued, "There's a lot of controversy because of the inflammatory nature of the missiles to have the tests held on the range. The cry is for the human race versus the missile race. By the time the controversy is over, the Cruise may become obsolete and we will be in the Star Wars Age."

"Now that you have completed the leadership course, and there are still several days before the second semester at High School begins, would you like to stay overnight in Cold Lake and see how the local population reacts to the Cruise testing by the Americans?"

"An excellent idea," Eddy said. "But first I want you to meet Monique Tremblay from Rimouski, Quebec. Come, I'll march you and Mom to see her as she's packing to leave home."

"You mean to say walk us, not march us?" Brenda said.

"No, Mom, while at the base cadets always march while in uniform. It's a tradition."

And when Eddy marched his parents to where Monique was packing, he introduced her to his parents. They had a brief conversation and then Eddy wished Monique the best of luck and an, "Au revoir."

Minutes later, after Eddy had packed also, he and his parents drove to the town of Cold Lake, where they registered at the Roundel Hotel overlooking Cold Lake that was frozen over.

Once registered, the trio had lunch and later stopped at the Lakeland Sporting Goods Store to visit the proprietors, Ethel and Randy Teague. As the Goalies entered the store, Mrs. Teague was receiving an order from a sporting goods salesman and the way she

Seeing Ham, Brenda and Eddy, Mrs. Teague said, "Well, welcome to Cold Lake! I'll be with you in a moment, but first I must pay for the order of tennis nets."

Turning to the salesman, she went on, "I have checked the nets over. There are two hundred. Thank you for the prompt delivery."

Ham's curiosity was aroused, wondering what a sporting goods store would do with so many tennis nets, especially when there was three feet of snow laying on the ground.

"We are going to build a Cruise missile catcher. The hot air balloons will be in place by midnight," Randy Teague, who joined in the conversation, said.

Mr. and Mrs. Teague, besides owning the sporting goods store and distributing Famous Okanagan Fruit Leather, were also anti–nuclear war and environment activists. Ethel Teague headed the Coalition for Nuclear Awareness and her husband was the local spokesperson for Greenpeace. Both organizations had drawn criticisms from the townsfolk.

Ethel and Randy Teague were concerned about Americans testing the Cruise missile over Canadian soil, and already knew how Brenda felt about the testing from a previous visit—she was in favor. "Peace through strength," she often said to her friends and acquaintances.

"What happened at this morning's testing?" Eddy asked Ethel politely, to which she replied, "The missile landed with neither a bang nor a whimper, just a thud."

The salesman who brought the nets into the store, by now had made his exit, which prompted Ham to say that he was surprised by the lack of protesters. "Usually at a time like this, they are out in droves."

"This is true," Ethel said and continued, "We could only muster a force of forty marchers this morning as the Canadian United States military have used a variety of tricks to minimize our effectiveness. Candidly speaking they got us in a corner."

"Why is that?"

"First, they gave us a short notice of plans for the tests and secondly they decided to hold the tests during the beginning of the week when few protesters can get away from work."

Following further conversation, Ethel said, "I wouldn't be surprised if a missile one day ended up in someone's living room. We have very few local people against Cruise missile testing anymore."

"Whatever happened to Dr. Helen Caldicott and Dr. Benjamin Spock?" Brenda asked after seeing them on television many times warning viewers about the dangers of a nuclear war.

"They are still active, but more so, on an international level. If we had been given proper notice about the testing they probably would have been here."

Brenda reminded Ethel that a year earlier there were many Cruise missile protests throughout the world. "In Canada, I recall marching protests in Toronto, Edmonton and Vancouver with up to fifty thousand people taking part."

"In Cold Lake, where we have the military, majority of the people, like you, are in favor of Cruise testing.

The bumper stickers favoring such tests outnumber those that don't, one-hundred to one," Ethel said and went on, "There are fifteen members of CNA and Greenpeace here still. We feel it's very important that we don't see the military people as being enemies, and that we maintain a good relationship with them."

Ethel said the group's peace marchers were akin to waving a red flag in front of the pro-Cruise community. "Often the pro-Cruise people don't understand what we are doing."

"But isn't it true that most of the trouble makers are from outside the immediate area?" Ham asked.

Ethel was noticeably upset by the words 'trouble makers' that H had used and replied, "If you believe those who want peace as trouble makers, as you call them, than you are right."

"Getting back to the tennis nets, what are you going to do with so many when it's February, there's three feet of snow on the ground and one apt to stay at home sitting by a fireplace?" Ham asked.

"As I said earlier, members of the Coalition for Nuclear Awareness and Greenpeace are building a Cruise catcher."

"A Cruise missile, catcher? That's ludicrous," Ham said.

"It isn't. Stick around. And mark my word, the catcher will disrupt the flight of the missile number two scheduled to be tested tomorrow morning."

That evening, Ham, Brenda and Eddy had dinner in the Roundel Hotel Restaurant, and then while in their room, on television, watched the movie *If You Want to Save Your Planet* and then went to sleep. They got up early in the morning and switched on the radio when an announcer said, "Now the 6:00 A. M. News. Members of the Coalition for Nuclear Awareness and Greenpeace are trying to catch the Cruise missile, which the United States Military is testing over Northern Canada today.

"A B-52 Bomber from North Dakota will release the missile over the Beaufort Sea that will reach the Cold Lake Military Weapons Range shortly before noon Cold Lake time. Yesterday's test according to the Military has been termed a success. It's expected today's test will be a success also. In other news, there are fewer protesters in Cold Lake than usual."

When Eddy switched stations a newsman was interviewing the Military and they were discussing the first missile landing. "It landed without difficulty. There were no problems. A parachute following the missile made it come to an abrupt stop without a hitch," the American military spokesman said.

The Canadian observer agreed and continued, "Yesterday's missile plunged down following a 2600 kilometer flight and produced no surprises."

The American Military observer went on, "I think all our people were well prepared for what was going too happened and the test went as expected."

Minutes later, the American Military observer said to the same interviewer, "We learned from yesterday's test to make certain we worked out most of the glitches of the test program. During this morning's test the Cruise will be on its own."

"How many tests will take place?" the interviewer continued.

"As worked out between Canada and United States, six."

Asked if the tests were necessary the American Military observer did not hesitate, "The tests in cold temperatures and topography similar to the Soviet Union over ice and snow, are necessary to provide data and missile reliability and accuracy. You see, your Canadian climate and terrain are comparable to that in the Soviet Union."

When the interviewer asked if any of the Cruise missiles being tested ever had gone off-course the American replied, "Several in United States have but most of the problems have been overcome."

After enjoying a breakfast, Ham, Brenda and Eddy were relaxing in the hotel lobby, and while looking out the window, noticed Ethel walking towards the spot where her husband and his helpers were working all night setting up the Cruise missile catcher. Seeing three multi-colored air balloons holding up a huge tennis net near the edge of the frozen-over Cold Lake, Ham went outside and said to Ethel, "This is the weirdest contraption I have ever seen."

The air balloons were three hundred meters in the air, each hooked on to large rectangular tennis net splice together from one's the Teague's had purchased the day before. The net extended for one-half kilometer in length and suspended from the air balloons that were anchored to the ice. The sight of the catcher made Moli burst out with laughter. The contraption was a strange piece of invention. "Your husband must have studied *Popular Mechanics,*" he said to Ethel.

When Moli stopped laughing Ethel readily admitted that her husband indeed got the idea after reading the magazine.

At the time Ethel was carrying two small dead spruce trees. In her left hand she held a tree that was still alive.

"What are the trees for?" Eddy, who joined in the conversation, asked and Ethel replied, "The live tree symbolizes life and beauty on earth."

"And the dead?"

"Death and destruction."

Soon, Ham, Brenda and Eddy were walking with Ethel towards the catcher and along the way other people joined in. By the time they reached the catcher site, about three kilometers from the hotel, there must have been two hundred people following them—some because of curiosity and others who believed the Cruise missile being tested, arriving in several hours, would be caught.

Once they reached the catcher site, Randy was finishing splicing the nets together with a thin wire so Ham said, "What makes you think that's the exact spot the missile will pass? The flight corridor is so wide that missile's path could be ten or twenty kilometers from here?"

"True," Randy said. "But following yesterday's test we calculated the approximate course that this morning's missile will take. Normally it should swoop down to approximately two hundred meters and land in a wilderness forty kilometers from here."

By now it was 7:30 A. M and dark outside. While waiting for the missile to arrive protesters made a bon fire on the ice to keep warm. As the flames crackled, Randy and his helpers made a final check of the missile catcher while others gathered around the fire and sang songs of peace.

Four hours later, Ethel said, "May I have your attention please. The Cruise missile has been released at the Beaufort Sea and should be arriving at Cold Lake any moment."

Randy took over and said to his helpers, "Please get ready to snag the missile."

Each took up his and her position.

Everyone appeared anxious and waited, looking in the northern direction. When there was no missile in sight, Brenda whispered to Ham, standing next to her, Eddy and Ethel, "I agree with you, using hot air balloons and a whole bunch of spliced tennis nets in order to snag a missile is ludicrous."

Minutes later, a Cruise missile did appear in the sky, led by an American Airbase Warning Central Systems aircraft.t and chased by two CF-18 Hornet jets. As the missile lowered in altitude, it struck the exact spot where the missile catcher had been placed.

This done, members of the Coalition for Nuclear Arms and Greenpeace, expressed joy. Even the guidance system and its power of four hundred kilometers an hour, the missile had failed to penetrate the net, veering to the left, towards a nearby house, where it smashed through a window, like Ethel predicted that it could.

American and Canadian military officials were outraged at the result of the test and members of the Coalition for Nuclear Awareness and Greenpeace snapped photographs of the missile. In all the previous tests no one had disrupted a Cruise missile while in flight. As soon as the weapon was recovered, it was crated and flown back to its point of origin in North Dakota.

"Thank goodness the missile did not have a warhead," Ethel said after realizing the destruction that could have been caused, if it had.

"If it did, we could have been blown from the face of Planet Earth." Eddy said.

That afternoon, the Coalition Awareness and Greenpeace held a press conference. By long distance telephone Ethel and Randy Teague were interviewed by reporters from the BBC in London and the *New York Times*. Other media followed with calls from Paris, Bonn, Tokyo and the Vatican. All wanted information on how such a feat could be accomplished and blueprints for the Cruise missile catcher.

NINE

A Letter to Eddy

Ham Bobek always had a love affair with books. Even when he played hockey for the Toronto Maple Leafs, he spent much of his free time at the public library reading biographies of famous people. Reading books made Ham, take stock of his life regularly.

Looking back at the years, Ham thought he should write a letter to his son who was one of eight students taking a CF-18 pilot training program at the CFB Cold Lake Military base in east central Alberta. The letter would assist Eddy in his career planning and a happy life.

Most of his life Ham enjoyed sports and was a successful entrepreneur, which he said, was a two-bit word for an independent businessperson, and CEO of Famous Okanagan Fruit Leather International Corp. Ham compared an entrepreneur to that of an artist who can look at everything—person, place or situation and find something that's interesting. Starting with the premise that the human being is the greatest resource on this earth, Ham picked up a sheet of writing paper, a pen and said to himself, "Schools, colleges and universities teach a wide range of subjects but offer little assistance on many topics I believe are of paramount importance to a student contemplating a career."

Ham, while alone in his paneled office at the Okanagan Tower, began writing a lengthy letter with love and affection.

Dear Eddy,

Mom and I miss you and hope you are enjoying your training as a pilot at Cold Lake. I'm not one for attending seminar's wanting to discover myself for an effective life but what I write, I write from experience. Through experience I can tell you that having faith in God is important. Beyond a doubt, He is the one we have to account to when life comes to an end and an epitaph is written on a tombstone.

First, are you at peace with yourself and God? It's an important question but some fail to ask themselves. You have to constantly monitor yourself. In my view, common sense is the best way to attack this world, which has many positive things, failures and rewards. One of my greatest rewards was when Dr. Bond delivered you at the Kelowna Regional Hospital. Without question, your Mom and I were looking forward to have a child and as it happens you turned out to be a fascinating individual.

Sure, there were times when you wiped your nose on your shirtsleeve, forgot to make your bed and clean the bathtub, forgot to take off your cap to show respect, chewed chewing gum while attending a church service, and played the ghetoblaster loudly in the entertainment room. There were times when I was irritated with your behavior, like the time you borrowed the car and didn't return it until 4:00 a. m.

"Or the time you skipped school, weren't dressed the way I thought you ought to be, or when you smoked a cigarettes and had a bottle of beer behind my back. But you know something, Eddy. I did some of those things myself. On the other hand, you were a great strength to me when Grandpa and Grandma Bobek died. You stood by me when Mom left us for a while, and when Grandpa was suffering with cancer and Alzheimer's disease.

Throughout the course of my life, I traveled frequently and had a burning desire to help other people. This is one reason why Famous Okanagan Fruit Leather International Corp. is such a success story. It's being creative and people helping people. In my travels I have found education very important. I know there are entrepreneurs who say they have only grade eight educations and own car dealerships, meat packing plants, and hockey, baseball or basketball teams, along with real estate, but believe me, your education is a valuable asset and a priceless possession.

Son, read books, all types of books. Read books for the sake of reading them to determine why you don't like what they are saying. Is it because of a different point of view, which you do not agree with? Also read editorials in newspapers and magazines. And remember, learning doesn't stop the day you graduate from High School and become a pilot. I caution you that no amount of reading or memorization will make you successful.

It depends on yourself.

In fact that is when real lessons are only beginning and they will require more emphasis, energy and study than ever before, if success is to knock on your door. Most people think of education as having gone to school. Well, that's a good place to start.

In your case, I know that you aren't complaining about your flight instructor. CFB Cold Lake is one of the best pilot training centres in the world.

By attending Cold Lake, you have seized an opportunity that many of your contemporaries didn't have. And by attending, the rule of thumb is the mark you get equals to the time and effort of studying you put in. Mom and I hope you put a fair share of time and talent into your studies in becoming a pilot, because if you give it your best shot, your most determined effort, you will have answered the knock on your door—the knock of opportunity.

When Mrs. Nichol was a child, she dreamt she was an angel in human form and stood in front of mirrors, hoping to see her wings sprout. Later in life, she dreamt she was God's daughter, the sister of Jesus, and she saw God's feet on the horizon and heard His voice in the stars. Later still, when Mrs. Nichol won the best red wine tasting contest

162

at the Septober Wine Tasting Festival she almost turned into a cannibal. Son, these are ridiculous dreams, but I know you have dreamt since you were six years old, that you wanted to be a pilot and I applaud you for that. I wish more people had similar dreams.

In your last letter you said you will stay in the military for five years and hope to fly a Jumbo Jet for a commercial airline after that. Avoiding any pitfalls I know an airline will hire you, but first challenge yourself and as Tim Rains of the Montreal Expos said, when he won the National League batting title, "You don't get to be a batting champion if you don't swing the bat."

Someday soon, we'll have lunch together and discuss your career but until then, set your goals in life—short, medium and long range. To reach your destination you need a map. Your plan lays out exactly what you have to do to achieve your goals. It's like being a pilot; you must first file a flight plan before you head for your destination. Have you such a plan? If your answer is **yes** you are on target and will be a success. A **no** answer probably means additional commitment is needed.

And once you become a pilot, have you got a Business Plan for when you get married and later retire? While your Business Plan is a general planning tool, your Balance Sheet and Profit and Loss Statement, must deal with more than just money. You must ask yourself for instance: Are my expenses cutting into profit? What lifestyle do I want to live? How much volunteer time am I going to give to my community, church and service club?

These are some of the questions you must ask yourself. And be smart, don't squander you money on loose women, booze, and what now seems to be fashionable with professionals, drugs.

Speaking of women, I would like to say a few words about Monique Tremblay, the girl you introduced Mom and me when we were at the Cold Lake Air Force Military Base, and the two of you received your cadet leadership certificates. At the time the Commanding Officer said he was proud of both of you, and that Canada was in good hands because of its youth. Well, I believe him, because youth is on your side and remember also, that leadership begins with good communication and rapport with people.

Sometimes I see you as a shy and hesitant boy, so when I saw you with Monique and you said you were interested in her, I hoped the friendship would continue and it has. I don't mind that Monique doesn't speak English well. You must remember you speak no French at all. If you get serious about Monique, however, I have several reminders. The first is that no longer is it a man's world only. And secondly I believe women these days are portrayed wrongly. Monique has her own dreams, cries and diets but she isn't passive, week, uninteresting and out of touch. Remember too that should you marry Monique chances are you will be a two-income family and while she works at home, you as a pilot, will be in foreign countries much of the time. You will have to communicate and trust each other.

If you are going to marry Monique, think out your marriage carefully, for not viewing it seriously, very often, your life ends in divorce, torn emotions one of which is anger, and a drained bank account. And if you have children they won't know whom to love.

They may become emotionally disturbed not loving either parent or end up as a ward of the government. It would be a tragedy if that happened to you because I know you are a kind and a sensitive person. On the other hand if your marriage is a good one, it can sweep you along to greater heights. One more thing, if you should marry Monique remember her on her birthday and wedding anniversary. This will tell her she's number one.

Today, as I write this letter, is an important day in your life because you are nearly halfway through your pilot training program. As soon as you make your solo flight, the next part of your training is navigation. I don't know if the Commander of 410 Squadron has told you or not that as soon as you make your solo a social event will be held for you and the other seven pilots. There will be a little bit of spirit naturally that evening, as the flight instructor makes a few jocular comments about your abilities. During the brief ceremony, which isn't a hazing ritual, the instructor will take off his hornet crest, the mark of a CF-18 pilot, and hand it to you. As part of the celebration, you will also swallow a *beverage* poured directly down your throat through the five-foot long CF-18 cannon-barrel, which roughly is the size of a baseball bat.

After you and your instructor mark the fact that the next part of your training is navigation, I'm certain the instructor will be proud of you and the entire team of trainees.

Soon, you will be in the real world, but before you get there, let me remind you that there are three levels of people that you will meet in your lifetime. Some people think they can't get past the first stage, the tangible stage, and you will have to prove to them that things which can't be seen do exist. Other people will talk about concepts, ideas and theories. I feel you belong to the third level and can create something. You can visualize something that has not happened; believe in something that is going to happen. You told me for example, years ago, that America was going to test the Cruise missile over Canadian soil from the Arctic to the Cold Lake Military Weapons Range, which it did.

One of the freedoms you have, is the right to choose, and you chose to become a pilot as your passionate profession, so doesn't stop now, falter and fail. Consider the purpose of your chosen career. My purpose at first was to be a hockey player with the Toronto Maple Leafs, but later I switched, because I wanted to market fruit leather and touch other people's lives.

I won't be upset, however, if you decide to change your career, because the most important trophies I get, are those when people walk up to me and say, "Thank you Mr. Goalie, for changing my life." These are the trophies

I cherish most, and not the Stanley Cup, which I helped the Toronto Maple Leafs to win.

And son, like in thinking there are three levels of maturity. In the first level a person says, "Please help me." I think it's an important level because until a person reaches out and says, "Help me," he hasn't matured at all, because he thinks he can do everything alone.

The second level of maturity says, "Can I handle it? I've got it now." But there's a third level of maturity, and which I think you belong too, because I have heard you say, when Mom was away, "Let me help you, Dad."

If you are thinking who you can help these days, think of those who feel nobody cares, like Santa once felt and Ogopogo helped distribute toys to the girls and boys, especially when life's problems are overwhelming: a terminal illness, a tragic accident, a marriage breakup, losing one's job. They all feel helpless and sometimes hopeless. If you can help when hope seems lost, your walls will be filled with all sorts of plaques, awards and trophies.

Recently, I read an article on the trials and pitfalls facing sons of successful fathers, the turbulence of growing up in a father's footsteps that are achievers. Don't worry about it and take a look in the sports you enjoy, baseball and hockey. Vance Law of the Montreal Expos is batting 303 and his father Verne, was an outstanding pitcher with the Pittsburgh Pirates. In the National Hockey League Gordie Howe's son, Mark, of the Philadelphia Flyers, continually made the NHL all-star team. In business there are similar parallels—the Bronfman's, Thompson's, Weston's and Irving's, come to my mind immediately.

Several days ago the principal of the Immaculate Regional High School asked me to speak at this year's graduation ceremonies and do you know what I'm going to tell the students? The same thing I told you in private, that one is rewarded in direct proportion he or she puts in, whatever they want. I'm also going to tell the students not to run down groups of people like their teachers, the policeman, the school bus driver and the garbage collector, and to eliminate the word *just* from their vocabulary. For instance our garbage collector is not *just* a garbage collector. Even if he has no PHD he still is as important as the next person.

As you know, Famous Okanagan Fruit Leather International Corp. has thousands of distributors throughout the world. The fruit leather we manufacture is a sophisticated meal replacement with magical qualities. I have discovered that people are still demanding personal service and that is important. Some say the trend is too high-tech and computers are culprits in making the service dead. I maintain that service is a valuable commodity and with computers we will improve service to a point where the Okanagan Fruit Leather computer database is going to be second only to the Pentagon's in Washington in capacity. Perhaps you have noticed how computers have improved the CF-18 Hornet over the XF-104 Starfighter, which by the way are still crashing.

Speaking of Famous Okanagan Fruit Leather distributors, I have noticed that many of them initially have a fear of failure.

One distributor I know personally, developed ulcers and had a nervous breakdown. When he recovered, and went into the field, he found it wasn't quite as bad as he thought it would be and now is a Master Distributor.

When I asked him about his success, he replied, and I want you to remember this, "We talk about a number of home runs Babe Ruth had but seldom about the number of strikeouts." So, son, when you become a pilot, don't be afraid to fly to the moon or outer space, if they ask you.

I met Charles Smith Sr. the other day, and he is still upset by people who are on welfare. I explained to him that jobs are difficult to find these days and asked if he was still prejudiced against people who weren't of English heritage and he said, "And I always will be."

Can you imagine Mr. Smith being a pilot and flying to India, Middle East or Asia? There's another quality you will have to develop is to love all kinds of people even from other countries whose customs are different than ours. I notice the phenomenon taking place in Canada and United States. I was in Banff the other day and wish I knew how to speak Japanese. Mark my word; Banff soon could be called Banff, Japan instead of Banff, Alberta.

People are not made out of clay and dirt although some are treated that way. That is why if you treat everyone fairly the results will be everlasting profits. And speaking of profits, which some say is a dirty word; don't invest in a Trust or Saving company whose deposits are not protected by Canada Deposit Insurance. Your mom and dad did and learned an important lesson. Before you start counting the millions you will make after you graduate, I have another piece of advice with no put-down intended. Get yourself a good accountant to help you steer your air-ship.

In your last letter, you told us that the military radio station in Cold Lake has invited you to do the Saturday afternoon shift as an announcer. I know you will enjoy broadcasting, but as a constant listener to the local radio stations, take my advice seriously and be yourself. Don't lower you voice to sound like Lorne Greene. Learn the correct pronunciation of words particularly with those of French, German, Russian, Italian and Spanish roots of origin. I have heard the names of Martina Navaratilova, San Jose and Quesnel, mispronounced so often that sometimes I wonder if these announcers went to school. Diction is very important and so is breathing properly. And if you are going to spin records, please don't scream while introducing them on the air. Be your normal self.

Since you will be working for the radio station during the weekend, the image you project will be important on and off the air. There are a few principles I would like to pass on to you about clothes, manners and the art of conversation.

Depending on the occasion, if it's not casual, there has been no formal education that I'm aware as to what to wear while at work, but from experience I know that a person should dress well but not flashy.

Choose neutral colors and make certain, since you will be wearing a uniform, that it is well pressed. As for manners always say, "Please,", "Thank you," and "You are welcome." And when using the telephone be courteous. As to conversation while in a group, try not to talk shop. Open the door for the lady and if one enters a room, stand up. When a group of men and women are socializing, don't rush away to where another group of men only, and are discussing sports, the stock market or politics.

I understand your recent application for a bank credit card has been turned down. I wouldn't fret because I think the bank did you a service. As you know banks charge high interest rates for the use of a credit card and if you neglect a payment they threaten to ruin your credit rating. That is while long ago, I cut mine in half with a pair of scissors, and returned it to the bank telling it to shove the credit card where it hurts the most.

As soon as you graduate as a pilot, you may have to deal with governments—municipal, provincial and federal. Last month I mailed an important document to one of the distributors in Montreal and the Post Office lost it. I have complained to postal authorities, Member of Parliament, the minister in charge of the Post Office and even wrote a letter to the Prime Minister but haven't had a response.

And more recently, we had to do some alternations at the factory in Kelowna, and had to go through nineteen departments before we were granted a permit.

I see by your letter that you have struck up friendship with several young men from other parts of Canada. Good. I have found comradeship is important during the peaks and valleys of life. What would I do, for example, without Ogopogo and Wong? They have left an imprint on my life, and I'm certain without them, there would be no Famous Okanagan Fruit Leather.

In the same letter you say you were criticized by some of your friends. I have found that constructive criticicisim is okay and not always fault finding. Before you lose any sleep over the critical remark consider the source. If the person is habitually critical of others it's a personality flaw of both the strongest and weakest human beings. Unhappily, it's the chief preoccupation of the weak, ill-mannered and the jealous.

Your mother was surprised when you asked for some spending money at a time when we sent you some as recently as last month. The first mistake people make, and that includes you, is that they haven't got a budget. If we didn't have a budget at Famous Okanagan Fruit Leather International Corp. can you imagine where the company would be? So Eddy, set up a budget.
Needless to say once you get your pilot's license and earn some money, you will deal with all kinds of investments: real estate, stocks, bonds and mutual funds. Beware of

buying on margin, because you should invest only what monies you can afford to lose. Avoid chances of your investment going sour.

It may sound strange no one advised me to buy stocks is wealthy. One would think with the knowledge they have on their fingertips they would be millionaires. Perhaps that's where the word *brokers* originated because they are broke themselves.

As your father, I have no right or indeed desire, to know what you do with your money. From experience after burying Grandpa and Grandma Goalie I suggest you carry life insurance to cover your funeral expenses. And I don't have to remind you that as a successful pilot you must be healthy and should stay away from tobacco, alcohol and drugs. In Saudi Arabia, for example, if you were caught with these items on your possession you could be flogged to death. Expect your heart to react if you are overweight. Eat nutritious food and include fruit leather in your diet.

I hear a lot about stress these days. I don't think it's new. Don't tell me there was no stress when I went into business. As a matter of fact I believe stress was around during the Biblical Age. Can you imagine how stressful Goliath must have been before David killed him with a slingshot or the time Jonah was swallowed by a whale? You can't tell me that wasn't stressful.

The trouble with scientists these days is that the use words for things that were happening centuries ago and are now trying to make us believe they discovered a new phenomenon.

In closing this letter, I must say that I'm looking forward to your graduation day at CFB Cold Lake. At the same time I write this letter with some trepidation because you chose to be a pilot instead of following my footsteps. I always thought you would join the company and operate Famous Okanagan Fruit Leather International Corp. when I retire.

I'm certain with your wisdom and the guidance of Providence you will be a success. One morning you will wake up and say, "There it is," and I will not wake up. The world will continue and you can mark on my marble tombstone that as a father, I loved you very much.

Before closing, here are several news items that may interest you. Kelowna had one of the largest funerals in its history last week for reverend Kubek. Remember, he's the priest who welcomed your grandparents, to Canada and baptized you and me. The new parish pastor is Father Frank Kurek. And speaking of replacements, Ron Pickens has been transferred to the RCMP detachment in Kamloops. The new RCMP honcho in Kelowna is Stretch Anderson who has been transferred from Prince George. And Lo Wong has received an honorary doctorate degree from the University of British Columbia.

All for now,

Much love

Your father,

P. S. Your mother loves you as much as I do.

Satchewan Roughriders win the Super-Super Bowl

Saskatchewan Roughriders of the Canadian Football League were having a difficult time. The team was so bad that it didn't make the playoffs in the last twelve years and a great number of fans were worrying about the clubs' future.

"Where is the Rider pride?" was a question often asked whenever fans met in shopping malls, places of worship and bars. There was more interest in the Roughrider demise than in Canada negotiating a free trade agreement under NAFTA with the United States or Americans testing cruise missiles on Canadian soil from the Arctic Ocean to the Cold Lake Military Weapons Range.

For instance, in Carrot River, one traveling salesman said to another over a cup of coffee, "Roughriders haven't won a Grey Cup since 1956. Oh, for the good old days when my wife and I would travel to Regina and watch the Roughriders play during the November freezing weather."

In Saskatoon, a politician seeking re-election said to a prospective voter, "If you vote for me and my party wins, I'll see to it that the Roughriders are subsidized with an annual grant, that's how much the team means to Saskatchewan."

In Moose Jaw, which is a short distance from Regina, an eight-year-old boy, Stevie Joseph, while lying in a hospital bed said, "Life in Saskatchewan would be more interesting if the Roughriders could win at least fifty percent of their games. Roughriders without winning, is like Christmas without Santa Claus."

In Regina, where the Roughriders play their games, the Mayor, a broad shouldered man in his early fifties, was so upset with the teams past performance, that on one cold February day, while big flakes of snow were whirling, summoned the Roughriders president to City Hall and said to him, "Casey Dandelion! You must do something about the Roughriders streak. The team is an embarrassment not only to the province of Saskatchewan but all of Canada. Last season for instance, the team won only three of eighteen scheduled games."

Dandelion, an elegant man with an oval face with little bags under his eyes, apologized, "You are absolutely right your worship. The Green and Gold are an embarrassment not only to Saskatchewan and Canada but also to the Canadian Football League. I admit the team is tying it best, but in a slump, and about to go into bankruptcy, if not extinction."

The Mayor looked at Dandelion to see the effect the warning on him and then continued, "I'm giving you three months to get a Roughrider team into shape for the forthcoming football season. If you don't, it's game over for you. Do you understand?"

With a quivering voice and a poker face, Dandelion replied, "I do your worship."

The Mayor continued again, "I warn you, Dandelion, if the Roughriders don't improve this season, I'll personally see to it that your company, Sanitation Disposal Ltd., doesn't get the city garbage collection contract when it comes up for renewal next year."

"Yes, your worship," Dandelion replied, perturbed by the reprimand. "I'll do my best to see that the Roughriders will be a team to reckon with. I promise you that much."

When a professional team keeps losing constantly it's not unusual in sports to blame the manager or coach. In this instance the blame was on both. Dandelion immediately invited a former Roughrider superstar, Speed Velocity, for lunch and hired him as the new manager. Velocity was allowed to hire a coach and support staff. Since the team was on the verge of bankruptcy, Velocity had a great challenge facing him, so he said to president Dandelion, "First, for the Roughriders operating, we need at least one-million dollars and an assurance that twenty thousand season tickets are sold in advance."

"And second?"

"That we do it as soon as possible."

"Besides being a former Roughrider, I understand that you are presently into public relations and marketing. I give you a free hand, but promise me one thing."

"What?"

"That the Roughriders, at least make the playoffs."

"Or else?"

"Your company will lose its contract in hauling away city waste."

Velocity rose early the following morning and contacted Saskatchewan radio and television station managers, persuading each to participate in a twenty four-hour season's ticket drive marathon. To help with the fund raising, Velocity solicited help from the Roughrider alumni and local entertainers to the restore Roughrider Pride program on the air, and accept pledges.

One ex-Roughrider to volunteer in the simulcast program was former quarterback great, Ron Lancaster, who was employed by Canadian Broadcasting Corporation as a football analyst and commentator.

As soon as the telethon began, Lancaster was one of a hundred volunteers who picked up the phone and said, "This is the Restore Roughrider Pride program. Line one. You are on the air. Where are you calling from?"

A viewer replied, "Biggar. New York is big but I'm calling from Biggar, Saskatchewan and pledge to purchase four season tickets. Do you accept Visa, Master charge or American Express?"

"We do."

The caller then gave the Visa number and expiry date.

"Thank you, sir." Lancaster said. There was a "clique" sound and then he continued, "Line two. Please tell us where are you calling from?"

"Yorkton," the caller replied. "There are more bankrupt farmers than football clubs, but I still pledge to purchase two season tickets as soon as I'm able to sell my wheat."

"Thank you, sir. Line three. You are on the air. Where are you calling from?"

Lancaster was surprised when a boy's voice said, "I'm calling from the Children's Ward in a hospital in Regina."

"What is your name, son?"

"Stevie Joseph."

"How old are you?"

"Eight."

"And why are you in the hospital?" Lancaster continued to probe.

"Because last November as I was on my way home from watching the Roughriders play, the streets were slippery, and a car struck me in a cross-walk. Doctors say I'll be in the hospital for another four months and in a wheelchair for a long time because of the injuries I received."

"I'm sorry to hear that. Was it a hit and run?"

"It was, but aside that, I would like to send the Roughriders five dollars that is part of my monthly allowance which my parents give me."

"Thank you Stevie. Is there a chance we'll see you at the football games?"

"I'll do my best to be there."

After speaking with Stevie for a minute, Lancaster continued taking phone calls. "Line five, where are you calling from?"

"Esterhazy," a female voice said and continued, "I have been a Roughrider fan for who knows, next season, because Americans have imposed tariffs on potash, our family can't afford to purchase season tickets, but here's what we'll do."

"Okay, what?"

"We'll start a quilt raffle and send the Roughriders the money."

"Thank you, if quilting is your fancy, then sew be it," Lancaster said.

There were similar calls throughout the day and night, but majority came from individuals and executives who promised to purchase blocks of tickets to be distributed among employees. As the telethon progressed, a camera zoomed each half hour on a billboard sign, which kept a computerized record of the amount of money pledged. By the end of the twenty fourth hours, the first objective of selling twenty thousand season tickets was met, and Velocity was on his way in rebuilding the Roughriders with a mix of college graduates and free agents.

"Thank you television and radio stations in Saskatchewan! Thank you football fans throughout our wonderful province!" Velocity said to his audience in the final hour of the program. "You have been wonderful. Mark my word, by July 1st; we will have a football team that will make Saskatchewan proud."

Confident that there was enough money in the bank to operate a football team, Mr. Velocity, several days later, hired a coach. Velocity did not hire an assistant coach from another CFL team or one coaching at an American college.

What Velocity did, was to surprise the media and historians alike, by hiring Lo Wong who invented fruit leather and was a vice-president of Famous Okanagan Fruit Leather International Corp whose headquarters were in Kelowna, B. C.

Inventing fruit leather was not the only credential Wong had: (1) Held an honorary doctorate degree from the University of British Columbia. (2) Coached Ham and Sam Bobek to stardom in hockey and baseball and (3), Wong had been given power to communicate with Saint Sam after the giant had entered heaven.

When the football season began in July, the Roughriders first game was against the Edmonton Eskimos, a powerful team and winner of seven Grey Cups in the past thirteen years.

The opening ceremony included a parade through downtown Regina and inside Taylor Field, a poompah band played tunes as cheerleaders did cartwheels. During the national televised CBC game that featured Lancaster and announcer Don Whitman, Lancaster said, "Well, folks, the first game of another Canadian football season is about to begin. Saskatchewan Roughriders is a new team from the manager down. Incidentally, an eight-year-old boy, Stevie Joseph, a victim of a hit and run, is watching the game in the wheelchair section of the stadium."

As a camera zoomed in for a close-up of Stevie, Whitman took over and said, "After twelve disastrous seasons the only way the Roughriders can go is up.

"I spoke to manager Velocity, and coach Wong, prior to the game, and both assured me that the Roughriders will win the Grey Cup. Now, there's confidence for you."

On the first play, an Eskimo kickoff specialist Gizmo Williams, picked up the all in his end, twisted and turned, hurdled over opposing players, and returned the football one hundred and fifteen yards for a touchdown. In the end the final score was a landslide: Edmonton Eskimos 51 and Saskatchewan Roughriders 0.

"It wasn't a game that restored Roughrider pride," Velocity said to the media following the game. We'll do better against the Toronto Argonauts when we play next week. But the Roughriders didn't. A Toronto safety made seven interceptions and the Argo defense came charging through sacking the Roughrider quarterback nine times. The other five passes the quarterback threw the football into the crowd intentionally. Final score: Toronto 42. Roughriders 11.

In Winnipeg, the following weekend, the game between the Bombers and Roughriders was close but in the dyeing seconds a wind blew up a storm so strong that when Winnipeg attempted a field goal from their own 20 yard line, the ball went through the uprights and landed near the intersection of Portage and Main. Final score: Winnipeg 27. Roughriders 25.

When the Roughriders hosted the Calgary Stampeders the following weekend. the Roughrider kicker missed five out of six field goal attempts and fans in Taylor Field Stadium sang "Ah Nana. Goodbye Roughriders." Final score: Calgary 25. Roughriders 23.

Fans weren't the only one's disappointed with the Roughriders performance, or lack of it, so was Dandelion who took Velocity and Wong aside and said, "Can't you see? What the Roughriders need is a punter and kicker."

"I have come to that conclusion too," Velocity said while Wong nodded his head, signifying he agreed with Dandelion and Velocity.

"Then find one," Dandelion said in a gruff voice, "And don't go over the budget by even one penny."

"Yes, sir," Velocity said and then while reviewing tapes of previous games, the following day Wong said, "I know where we can find a punter and kicker who may help our team and it won't be expensive."

"We need someone that's experienced."

"He is, and because of his height, strength and speed, not only can he kick the football the length of the entire football field, but also return one without being touched by opposing players. He's versatile and can block punts if necessary."

"Unbelievable! He must be an exceptional athlete if he can do all these things."

"I assure you he can. And do you want to know something else?"

"What?'

"He'll make the CFL All-Star team in his rookie year."

"Okay, don't keep me in suspense any longer. Who is it that you have in mind?"

"His name is Ogopogo."

Hearing the name, Velocity burst out with laughter. When the laughter subsided, he said, "Ogopogo, the creature who lives in Okanagan Lake and a fruit leather entrepreneur."

"So help me, Jackie Parker, or is it, Sam 'The Rifle' Etchevery, that's him," Wong replied and following a brief discussion on how Ogopogo could help win, Wong was given permission to summon the serpentine-like monster to Regina for a tryout practice

"I'll be on the first flight available," Ogopogo said as soon as Wong phoned him.

During the next game, Ogopogo was in the Roughriders lineup against the Hamilton Tiger Cats. For this particular game, Ogopogo shrank one-third his normal size, which was six feet, eight inches tall, when Ogopogo stood on his hind legs. The height was not unusual for a football player.

As soon as the National Anthem was sung, Wong said to his team, "Remember, we have lost four straight games and must win this one if we are to make the playoffs." Turning to Ogopogo Wong continued, "Welcome to the Canadian Football League and best of luck against the Hamilton Tiger Cats."

Ogopogo's debut in the CFL wasn't a favorable one, because near the end of the first half the Roughriders were on the Hamilton 12 yard line.

When Ogopogo attempted a field goal, he slipped, fell and fumbled the ball as soon as it was snapped to him. A Hamilton player picked up the loose ball and ran the length of the field to score a touchdown.

When the second half began, the Ticats filed a protest with the referee, complaining that Ogopogo wasn't a homosapient and therefore not eligible to play in the Canadian Football League. Whitman and Lancaster described the protest this way:

Whitman: "The referee is ordering Ogopogo to get off the field because he's ineligible to play, but the Roughriders are countering the protest. Strange as it is, Ogopogo must have ingested a strip of fruit leather because he's one-third normal size when standing on his hind feet. Ordinarily Ogopogo is twenty feet in height or length. Can you imagine him after a good hang time of the ball, retrieving his own kick?"

Lancaster: "You are right, Don. That's an interesting observation. Hold everything! The Saskatchewan and Hamilton managers and coaches are huddling near centre field and are now reviewing the CFL Rule Book. Candidly speaking, I don't think the rules define what is a football player."

With that assessment Lancaster was correct, because after a five-minute game delay, one could hear Velocity delightfully say to the referee, "Show me in the rule book where a *player* is defined and Ogopogo can't play."

When the referee couldn't find such a rule, he said to the respective teams, "On with the game. Ogopogo stays!"

As the game progressed, Ogopogo had an opportunity to kick another field goal but failed when the ball hit the uprights. In the final quarter, however, Ogopogo overcame his nervousness and after swallowing a strip of peach-flavored Famous Okanagan Fruit Leather, he was energized and set a CFL record by kicking nine consecutive field goals by defeating the Hamilton Tiger Cats 27-14.

After the 9th field goal Ogopogo retrieved the football and brought it to Stevie Joseph, who was watching the game in the wheelchair section. Ogopogo said to Stevie that he could keep the ball forever.

Following the initial victory, the Roughriders went on to defeat the Ottawa Roughriders and the British Columbia Lions. Following the game against the Lions, the usual after-the-game press conference was held and Wong was bombarded with questions from media reporters.

Wong answered one reporter question with, "The Roughriders can smell first place in the CFL since Ogopogo joined the team. Ogopogo is a tremendous athlete and inspiration. The Roughriders have momentum. There's a level of exhilaration and intensity among the players that is unbelievable. They play with a vision to see a dream come true."

At the same press conference the B. C. Lions coach said, "There is no question if teams are going to win against the Roughriders they'll have stop Ogopogo kicking field goals from ninety yards out."

And when the other games did take place, the Roughriders winning streak continued. The team won fourteen games in a row and the right to meet the Edmonton Eskimos in the Western finals with the winner playing Toronto Argos for the Grey Cup. In a televised game against the Eskimos Lancaster said, "It's a dream come true for the Saskatchewan Roughriders to play in the Western CFL finals.

"They are the Cinderella team of the year, but I believe, because of Edmonton's experience and scouting system, that Ogopogo doesn't kick a field goal. The Eskimos are a mean bunch and are psyched up for this game."

As it turned out the Eskimos dominated the game for 59 minutes and 30 seconds and seemingly had c certain victory, when it vanished into never, never land in the final thirty seconds. The Eskimo quarter back had a reputation for never winning the big games.

First a 104 yard, three play drive, capped by a two yard toss from the quarterback to the receiver, with just one second remaining in the game, gave the Roughriders a 33–32 victory and the right to play Toronto Argos in the Skydome for the Grey Cup.

As a result of the part Ogopogo played against the Eskimos, he was honored by Canadian International Airlines as the CFL player of the year, and given a trip for two, to any destination in the world.

"In a season of ten percent cutbacks, that's a nice prize," Ogopogo said to the president of Air Canada. In addition to the trip Ogopogo was named rookie of the year and presented with a $5000 cheque.

The following day newspapers wrote about the Saskatchewan Roughriders. Some of the headlines were: Roughrider Pride Restored, Roughriders Blast Eskimos, Big Day For Wong and Ogopogo, Roughriders Not Losers Anymore, Roughriders Meet Argos in Grey Cup.

Prior to the Grey Cup game, which took place several weeks before the Christmas holidays began, Lancaster said from his television booth at the Skydome. "Both Roughriders and Argos are evenly matched that if I don't have a heart attack while commenting on the game, I don't think I'll ever have one." And in a softer tone of voice continued, "Incidentally, Stevie Joseph and his parents from Moose Jaw, Saskatchewan, are guests of Ogopogo. With the airline ticket and the $5000 he had won, Ogopogo flew Stevie Joseph and his parents to Toronto covering all their expenses."

As a camera panned the Skydome and later zoomed in on Stevie and his parents, Lancaster continued, "That's generous of Ogopogo."

As for the game itself, Whitman said, "This should be an exciting game as the West is matched against the best in the East. Despite a general lack of hoopla compared to previous Grey Cup games this one is interesting because of the extraordinary football talent.

Fans have come to see the Toronto Argos, some the Skydome, and some to watch football's phenomenon, Ogopogo, kicking field goals. By the way, the crowd is sixty thousand and in a festive mood."

The highlight of the first half of the game was when Toronto returned an Ogopogo punt for ninety yards and a touchdown. Near the end of the game the Roughriders were trailing 33-28 and needed a touchdown desperately in order to win. A field goal would not do it.

During a huddle Ogopogo slipped a strip of fruit leather from his uniform, swallowed it, and while changing in height from six feet six inches to his normal height or length of twenty feet, he said to his teammates, "Watch me."

As soon as the ball was snapped to him, Ogopogo kicked it so high that the ball's trajectory almost reached the Skydome roof. With seventeen seconds hang time and twenty seconds left in the game, it was perfect timing. By the time the football was landing at the opposite end, Ogopogo was already waiting on the ten-yard line.

Because of Ogopogo's tremendous height and speed, he was the only player able to catch the ball, and when he did, run for a touchdown. Following a convert the video screen board flashed:

Roughriders 35. Argos 33. Saskatchewan Roughriders New Grey Cup Champions!

Naturally Argo fans were disappointed but not the coach. When the Argo coach was interviewed in the dressing room by Lancaster he said. "Our team played with verve, discipline and enthusiasm that we didn't deserve to lose but what can I say? Ogopogo came up with another of his tricks. I'll have to say the game will go down in history as a classic."

There was pandemonium in the Roughriders dressing room as champagne bottles kept popping. Above the triumphant sounding noise Wong said, "This was the kind of a game the National Football League would like to have on TV."

Velocity agreed. "It was awesome to see Ogopogo in the dying seconds return his own kick and scramble for a touchdown. I challenge the National Football League for the winner of the Super Bowl to play the Saskatchewan Roughriders, champions of the Canadian Football League."

Meanwhile, in Regina and other Saskatchewan cities, towns and villages, Roughrider fans paraded through the streets less than an hour after Roughrider pride was restored.

In Regina, where Christmas lights and decorations were in place and carols emanated from loudspeakers, fans wearing their team regalia chanted, "We are number one. Now the Super-Super Bowl. Giants, Bears, Packers, Dolphins, Jets, Cowboys, it doesn't matter."

At the same time, a Regina radio station was interviewing fans at a night club for their reaction and one in a frenzy state said," This is the sweetest victory ever. I knew right along that with Wong at the helm and Ogopogo as our kicker, we could win the Grey Cup."

Another fan said while clutching a beer bottle, "I agree with Velocity that Canada and America should have a Super-Super Bowl."

Several days after the Roughriders returned to Regina, the team was honored with a parade and a public reception where the Mayor said, "Thank you, Roughriders for winning the Grey Cup and restoring Roughrider pride." As a side remark, the Mayor said, "Dandelion, you'll get to keep your garbage hauling contract."

The Mayor then paid special tribute to club manager Velocity and Coach Wong, and congratulated Ogopogo for being named the CFL Player of the year. As Ogopogo acknowledged those applauding, Stevie Joseph, who was in a wheelchair next to him, said, "I want to congratulate you too, Ogopogo."

Ogopogo and Stevie Joseph had struck up a friendship since Ogopogo's arrival in Regina and the two seemed inseperateable as they were for most of the time during the football season, because Ogopogo boarded with the Joseph family. It seemed no other family wanted Ogopogo to board with them and it's still not clear if the reason was because of Ogopogo's color, shape, unorthodox habits or that he wasn't a human being.

At any rate, the Ogopogo phenomenon, on and off the field, did not go unnoticed by the media, particularly in America where as a rule things are first, the biggest or the best on the entire Planet Earth. Ogopogo made the front cover of *Sports Illustrated, Time* and *National Geographic. The Miami Herald, Washington Post, and San Francisco Examiner* featured articles about Ogopogo and appeared as a guest on *Good Morning America, Nightline, Larry King* and *David Letterman* shows.

Ogopogo also appeared as a guest on the televised NFL game between the Chicago Bears and San Francisco 49rs, hitting Super Bowl stride.

Well known American journalists suggested they collaborate with Ogopogo in doing his biography, and book on cooking, physical exercise and Ogopogo's favorite bird calls. One author even suggested that Ogopogo write a weekly column on how to kick field goals.

Advertising agencies clamored for Ogopogo to endorse various products but he declined with the exception of advertising Famous Okanagan Fruit Leather. Ogopogo agreed however, to become a honorary member of the Handicapped Children's Association of Saskatchewan and to work part-time as a Santa Claus at Sears Department Store in Regina.

It was a time when Ogopogo was playing the role of Santa that a girl, about seven, climbed on his knees and said, "I would like a teddy bear for Christmas that looks like Ogopogo."

"If you are good I'll see that you get one," Ogopogo replied in a disguised voice.

When it was Stevie Joseph's turn to speak to Santa, Ogopogo said, "Is there something else that you want more than anything else for Christmas?"

"I do."

"And what may that be?"

"I want to see the Saskatchewan Roughriders play the National Football League champions in a Super-Super Bowl."

"You, what?"

"I would like to see the Saskatchewan Roughriders play the National Football League champions in a Super-Super Bowl," Stevie repeated.

"That is a different request. I'll do what I can," Santa Ogopogo said at the same time realizing that he was speaking to Stevie Joseph.

For a moment, Ogopogo had wished he had not taken a part-time role-playing Santa Claus at Sears Department Store.

Ogopogo buried his head in his hands (legs) and said to himself, "I hope Stevie isn't disappointed this Christmas. I wonder if the CFL Commissioner can help. I'll call him."

As soon as the store closed for the day Ogopogo discarded his Santa suit and went to the nearest public telephone booth where he placed a long distance call to the Commissioner in Toronto.

As soon as the Commissioner picked up his phone and said "Hello," Ogopogo identified himself and said, "Mr. Commissioner, I have just finished playing a role of Santa Claus at Sears Department Store in Regina, and had a most unusual request from an eight-year-old boy. Perhaps you can help this boy fulfill his lifetime passionate dream? Tell me, have you got children of your own?"

"I do. Three, of them."

"And you wouldn't want them to be disappointed at Christmas time?"

"I wouldn't."

"To let down a child at Christmas would be a traumatic thing, especially when the child is a wheelchair victim," Ogopogo said.

"It certainly would," The Commissioner replied, "What is the special request?'

"The request is that Stevie Joseph would like to see the Saskatchewan Roughriders, they are the Grey Cup

Champions as you know, play the National Football
League Super Bowl winners in January."
"This is an unusual request from an eight-year-old boy
I admit, but since it deals with football, I'll speak to
the National Football League president and see what he
thinks about the idea. I'll call back tomorrow."

The Commissioner kept his promise, but when he phoned
back he said, "No such luck."
"Did the NFL president give a reason?'
"He did."
"Well, what was it?"
"There will be no Super-Super Bowl game because only a
handful of people in America have heard of Saskatchewan
and many can't pronounce the name. If it was Toronto,
there could be a fifty-fifty chance."
"Then I'll call the Prime Minister of Canada, perhaps he
can use his influence?" Ogopogo said.
"And you may also call the North Pole to the real Santa.
But I warn you, don't get your hopes up because Santa
has problems of his own dealing with issues like parking
problems for his sleigh and reindeer and small chimneys
caused by children's demands for unusual and larger gifts
than before. At any rate give the real Santa a call."
And that is what happened. Ogopogo called the real
Santa and went on to give the jolly bearded man in full
detail the Stevie Joseph story and his unusual request to
see the Saskatchewan Roughriders play the Super Bowl
champions. Ogopogo ended his conversation by saying
that Stevie's parents weren't wealthy and above everything
else, the boy's health condition was deteriorating.

Santa said it would take a miracle for Stevie's wish to come true and wished him a speedy recovery. "But if you wish to call the Prime Minister of Canada and see if he can help us, please do."

When Ogopogo called the Prime Minister's office the PM was out of town so Ogopogo left a message with his secretary. Two days later Ogopogo had a paid plane fare and summoned to Ottawa.

When the Prime Minister finished listening to Ogopogo, he immediately got on the **hot line** to Washington and called the American president at the White House.

When the president was handed the phone, he said all his aides had already left the White House so they could spend Christmas with their families. But when the Prime Minister said, "Stevie Joseph desperately needs you."

The President changed his mind and said, "In that case I'll speak to the people who run the National Football League and call you back as soon as I'm able too."

The president kept his word and returned the call the following day. "The NFL clubs had taken a poll and agreed to play the Saskatchewan Roughriders, but on two conditions."

"Conditions? What conditions? The Prime Minister asked.

"That the game be played according to National Football League rules."

"And what is the second condition?"

"That the game be played in Florida where it is warm, instead of cold Canada."

"We got ourselves a deal," the Prime Minister said and then bet the President a box of frozen trout caught in Cold Lake if the Roughriders lost and in turn, the President send him a crate of Florida oranges if the Roughriders won.

By the time Santa heard about the confirmation, it was Christmas Eve so on a piece of paper he wrote a note, stuffed it in an envelope that was placed into a bag with other presents he had to deliver to the good girls and boys.

Next, Santa hopped into his sleigh and as the reindeer were pulling it towards the sky, he hollered, "I hope there's no storm tonight as I have deadline to meet and deliver a present to Stevie Joseph in Regina, Saskatchewan and to other girls and boys throughout the world. On Comet! On, Cupid, Dasher, Dancer, Vixen and Rudolph!"

Christmas morning, after Santa had distributed the toys, Stevie sat with his parents and Ogopogo near the fireplace opening packages. When Stevie came to an envelope Marked, "To Stevie Joseph from Santa," he hollered with excitement. "Look Mom and Dad. Look Ogopogo! Here's an envelope addressed to me from Santa Claus!"

"What does it say?" Stevie's mother asked in a tone of voice that was as exciting as Stevie's was.

Stevie opened the envelope quickly and the read the contents out loud:

"To Stevie Joseph

Regina, Saskatchewan

Arrangements have been completed for the Saskatchewan Roughriders to play the winner of the Super Bowl in January. Have a Merry Christmas.

Signed—Santa. North Pole—Postal Code: HOH OHO.
"I can't believe it. Some of the kids even said that the Santa
at Sears wasn't real," Stevie said, as soon as he finished
reading the note and placed it on top of his bed.
Looking towards Ogopogo who was standing between
the Christmas tree and a burning fireplace, Stevie then
asked where the game would take place.
"In Miami, Florida. January 25." Ogopogo replied. "And
I'll see to it that you and your parents are there to watch
the Roughriders play."

Between Christmas and January 25 the Chicago Bears
defeated the Denver Broncos in the Super Bowl and in
that space of time the Roughriders had many practices
studying the four downs rule.
It was a beautiful day with plenty of sunshine in Miami
as the Roughriders and Bears were to clash in the Super-
Super Bowl the following day. The Roughriders had
checked into the Miami Holiday Inn where a large banner
with the words *RIDER PRIDE* greeted everyone.

The hoopla at the Holiday Inn was all-Canadian with all
sorts of parties and guests in costumes as beavers, Canada
geese, whooping cranes, miners, oilmen, cowboys and
snowmen. Many of the guests booked into the hotel
as part of their regular *Snowbird* holidays and watched
entertainers and cheerleaders perform.
Miss Grey Cup was there, along with Miss Canada and Miss
Saskatchewan. They were accompanied by cheer leaders
and two Mounties dressed in scarlet tunics whose job was,
besides promoting the province of Saskatchewan, keeping

semblance of law and order in the hotel and to be stationed near the Roughrider bench when the game was played.

It was during the hotel festivities that an unusual thing for Saskatchewan but not Florida, happened. While Ogopogo and Stevie Joseph were sitting on a bench, near the beach, when a blue colored van with two unshaven strangers speaking in a thick foreign accent, stopped in front of them. Pointing to Ogopogo the first stranger said to the second, "That's him. You take Ogopogo by de arms and I'll him by the legs," which they did, and shoved Ogopogo in the back of the van and drove away at great speed. It was a moment when Ogopogo was relaxing and his size was one-third his normal height/length.

Seeing what had happened, Stevie wheeled into the hotel lobby where team manger Velocity and Coach Wong were discussing football strategy and shouted, "Somebody stole Ogopogo! In order to win the Roughriders need Ogopogo!"

"Let's call the police!" Wong said and dialed a 900 number.

Between the time Ogopogo was kidnapped and game-time the following day, Miami police were in contact with the RCMP, FBI, Canadian and American embassies but there was no trace of Ogopogo. An hour before game time the two kidnappers were in a ramshackle house on the outskirts of Miami. Having hidden Ogopogo in a room, they were placing a bet with a gambling bookie on the outcome of the Saskatchewan Roughriders vs. Chicago Bears game.

"What are the odds now?" the first kidnaper asked the bookie on the other end of the telephone.

"With Ogopogo out of the Roughrider lineup the odds are 100 to 1 the Bears will win the Super-Super Bowl by three touchdowns," the bookie replied.

"Correct me if I'm wrong. The odds are 100 to 1 the Bears will win by three touchdowns?'

"Those are the exact odds."

"Good. Then I'll bet $1000, that's enough money should we win, to buy guns and ammunition for our next robbery."

"Quiet, not so loud, Ogopogo may hear you," the first kidnapper reprimanded his friend.

Although Ogopogo was locked in solitary confinement in the same house where the kidnapers lived he wasn't harmed in any way. Unfortunately Ogopogo didn't have any fruit leather with him. Under normal circumstances he would ingest a strip, get energized, and get himself out of a predicament like this. Ogopogo, however, had another possibility of escaping but it meant communicating with Saint Sam Bobek in Heaven.

Again, unfortunately, Ogopogo did not have the power to communicate with the saint but coach Lo Wong did.

When all avenues to locate Ogopogo were exhausted, Wong did indeed make contact with Saint Sam. At first however, the newly canonized saint was reluctant to do anything but when he heard about Stevie's predicament said, "I'll even get all the other saints and angels to search.

As soon and we find Ogopogo I'll notify the two RCMP constables accompanying you to Miami."

When the Super-Super Bowl broadcast began Whitman said, "Well, football fans in Canada, there's gloom among Saskatchewan Roughriders players, as well as their supporters in Miami, because Ogopogo is missing from the lineup.

"Chicago Bears are huge, strong and fast with tacklers as furious and grizzly bears in the Yukon. They are explosive."

Lancaster continued: "You are right, Don. The Chicago Bears are an explosive team and one of the fiercest in the National Football League. Without Ogopogo in the lineup the Roughriders haven't got a chance in winning."

Lancaster was correct with that assessment and in the space of time that the game began and end of the first half, Saint Holi made contact with the two RCMP constables in the stadium and pinpointed the exact location where Ogopogo was kept as a hostage.

'Come, lets go!" the first constable said to the second, and then the two policemen fought their way to street level and the second hollered, "Taxi! Taxi!"

Within minutes the two Mounties, in scarlet tunics, were knocking on the door of the ramshackle house. Hearing an unexpected knock the first kidnapper said, "Who is it?" but the Mounties did not answer.

The kidnappers' curiosity was aroused, so the second went and opened the door and this time the second Mountie said, "We are members of the Royal Canadian Police."

The first kidnapper put a hand to his ear, "Mountain what?"

"They are members of a lodge like the Moose, Elk and Shriners," the second kidnapper, who joined his friend at the door, said.

The first Mountie corrected his adversary. "We are Canadian police."

"Like in the Sunday morning cartoons?" the second kidnapper said but this time the two Mounties did not correct him.

"We are searching for the Saskatchewan Roughrider football player Ogopogo," the second Mountie continued.

"We are no fan of his," the first kidnapper replied but the two Mounties disregarded his comment and upon a mutually signal handcuffed the two bandits and rescued Ogopogo. Miami police were on the scene within minutes.

As Miami police were pushing the two kidnappers into their patrol car, the first Mountie said to the waiting taxi driver, "Let's hurry to the Joe Robbie Stadium, but Ogopogo corrected him, "No, please, first to the Holiday Inn."

The Mountie was surprised. "The Holiday Inn? What for? The game will soon be over."

"To the Holiday Inn, so that I may pick up a supply of Famous Okanagan Fruit Leather that I left in my room."

The taxi driver negotiated his way through streets and avenues filled with heavy traffic, coming to a stop in front of the hotel where Ogopogo picked up a package of fruit leather. On the way down the elevator was busy so he slid down the banister stopping in the lobby for several seconds to learn from a television set that the Bears were leading 21-0 near the end of the third quarter, and were about to score another touchdown.

"There's still time for me to play and the Roughriders win," Ogopogo said to the two Mounties and to the taxi driver, "Please hurry, to the stadium."

As the taxi driver stepped on the accelerator Ogopogo asked the two Mounties an important question, which was, "Is Stevie Joseph at the game?"

Ogopogo was assured that Stevie and his parents were but saddened that Ogopogo wasn't in the lineup.

When Ogopogo arrived at the stadium he could hear a deafening uproar, the Bears had scored their fourth touchdown.

Ogopogo rushed to the dressing room, put on his gear and a Saskatchewan Roughrider uniform. By now the two teams were in the final quarter and the Bears were about to kick a field goal but the play was temporarily interrupted when Ogopogo appeared on the sideline and Roughrider fans acclaimed him applause reserved only for a hero.

"Can we pull it off?" Wong said to Ogopogo as soon as they were within speaking distance.

"I think so. As soon as I enjoy my strip of Famous Okanagan Fruit Leather," Ogopogo replied and when he did, his size increased from six-foot-eight inches to his normal length/height of twenty feet, in other words he was two stories high.

When Ogopogo stood on his hind legs, the Bears and their supporters were awed by the gargantuan figure and led the Bear coach to pull out a pistol. "I'll stop chewing tobacco! What is this? A creature from the Ice Age?" the Bear coach said as he was about to fire a shot but seeing the two Mounties nearby, changed his mind, and instead threw the pistol into the stands and said to his players, "Go, get him Bears!"

While the Bears coach said, 'Go, get him Bears.' On the other side of the field Wong said to Ogopogo, "Do you think you can block the field goal attempt?"

Ogopogo did, and then picked up the loose ball and ran it for a touchdown. Following a convert the scoreboard read: Chicago 28—Saskatchewan 7.

Silenced hushed the stadium, but silence turned to an uproar several minutes later when a Bear fumbled the ball and again Ogopogo scooped it up scrambling for another touchdown. Following a convert the scoreboard read: Chicago 28—Saskatchewan 14.

Halfway through the final quarter, Ogopogo did what he did during the Grey Cup game against Toronto Argos. When he had a hold of the ball, he quick-kicked it into the air after the second down. While the ball was afloat, Ogopogo ran behind the Bears' goal line.

The trajectory was perfect and with the ball hang time of seventeen seconds, Ogopogo grabbed the ball as it was landing. Even the fiercest of the Bears could not stop Ogopogo catch the ball for another touchdown that was converted without difficulty. The scoreboard read: Chicago 28—Saskatchewan 21.

The Bears' misfortune continued when minutes later, an errant Bear pass was intercepted by a Roughrider who returned the ball for a 30 yard touchdown. Following

a successful convert, the Score Board read: Chicago 28—
Saskatchewan 28.

Whitman and Lancaster described the final seconds of the
Super-Super Bowl this way;

Lancaster said to his TV audience, "Unbelievable. What
a comeback by the Roughriders. The score is tied 28-28
and there are thirty seconds left in the game. After a
Roughrider kickoff, the Bears will have the ball in their
own end and anything can happen."

Whitman: "Since Ogopogo returned to the lineup in the
final quarter Bears have looked like a team of futility with
eight penalties, three missed field goals, five fumbles, three
interceptions and I wouldn't be surprised if something
unusual happened."

Lancaster: "Hold it! The Roughriders have just kicked off
and guest what? Guess what?

The Bears fumbled again. Ogopogo has the ball and he's
going, going, going and he's gone. No Bear can stop
him. Touchdown! Saskatchewan Roughriders win the
Super-Super Bowl game. There's pandemonium in the
Joe Robbie Stadium"

That memorable day, not only did the Saskatchewan
Roughriders win the Super-Super Bowl, but also it's a
day that Stevie Joseph will never forget. As soon as the
game was over, young Stevie discarded his wheelchair and
began walking with the use of a cain.

Flashbulbs popped and film cameras followed Stevie as he
hobbled his way across the stadium to congratulate Ogopogo
who by now was in the dressing room celebrating an upset
football game and Stevie Joseph's Christmas present.

Tempo Shlikaput

Although Tempo Shlikaput isn't as famous as 'General' Tom Thumb, the most famous midget in history, he still brought delight to thousands of people, young and elderly, in Kelowna and the Okanagan Valley of British Columbia. Tempo was eighteen-years old when herbalist Dr. Lo Wong discovered the thirty six-pound, thirty six-inch tall midget, a son of poor and medium height parents. Dr. Wong had already discovered Famous Okanagan Fruit Leather and Ogopogo, who at first people said was a fake but with the passage of time, discovered that he became a permanent fixture in and around Okanagan Lake which the entire Planet Earth was reading and talking about. Wong hoped the world would soon get to know Tempo Shlikaput too.

When Shlikaput made his first public appearance in Kelowna skeptics couldn't believe that this small person's weight was the same as his height. Years earlier, when his parents showed their son to Dr. Paul Bond the doctor could not offer them little hope that the child could ever grow to normal height, nor did he. Apart from his small size Tempo was perfectly proportioned and did what normal male people did: play catch, eat junk food and chase girls. At parties he was tossed from one person to another.

It was at such a party that Wong first saw the tiny man's potential as a great entertainer so he asked Tempo to live with him. Dr. Wong was chairman of a committee to build a small people's village in Kelowna and thought this tiny man's talents could be used in a fund-raising campaign.

When Tempo first met Wong eye to eye, he was exceedingly bashful. He had light colored hair, muddy cheeks and was in best of health. Tempo lodged with Wong in the Okanagan Tower, a high-rise situated next to the Famous Okanagan Fruit Leather International Corp. factory. Every free moment Wong could find to be away from his laboratory he tutored his tiny protégé and Ogopogo, for their roles in the fund-raising *Big Show*. Wong taught Tempo and Ogopogo songs and jokes, monologues, how to pose and strut and impersonate celebrities such as the Queen giving her annual Christmas message,

Tempo, thrilled by the attention he was getting and the colorful costumes Wong provided, soon lost his bashfulness. Together with Ogopogo and Wong's direction, he worked day and night for the greatest extravaganza Kelowna was to witness—much greater than the Annual October Wine Festival.

After a week of rehearsing, Tempo and Ogopogo became attached to each other and Kelowna was flooded with radio, TV, newspaper and handbill advertising.

The theme was always the same:
SEE TEMPO SHLIKAPUT AND OGOPOGO DISPLAY THEIR TALENTS—PROCEEDS TOWARDS CONSTRUCTION OF A SMALL PEOPLE VILLAGE

Before Tempo and Ogopogo appeared on a specially constructed stage in Karry Park, Wong, who appreciated the value of publicity, made the rounds of newspaper editors and talk-show hosts, with the midget on his shoulder and Ogopogo by his side. Tempo, no bigger than a large doll, was deposited on their desks and together with Ogopogo, recited poems, impersonate people, danced and sang to their hearts content, which lead the editor of the Kelowna Currier newspaper, to write: "The Tempo Shlikaput and Ogopogo charity show in aid of construction of a Small People Village In the city of Kelowna is Worthy of a crowd off at least one hundred and twenty five thousand, which is Kelowna's entire population.

Tempo's and Ogopogo's performance on a June full-moon night was an instant success and raised $50,000. Wong, an incorrigible punster, wrote most of the introductory lines as there were dances, comedy, singing routines that made Karry Park ring out with laughter and applause. Kelownaites and their cousins from Penticton and Vernon flocked to enjoy Wong's new stars.

One visitor at concert was the entertainment critic for the Vancouver *Sun* newspaper, who after witnessing the performance wrote: "Shlikaput and Ogopogo were lively and sprightly with no deficiency of intellect—their song-dance and standup comedy routine deserves exposure beyond the province of British Columbia."

Tempo and Ogopogo were an answer to a showman's prayer. Their charm, their natural talent as performers, their quick wit, and above all their size variance, made them celebrities overnight but there were, as yet, no Shlikaput/Ogopogo T-shirts for sale.

Wong signed the new-found entertainers to a one-year contract which made Wong and Ogopogo pleased, but not nearly as much as rest of Kelowna who realized Wong had found a gold mine in that the village for midget people would be completed the following year.

Tempo and Ogopogo were sent on a tour throughout Canada and their fame spread from Victoria, B. C. to St. John's, Newfoundland. During a St. John's performance Wong had an idea, why not America and have Tempo and Ogopogo perform there with equal success?

"Where do we start?" Tempo excitedly asked.

"New York City."

A week had elapsed, before Wong, Tempo and Ogopogo arrived in New York to perform at the Lincoln Center.

Word of their coming reached the city after Wong appeared on the *Larry King Live* show and a crowd was waiting to catch a glimpse of them at the Grand Central Station.

Tempo's and Ogopogo's debut in America was a disappointing one, however. Very few patrons showed up at the Lincoln Center.

Next day, the manager of the Center said to Wong, "Freaks of Nature and human oddities should appear only at a circus or a zoo and not a place of culture."

But to Wong, Tempo was a human marvel and was determined to have a village in Kelowna built.

Sadly, Ogopogo said, "A hunter does not at all time bring home game."

"And a baseball player does not always hit a home run," Tempo said.

Wong had hoped to present Tempo and Ogopogo to the Mayor of New York City within several days of their arrival as Americans have a profound interest for the unusual.

Wong reasoned that once the Tempo/Ogopogo team had been received at City Hall, all of New York would be lining up to see and hear them perform. But there had been a serious accident in the Mayor's family so he could not receive them. A hall was rented off Broadway and Tempo and Ogopogo presented a concert that brought them fame in Canada in which the highlight was Tempo playing the kazoo and Ogopogo a comb with a fruit leather wrapper.

Soon, New Yorkers found Tempo and Ogopogo irresistible and when Wong suggested a London engagement both accepted. Tempo also accepted an offer from the manager of the New York Yankees for a one-game stint against the Detroit Tigers.

It seems that the Yankees were at the bottom of the American League standings at the time and the manager wanted to motivate his players. On that particular afternoon Tempo was assigned as the designated hitter.

Tempo was not a good baseball player but he had a very small strike zone. As a matter of fact the Yankee manager instructed Tempo never to swing at the ball because he could be relied upon to earn a walk, a base on balls.

After seven innings, the Tiger pitcher became frustrated and said to Tempo, "Shlikaput, If you don't swing at my pitch I'll hit you," which he did, during the next pitch. Tempo made it to first base another time after being struck by a pitch. In the end because of Tempo not swinging the bat, the Yankees got out of their slump and went on the defeat the Tigers 11-0.

Tempo and Ogopogo completed their last performance in New York the following night and the following day, ten thousand admirers watched them board a ship due to sail from New York to London. As the vessel swung seaward a brass band played *O Canada*.

After Tempo, Ogopogo and Wong arrived in London, and like in New York, their first contact with English show biz was a disappointment. The proprietor of a London theatre offered them one-hundred pounds a night. Wong declined the offer. Next the Mayor of London told Wong that the usual place for seeing midgets and monsters in England was at a circus and not in a theatre or a park.

Wong began to think that he had made a serious mistake in coming to England but was determined to have a village for little people built in Kelowna.

"England will pay in gold to see Tempo Shlikaput and Ogopogo perform," Wong said to the Mayor of London and hoped to present his treasures to the Queen and her husband in Buckingham Palace within a week of their arrival. The English had a high respect for royalty. Wong realized this, and once the Queen might receive Tempo and Ogopogo all of London would be lining up to see them perform.

Unfortunately there had been a scandal in the royal family, and any kind of entertainment was out of the question. So a theatre was rented in the West end of London and Tempo and Ogopogo presented their routine that brought them fame in Canada and America.

Wong's first step was to send letters of invitation to the nobility, editors of newspapers and talk-show hosts. Before long, limousines were lined-up outside the theatre. The Canadian ambassador was so impressed with Tempo's and Ogopogo's performance that he promised to use his influence to have the two Canadians presented to the Queen.

Two days later, the Baroness Rothschild, wife of a wealthy banker, sent her chauffeur for Tempo, Ogopogo and Wong. At her mansion they were ushered up a light of marble stairs to find a party of at least fifty ladies and gentlemen waiting with the baroness. For two hours Tempo and Ogopogo kept the company in stitches.

As Tempo, Ogpopogo and Wong were leaving, a cheque with six figures was slipped into Wong's hand. There was a note attached that read: "Towards The Construction of a Small People Village in Canada."

The time now seemed ripe to present Tempo and Ogopogo to a larger audience but this did not happen until later, because an elegantly uniformed officer of the Life Guards knocked on Wong's door in the hotel where he stayed. On an appointed time Tempo, Ogopogo and Wong arrived at Buckingham Palace in attire suited for the occasion.

The tiny Tempo Shlikaput and the gargantuan Ogopogo, made a quaint pair. The Lord in Waiting gave Wong and his two entertainers a quick course in court etiquette.

They were forbidden for example, to address the Queen unless she spoke first. In the great picture gallery at Buckingham Palace the three visitors found one hundred and fifty members of nobility along with ambassadors and their wives, from other countries waiting.

The Royal party and foreign dignitaries were thrilled at the first sight of the tiny Tempo and tall Ogopogo striding towards them. During the tour Ogopogo shrunk to a seven-foot height. When they were close enough the two entertainers bowed and the Queen said, "Welcome to Buckingham Palace."

"Good evening your majesty, ladies and gentlemen," Tempo answered in his high-pitched voice.

The gathering burst out into laughter when Ogopogo in a deep voice said, "It's a pleasure to be your guest."

Taking Tempo by his hand and Ogopogo his front foot, the Queen led the couple and Wong around the gallery. The queen was curious about the Small People Village that was to be built and fielded questions at her guests about the project.

The replies kept the Queen laughing constantly. Tempo said to her majesty that she was pretty and enjoyed listening to her annual Christmas message to the Commonwealth.

Then, Tempo and Ogopogo gave a performance of their best songs, imitations of famous people that included the Queen giving her annual Christmas message to the Commonwealth, a comedy routine and dances. Those present found their act interesting and burst out laughing many times.

What made the scene even more interesting was when the Queen's favorite poodle got excited by the unorthodox appearance of two entertainers and began to bark, and then snapped at Ogopogo's hind leg. This time the Queen and her companions burst out with laughter till tears came down their eyes.

The following day, all of London's media carried an account of Shlikaput's and Ogopogo's visit to Buckingham Palace. The account distributed by a court official, actually had been written by Wong himself and in part read; "After Shlikaput and Ogopogo performed for the Queen and foreign ambassadors, a large amount of money was delivered to Kelowna, B. C. Canada towards the construction of a midget village in that community."

Tempo and Ogopogo were doing a thriving business in London. Their photographs were frequently seen in tabloids and on television. The BBC and even Dame Edna interviewed the couple. Children bought paper dolls representing the couple in costumes they were in their most celebrated roles. Musical compositions were dedicated or written about them.

The Shlikaput and Ogopogo Polka were played everywhere. Their life-like figures were even made for the Wax Museum.

The highlight of Shlikaput's and Ogopogo's stay in London was invitations by foreign ambassadors to appear in their country, and a satellite performance at Wembly Stadium where seventy thousand screaming-cheering fans attended. The TV performance was beamed throughout the Commonwealth with an estimated audience much larger than that of the Super Bowl or Academy Awards in America.

After a stay in London, Tempo and Ogopogo embarked for Paris where their performance eclipsed all that had taken place before. Valuable gifts where showered on them including French wine, perfume, diamonds and emeralds. The crowd that packed both sides of Champs Elysees cheered widely as the three Canadians rode in an open convertible bowing left and right with all the aplomb of a conquering hero.

Wong had engaged the Paris Opera House for Tempo and Ogopogo to perform in. Their popularity was so great that tickets for their performances were sold out a month in advance. Poems and songs were written about the couple.

Children munched chocolate figures like their image. The French also named cereals after the two entertainers— Shlikaput Flakes and Ogopogo Fishcakes. Plastic statues of the couple appeared in boutique shops. Wine bottles with their picture on the side became popular in restaurants and bars.

A bank had a poster in its window say the couple had an account there. Coached in French. the couple even performed a comedy routine in the French language entitled *Le Petit Poucet Et Gros Monster.*

Next, having received an invitation from the Spanish ambassador to England, Wong took the entertainers to Barcelona where their performances outdrew bullfights. There were also comic books sold in shopping malls where Shlikaput was a toreador and Ogopogo a flamenco dancer. To commemorate Tempo's and Ogopogo's visit to Spain, the Mayor of Barcelona presented each a box of cigars that included writing in Spanish. Neither of the entertainers smoked nor spoke Spanish, so they asked the Mayor to translate the writing.

"Sure thing," The Mayor replied, "It says smoking this cigar may be dangerous to your health."

But that did not matter, what did, was that Tempo and Ogopogo kept on being non-smokers and on the following day were on flight bound for Italy.

In Italy the two entertainers watched the Leaning Tower of Pisa nearly fall over. In Rome they dined with the Italian ambassador to Canada.

On the menu was spaghetti Bolognese but since Wong was a vegetarian he didn't eat it. The ambassador's cook offered him a pasta and prawn entrée instead. Even before their performance at the Opera House Tempo's and Ogopogo's fashion trend rivaled that of Gucci's.

After a week of sold out performances in Rome, the three Canadians had a private audience with the Pope at the Vatican who to each of them said in a poetic manner, "Kelowna is your cradle. Kelowna is your nest. Kelowna is where your bones should rest."

Wong took the Pope's advice seriously and returned to Canada. With the money raised Wong put it into a savings account at the Kelowna Savings Credit Union.

The Kelowna entertainers were delighted with the warm welcome they had received at home, but shortly afterwards, despite his success as an entertainer, Tempo found something missing in life—a female companion.

One day while carpenters were building Midget Village Tempo stopped at Wong's laboratory and became attracted to a new 'Wonder' who Wong introduced as Edith Tomatoot, his receptionist. Edith stopped growing at age ten. She was thirty two inches tall and weigh thirty two pounds. No one knew she was a midget when she answered a phone unless they came to see her in person.

When Tempo was alone with Wong he said to him, "Please, introduce me to the most charming little lady I ever saw. I believe she was created by God to be my wife." Wong smiled as Tempo and continued, "Look, you are a friend of mine.

I want you to say a good word for me to Edith. I'm financially secure and want to marry her and settle in the Little People Village. I feel as if I must marry the young lady."

To Wong, a bachelor, Tempo seemed unusually excited and urged him to calm down and to proceed with caution as he could hardly expect to win Miss Tomatoot's affection overnight. "And one thing more," Wong said.

"What?"

"Marriage is no trifle thing," Wong said and revealed that Shlikaput had a rival for the young lady's heart.

"Who?"

"Another little person who works for Famous Okanagan Fruit Leather International Corp. as a salesman. His name is Gregory Littleman and although he's little, he's muscular and larger than you."

Shlikapoot got excited, took several steps forward and said, "Gregory Littleman? I know him. I'll fight him if necessary."

As usual Wong found a way to turn an unpredictable situation into an advantage. He invited Tempo and Ms Tomatoot to accompany him on a trip to Victoria where Wong had an appointment to meet the premier and his cabinet about the possibility of obtaining a government grant towards the construction of Midget Village.

"What a tiny but well-matched couple," the Minister of Housing said as soon as he saw Tempo and Tomatoot on Wong's shoulders. They had already become acquainted while riding in the car to the point that Tomatoot said to Tempo, "You may call me Edith instead of Ms. Tomatoot."

"And you call me Tempo."

As the meeting progressed, Tempo and Edith sat by Wong's side. At one point during the meeting Wong said to the premier of British Columbia, "Once completed the Midget Village will be a far greater tourist attraction than skiing at Big White Mountain, swimming in Okanagan Lakes, the Alice Nichol Bird Sanctuary or the Game Farm IN Penticton, operated by Dr. Paul Bond."

In reply the premier who enjoyed skiing, swimming and dancing, said, "The cabinet will discuss your request immediately. And when the cabinet did, it passed an order-in-council allocating a sum of money as the government's share to public housing for little people.

During the weeks that followed, every time Tempo came to Wong's office he would never fail to bring Edith a bouquet of flowers. Gregory Littleman was not indifferent to Tempo's presence. Whenever he saw Tempo approaching the Famous Okanagan Fruit Leather International Corp. complex Littleman would strut like a bantam rooster.

One day Tempo and Littleman got into a scuffle. The heavier Littleman was a peaceful man while Tempo on the other hand had taken Korean martial arts for self-defense.

Before Littleman knew how to say "You'll never take Ms. Tomatoot away from me," he had been thrown on his back and given a whack. In all future meetings Gregory Littleman was careful to keep his distance and Tempo kept on wooing Edith.

Fearful that his parents would not approve his plans to marry Edith, Tempo was eager to have them meet her under favorable circumstances. And when they did meet, they gave their son their approval.

The following night, Tempo and Edith met again and discussed how Wong had appointed Tempo 'supervisor' during the construction of the little People Village, and that Tempo hoped to be the Mayor once the village was completed. They also talked about a trip Edith was to take to London.

"I wish I was going with you for I know a great deal about foreign countries. I could explain them to you," Tempo said and added that he had been to New York, London, Paris, Rome and Barcelona.

"I thought you remarked the other day that you were tired of traveling," Edith said and he replied, "That depends on my company while traveling."

"You may find my company not agreeable."

"I would be glad to take the risk," Tempo said and slipped an arm around Edith's waist.

In reply she said, "Tempo, of course I would."

The little arm clasped the little waist closer and finally Tempo said, "Don't you think it would be pleasanter if we were man and wife?"

"That," Edith told her suitor was an odd way to joke.

"The matter," Tempo replied was much too serious to joke about and went on, "The first moment I saw you I felt you were recommended to me by Saint Holi to be my wife."

"I think I love well enough but I always said I would never marry without my parents' consent."

"Is that so? Then I will ask them." And when Tempo did, they too gave their approval.

News of the approaching wedding set Kelowna on its ears. When Wong heard of the wedding plans he offered them a sum of money to wait until the month of October when most of the fruit in the Okangan Valley was picked and vacationers had gone home.

'Not for one hundred-thousand dollars. We'll get married during the month of June," Tempo protested.

The bride-to-be nodded her vigorous approval.

Wong promised the tiny couple that he, Ogopogo and Wong would pay the wedding bills and the promise was kept.

During the month of June at the No Name Universal Church Tempo Shlikaput took Edith Tamatoot to be his bride as soon as Pastor Kurek intoned, "I pronounce you husband and wife."

Ogopogo was best man and Edith's sister, Mimmie, was maid of honor. Five-hundred guests were invited, some from foreign countries. There were millionaires, generals, senators, academics and society leaders. Gifts poured in from everywhere.

The New York Yankees heard about the wedding and sent the bride and groom a baseball along with a congratulatory note wishing them a happy marriage. Even the local Okanagan Indian Band presented the couple a totem pole, which was especially carved for the occasion.

Shortly after the vow taking, a reception was held in the ballroom of the Holiday Inn. Mr. and Mrs. Shlikaput stood on top of a piano and greeted a long list of guests. The wedding cake was 36 inches in height, the same as the grooms and his weight.
Interest in the wedding was worldwide and so intense that it pushed news of a severe earthquake in California off newspaper front page.

For their honeymoon the bride and groom traveled eastward in a rented car that had been adjusted to fit their height. The first stop was in Banff, then Calgary, Regina and Winnipeg. In Ottawa they were invited to the Governor General's residence where the queen's representative and his wife gave a reception in the couple's honor. Fashion editor Melody Grace, who was among the guests, wrote in the Toronto *Globe and Mail*: "Mr. and Mrs. Shlikaput looked like a couple from fairyland."

Following the reception in Ottawa the two tiny people were off again, this time not to Montreal or Halifax but a world tour that was to take them to Australia, Philippines, Japan, China, Soviet Union, Egypt and Israel.

In Australia, they enjoyed watching kangaroos jumping, koala bears climbing trees, sheep being sheared and wool made into clothing. The couple also attended an operatic concert in Sydney featuring coloratura soprano, Madam Wawa.

The following day Mr. and Mrs. Shlikaput traveled to the Philippines where they rode the Pagsanjan Rapids, watched religious re-enactments, a cockfight and for more excitement rode in a jeepney in Manila

It was while the tiny couple was in Japan, that they were welcomed by Prince Ahahito. The couple then rode in a rickshaw and while in Tokyo agreed with a high-tech company to have robots made to their likeness and named after them.

In India the couple was received by a maharaja who offered the honeymooners a hunting elephant but the animal was too large to pack in a suitcase so they instead accepted a literary book entitled *Ten Good Reasons Not to Be a Leader in India* by the late Mahatma Ghandi.

From New Delhi Tempo and Edith were on their way to China when a monsoon with hurricane-force winds and ten-meter high waves hit the coast. The honeymooning couple did not want to risk their lives so they flew to the Soviet Union and Moscow.

In Moscow, the Mayor greeted the couple with a bottle of vodka. Here is where the newlywed couple made a mistake and got slightly intoxicated.

"After all we are like big people," Tempo said to the critics and then, after touring Moscow and taking in a performance by the Bolshoi Ballet, the couple continued their trip to Egypt and viewing the Pyramids.

In Cairo the Khedive of Egypt lent the two tiny people his private train so they could visit Israel and its seaside resorts, have a desert adventure and tour Biblical sites.

It was while Tempo and Edith were in Tel Aviv, Israel, that they studied Hebrew in five-easy lessons. Such knowledge they thought would be beneficial when they would soon move into the Kelowna Midget Village.

As soon as Mr. and Mrs. Shlikaput returned to Kelowna from their honeymoon, inspired by Jonathan Swift's tale of the midget kingdom of Lilliput in *Gulliver's Travels*, almost one hundred years earlier, contractors were nearing completion of the village.

If people find a midget fascinating to watch, looking at a group of tiny people is even more fascinating as little carpenters, masons, plasterers, brick men and electricians worked day and night. Over the years there have been several Little People towns that earned fame. Peter the Great built one on ice covered Neva River at St. Petersburg as far back as 1710. Since the village was made of snow it did not last long.

Later in 1904 a permanent community was erected on a more appropriate location, Coney Island, New York. And Leo Singer had one in Vienna.

As soon as construction of the Little People Village was completed, Wong let it open for public inspection. It had a village hall, a museum, theatre, credit union, restaurant, bakery, library and private homes, all scaled down to midget size. The Village was built to accommodate one hundred midgets from throughout Canada.

As soon as the official opening and ribbon-cutting ceremonies were over the village was jammed with visitors from outside Kelowna.

It was at the opening that Wong thanked everyone who contributed to it, "I particularly want to thank Tempo Shlikaput and Ogopogo who entertained audiences in Canada, New York and Europe and with the funds available and assistance from the provincial government, we are now able to have our own Little People Village in Kelowna."

A week after Midget was officially opened and occupied by little people and election was held, Tempo Shlikaput declared as its first mayor.

Halfway through the winter, however, Kelowna experienced a blizzard and Mr. and Mrs. Shlikaput narrowly escaped death when their home caught on fire. Ogopogo, who was nearby at the time, carried the couple to safety but somehow Tempo was never the same. His health began to deteriorate and early one morning he suffered a stroke and died.

Thousands attended the funeral. Most were women and students from nearby schools. Wong and Ham Bobek rushed home from China where they were opening a factory for Famous Okanagan Fruit Leather products, to be present for the burial. The four-foot coffin was buried at the Kelowna Memorial Park Cemetery.

Later, a tall marble shaft was raised over the grave. On it stood a life-size statue of Tempo Shlikaput, which he posed when he was eighteen years old and Wong discovered him as an entertainer.

Tempo Shlikaput had been in the grave only three months when Edith devoted much her spare time to the promotion of better access to public buildings for little people.

In Kelowna for example, she said to the local Member of Parliament. "Your government has helped those using wheelchairs by slanting curbs on corner sidewalks but nothing about placement of telephones in public buildings. A little person has to stand on a stool or an empty box to pick up a receiver, which is large for little hands to hold."

Later, Edith changed religion and became a new-reborn Christian. When it came to her newfound faith she was against having a totem pole, which the Okanagan Indian Band, presented her and her husband as a wedding gift, placed at the entrance to the Little Peole Village.

"The totem pole I hate with a passion. Faces of birds, fish and animals stacked one on top of another. It's sorcery. It's witchcraft. The totem pole is evil," she said to her neighbors. But others within the Village community didn't agree with Edith and suggest she back off and mind her own business, which she eventually did. Rather than propagate the totem pole controversy Edith Shlikaput wrote her husband's biography and in it reminisced about his and her own triumphs and problems. She recalled how Tempo, while campaigning for funds to build the Village, had kissed thousands of ladies throughout the world and was photographed more often than any other male in Canada.

Edith in her book said the life of a midget wasn't an easy one. In one of the chapters she wrote: "If nature endowed me with my superior personal attraction it was comparatively small compensation for the inconvenience, trouble and annoyance imposed on me and Tempo by our diminutive stature. In that restrained sentence throbs all the hurts and pathos of those who have been selected by fate to be among the little people."

A year after Tempo Shlikaput's biography was completed, Edith died. While it is known that midgets lived until their nineties, Edith and her husband died at an early age. Her single headstone, next to her husband's, simply read with three words:

TEMPO SHLIKAPUT'S WIFE.

In Search Of Canada

During the month of June in 1996, Kelowna was hosting the annual convention of the Canadian Independent Advertising Association. Among those attending were chief CIAA executive officers and accountants. The guest speaker was the renound Canadian film director, Jean Croteau, from St. John's Newfoundland. His topic was, 'The 500 Anniversary of explorer John Cabot, sighting Canada' and explained how Film Canada, in conjunction with the Government of Canada, were going to produce a movie commemorating the occasion.

During an evening intermission, Monsieur Croteau was canoeing on Okanagan Lake and came upon herbalist, Dr. Lo Wong, relaxing on the sandy beach strumming his guitar and singing a Chinese folk song. While approaching Wong, Choteau's curiosity was aroused. Croteau enjoyed the song Wong was singing so much, that he said to himself, "I probably can use him in the movie I'm going to direct."

Within minutes, Mr. Croteau paddled within speaking distance, introduced himself and said, "Sir, you have a distinctive voice, why don't you audition for the movie I'm about to direct?"

Wong, although startled, was not upset by the intrusion. "What movie?" he said.

"It's called *From Sea to Sea*."

"What is the move about? With a title like that, it must have battle scenes? Perhaps it's about the *Titanic*?"

Croteau's reply was: "No, not the Titanic. In 1997 Canadians will mark the quincentennial of Giovanni Cabato, also known as John Cabot, an Italian navigator and captain while sailing the *Matthew* under the British flag and landed in Bonivista, Newfoundland. Cabot planted the first British flag on North American soil June 24, 1497, five years after Columbus's first voyage in 1492. The movie, oh yes, the movie covers five centuries of Canadian history featuring explorers, homesteaders, missionaries, entrepreneurs, politicians and sports celebrities, who created an influential nation called *Canada*.

Wong was perplexed with the reply. "Will the movie also deal with Canada's bootleggers, making of the Canadian Pacific Railway and the Klondike Gold Rush?"

"It certainly will," Croteau said and from his wallet pulled out a clipping from the *Currier* newspaper covering the speech he gave that morning. Croteau then read the pertinent part aloud.

"Auditions for the movie *From Sea to Sea* are being held in St. John's, Newfoundland. The closing date is July 8, 1996."

After taking a second breath, Croteau went on, "For more information why don't you and I meet me at the Hotel Sandman Inn? I'll be free at nine."

"I'm certainly interested to meet with you but on one condition."

"What's the condition?"

"That I bring along a friend of mine. He's a better actor than I am. As an entertainer he has toured Canada, New York and Europe."

"If you wish, your friend can come too. I'll need all the help I can get."

At that point in the conversation, Ogopogo was swimming towards shore and as he approached Wong and Croteau, Croteau got frightened and said. "Quick, let's run for cover, there's a lake monster approaching us!"

Wong burst out with laughter. "That won't be necessary. This is Ogopogo, the friend of mine I was talking about. Ogopogo won't harm you."

Formal introductions followed.

It was half-past moonrise, by the time Wong and Ogopogo concluded their meeting with Croteau at the hotel. As they were about to take an elevator to the lobby, two well-dressed strangers approached them.

"Good evening. My name is Rex Widespread of Best Advertising Agency," the first stranger said, and the second, was introduced as Bob Dean, the agency's accountant.

As soon as the formal introductions were completed, Widespread continued, "Can Mr. Dean and I have a chat with you in private?"

"To discuss what?" Wong asked.

"An offer."

"What kind of an offer?"

"One that will make you and Ogopogo well known celebrities."

"Is that so? Tell us more."

"We want you and Ogopogo to sign a contract with our advertising agency, endorsing various products. We heard and read about both of you, Famous Okanagan Fruit Leather and the time the little person, Tempo Shlikaput, and both of you entertained in Europe. What else can I say?"

"You can say that at the moment we are not interested and to leave us alone," Wong said.

Widespread seldom took *No* for an answer and persisted, "Our offer is tem thousand dollars for each product you endorse."

"There is no limit to how much money you can make endorsing various products that come on the market these days," Dean continued.

"In reply, Wong said, "Look. We are famous already if one is in search of fame. At the moment our only interest in getting to St. John's, Newfoundland by July 8th." Widedespread was curious so he asked, "What's happening in St. John's on that date?"

"Ogopogo and I have an appointment to audition for a movie."

"Of course, Monsieur Croteau spoke to us this morning about the project."

No matter what amount of money Widespread and Dean offered, Wong and Ogopogo refused to sign an endorsement contract, which eventually led Widespread to say in an unpleasant manner, "Mark my word, this is a day the two of you will regret."

Dean followed, "Think it over. Can't you visualize your names and photographs on billboards along the Trans-Canada Highway?"

"And in newspapers, magazines, radio and television," Ogopogo replied. "We know the routine."

"Thanks, but no thanks," Wong said, and along with Ogopogo made their exit.

Then in the morning, Wong and Ogopogo woke up the same time the sun rose, packed their camping gear into Wong's antique sports car, made certain they had an ample supply of fruit leather, and were on their merry way across Canada. Can you imagine their joy as the couple in sunshiny weather drove uphill, downhill and around a bend along the scenic British Columbia Highway 97?

They drove past fruit stands, orchards and vineyards, viewpoints and Okanagan Lake itself, until the city of Vernon, where they stopped at the Tourist Information Centre and picked up a copy of the *Tourist Guide of Canada*.

The Guide had maps and articles about Canada's geographical features for the remainder of the journey: mountains, lakes and rivers, prairie, locks and canals, forests and cities. Next, they passed by Mara Lake and then at the junction of 97 and Trans Canada Highway at Sicamous, they came to a totem pole that stood one hundred feet high. with figures of humans, animals, birds and fish standing one on top of the other. Here, the Trans-Canada Highway as well as the Canadian Pacific Railway took over in an easterly direction towards the Rocky Mountains, Banff and Calgary. Along the way one crosses several mountain ranges: the Monashee, the Selkirk's, the Purcell's and the Great Divide at the Canadian Rockies, each one more splendid than the one passed.

At nearby Craigellachie, Wong pulled to a curb, stopping at the historical monument, where the last pike was driven commemorating completion of the Canadian Pacific Railway in 1855 as Canada's first rail link. Pointing to a monument Wong said, "That's where I fit into the proposed movie. It was during the building of the railway that my ancestors were treated as second-class citizens."

Before Wong and Ogopogo reached the town of Revelstoke, and began climbing a chain of mountains, they came upon what appeared to be a tragic railway accident.

An engineer and a crew were trying to hook up to a caboose, which had sprung loose and turned on its side.

"I'll help you put the caboose back on track," Ogopogo said to the engineer who introduced himself as Gaston Hamel.

"We can use all the help we can get," Hamel said. "There's a passenger train heading this way from Calgary to Vancouver. It should be here any moment."

Ogopogo popped a strip of Famous Okanagan Food Leather into his mouth, became his normal 20-foot height size, flexed his muscles, picked up the caboose and with the engineers and Wong's help, placed it back on track just in time averting a major railway accident.

"Thank you. Thank you. I'm greatly indebted to you," Hamel said and during a chat that followed, said that ordinarily he was an engineer on the Montreal to Quebec City run.

It was during the conversation that a passenger train came from the opposite direction at great speed.

"Whew! That was perfect timing," Hamel said as the train sped by. "Thank you Mr. Wong and Ogopogo, for your help and best of luck on your journey to Newfoundland.

"The engineer I replaced has another week of vacation, and then I'll return to Montreal," Hamel said.

"And we may cross paths again?" Wong said.

"We may."

As soon as Ogopogo shrunk to his one-third normal size, Wong continued driving. They drove through Roger's Pass and about to reach the Continental Divide, when a sudden blizzard erupted. As the elevation became higher, winds stronger and snowflakes larger.

Ogopogo and Wong met transport and logging trucks, pickups, cars and mobile homes waiting out the storm, but they kept on driving.

They also saw elk, bear, deer and mountain sheep searching for food along the Trans-Canada highway. As soon as they reached the summit and began going downhill, the sun began shining, birds singing and fish in streams and rivers jumping. As they drove past Lake Louise and through Banff National Park, they soon came to the Banff town site, where a billboard sign in bold letters read: *WELCOME TO BANFF, ALBERTA.*

"Let's camp overnight in Banff," Wong suggested and Ogopogo agreed. Together they set up a tent near a high cliff in a campground that had a panoramic view of Lake Minewanka and snow covered mountain peaks behind it.

Before bedding down for the night Wong and Ogopogo drove along the streets of Banff and did what most tourists do. They rode the gondola, visited the museum and the hot springs mineral pool. As the sun was setting they had dinner at the Banff Springs Hotel. Everywhere they went, there were signs in Japanese. Once seated in the hotel restaurant, Ogopogo spotted Widespread and Dean at a nearby table having their dinner.

"Guess who is behind us?" Ogopogo whispered to Wong as a pretty waitress of Japanese heritage handed them a menu.

"Who?" Wong said, keeping his voice down.

"Rex Widespread and his accountant, Bob Dean."

When Wong looked back he was surprised. "Widespread and Dean are following us and must have flown into Banff by private aircraft," he said.

As Wong and Ogopogo were enjoying their dinner, Widespread, dressed in a hand cut blue suit that was neatly pressed and, Dean, well dressed also, walked up to their table.

Following a brief conversation Widespread said, "Well, Ogopogo and Mr. Wong, how about an endorsement contract with Best Advertising Agency? Have you reconsidered?"

'We haven't. And have no plans to sign a contract with your agency," Wong said.

"And once you sign, believe me, you will be famous. Take Wayne Gretzky, since he was traded by the Edmonton Oilers to the Los Angeles Kings," Widespread continued.

"What about Gretzky?" Wong asked, losing his patience also.

"Gretzky makes more money endorsing products than from playing hockey. His name is on television, radio, billboards and in newspapers and magazines."

"And in Edmonton, they even built a statue to his likeness," Dean continued.

"And he's good at opening shopping malls," Ogopogo said.

No matter how persuasive Widespread and Dean may have been, Wong and Ogopogo refused to sign a contract, which eventually led Widespread to become furious and say, "You will be sorry. I'll do everything in my power to have the Canadian government cancel production of the movie *From Sea to Sea*."

When Widespread made the threat, Wong didn't think the CEO could do that. Widespread burst out with laughter and said, "Just watch me. You are forgetting that besides being CEO of Best Advertising Agency I also advise the Federal government on heritage and culture."

Shortly after Wong and Ogopogo had their dinner, they returned to the campground, where they crawled into their tent. Before falling asleep, through the open door, they listened to coyotes howling in the distance. They also heard footsteps near the tent, but were too tired to see who or what it was. They wished they had, when the sun rose in the morning and found that Wong's antique sports car had been rolled down a mountain cliff, shattering into hundreds of pieces.

"Not only is my antique sports car crushed into smithereens but my walle.t that I had locked in the glove compartment is missing!" Wong exclaimed.

A black talking bear heard Wong, came up to him and said, "What you are saying sir, is that now you have no transportation and have been robbed."

"Exactly, I couldn't have said it better," Wong said.

Wong and Ogopogo then told the friendly bear, what had happened, and why they were going to St. John's, Newfoundland. They also suggested the bear accompany them

"I would like to but my contract with Banff National Park obligates me to stay here at least another year," the bear said.

"Why so?" Ogopogo asked.

"So visitors from throughout the world can have their picture taken with me. As you may know bears and Mounties are symbols of this park. and appear on post cards."

"Besides ordinary visitors, have you been photographed with anyone else?"

"I have, Hollywood celebrities and even with the Queen of England, but more recently with hundreds of Japanese who vacation here," the bear said, and went on, "Since the two of you are without money and transportation, I suggest you go and see Father Jim Shepherd at Our Lady of Perpetual Help church, which is situated on Buffalo street."

Father Shepherd is a charitable clergyman knows how to help those who get into difficulties, while in Banff."

"Thank you, we'll do that," Wong said.

And when Wong and Ogopogo found Father Shepherd's church, they knew instantly he was dedicated to his priestly duties when he said, "Food and overnight lodging I can provide. Blessed are those who find themselves in difficulty while in Banff."

Impressed by Father Shepherd's charitable qualities, Wong said, "In exchange for the food and lodging overnight is there something that we help around the rectory or church?"

"Handyman, repairs. Even assist you in saying mass," Ogopogo said.

Father Shepherd burst out with laughter at the mass part and handed Wong a list of chores they could do.

Next morning Ogopogo and Wong, dusted and polished the pews in the church. In the afternoon they repaired the plumbing as the toilet constantly kept running. When the evening mass was about to begin the altar boy and lecterer failed to show up. Father Shepherd suspected their absence was because of a *TV Special* that night, so he called on Ogopogo and Wong to assist with the mass too. Ogopogo was the altar boy, and Wong as a lecterer, read two verses from the *Bible*.

Ogopogo and Wong's fortune did not last long, however, because Widespread and Dean were in the habit of attending evening church service too. As soon as Father Shepherd said, "Go in peace. The mass has ended," Widespread was furious. He met father Shepherd in the sacristy, and tore a strip of him for allowing "Two freaks of nature" to assist him in celebrating mass. Widespread even threatened to the report the priest to the Bishop who had a reputation as a cantankerous old man. This was prevented however, when Wong approached Widespread and said to him, "Be patient. That won't be necessary."

Encountering difficult situations before and knowing that advertising executives were constantly searching for models, Wong told Widespread about an attractive waitress he had met at the Banff Springs Hotel. "We'll take you there," Wong said.

"Okay, let's go."

While Widespread and Dean were in conversation with the waitress at the Banff Springs Hotel, a train was about to leave for Calgary so Ogopogo and Wong stepped inside. Most of the passengers did not recognize Ogopogo because of his size or unusual shape. Ogopogo did, however, because of his clumsiness, accidentally release the trains brakes and at the same time, insulted a passenger when Ogopogo said, "Edmonton Oilers are a better team than the Calgary Flames."

Unable to pay for their fare the conductor was about fling Wong and Ogopogo out the door. Fortunately this wasn't necessary because Ogopogo discovered that the person he insulted earlier was the Mayor of Calgary who had a large lump on his head because when the brakes were released, the train began moving with a sudden jerk.

"I can make the lump disappear. You'll never get re-elected like that," Wong said to the Mayor.

"You are a medical doctor?" the Mayor asked to which Wong replied, "Although I have a doctorate degree I'm not a medical one. I have Okanagan Famous Fruit Leather with me,, which some doctors prescribe for injuries like yours. Here, enjoy a strip."

"Thank you," the Mayor said, and after he swallowed a strip of fruit leather, continued, "I'm scheduled to attend a Grand 'Ol' Opery concert at the Saddledome as soon as we reach Calgary, but with this lump on my head, I better excuse myself."

"The lump will disappear shortly, but first, can we impose on you sir, to pay mine and Ogopogo's fare to Calgary?"

"Certainly," the Mayor said, and when the lump disappeared and the fare was paid, the Mayor became ecstatic and invited Ogopogo and Wong to be his guests at the Grand 'Old Opery concert held in Calgary. But when the trio arrived at the Saddledome, they were informed that the Opery stars that were scheduled to perform were involved in a major traffic jam in downtown Calgary, and would be late. The crowd became restless and impatient. Many wanted refunds.

"Ogopogo and I can entertain the crowd until the Opery stars arrive," Wong said to the Mayor. "We have entertained crowds before."

"Wait, I'll speak to the promotions manager," the Mayor said, and when he did, Ogopogo and Wong were given cowboy hats. As the curtain went up, the master of ceremonies intoned to a microphone at centre stage, "Ladies and gentlemen. Until the Opry stars arrive, you will be entertained by Ogopogo and Wong from Kelowna, British Columbia."

Ogopogo and Wong did an act comprising of monologues, tap dances, imitation of celebrities, slight of hand, juggled tennis balls and then played on a kazoo and comb until the Opery stars arrived. In the end Wong and Ogopogo were given a thunderous ovation.

When the Opery stars were through with their concert the promoter of the concert, said to Wong, "Your and Ogopgo's performance was tremendous. Not only have you saved our reputation but also the crowd loved you. It is only fair that you keep a portion of the gate receipts."

"In the meantime we are on our way to St. John's, Newfoundland to audition for a movie commemorating five hundred years since explorer John Cabot saw Canada."

"And thank you for one-quarter of the gate receipts. You are generous," Ogopogo said. "With part of the money we will buy ourselves a vehicle so we can continue with our journey."

In the morning, Wong and Ogopogo purchased a yellow-colored station wagon from Honest Ralph's Used Cat Lot and then while on a straight stretch of the Trans-Canada Highway, near Regina, Ogopogo looked out the back window and said, "Hey, Mr. Wong, look! You must be speeding because there two cops on motorbikes chasing us."

Wong glanced at the speedometer gauge. "But I'm not speeding."

When the motorbikes approached closer, one of the policemen signaled Wong to pull off the highway, and when he did, Wong and Ogopogo realized the two men on motorbikes were Widespread and Dean.

"Now we got you," Widespread said to Wong and Ogopogo, and then, motioning to Dean went on, "We'll take the couple to a remote abandoned farm house and get their signatures to an advertising contract."

At that same moment, a police cruiser coming from the opposite direction pulled up to the station wagon and asked Wong if there was anything the matter.

"There is," Wong replied pointing to Widespread and Dean.

The real policemen questioned the imposters for several minutes, and then ran their names through a computer. Finally the real officers said, "Widespread and Dean, you'll have to come to detachment headquarters for further questioning."

As Wong and Ogopogo continued their journey, it got wild and stormy. The thunder was loud; the lightning lit the sky as if it was on fire. The thunder and lightning were later accompanied by a blusterous wind that whistled angrily raising clouds of dust over the entire prairie in front of them.

It was at the height of the storm that Wong and Ogopogo came upon a huge bird that was struggling by a barbed wire fence. The bird, had a large neck, short tail, about sixty inches in length, snowy white in color with a large yellow orange bill pouch and a wing span with black tips of about six feet.

"It must be a ravenous bird of prey," Ogopogo said, but when the vehicle came closer Wong corrected him and said, "It's a pelican. One doesn't see pelicans often anymore."

As the station wagon approached closer still Wong said, "Last week I watched Dr. David Suzuki on the program *Nature of Things* and he said at the time that pelicans were endangered species until recently.'"

Wong pulled off the highway, stopped at a curb and said to the huge bird, "You look wet and cold. Do come inside the station wagon where it's warm and comfortable."

"Thank you, sir," the pelican replied and once inside, Ogopogo said, "Tell us who you may be."

"I'm a talking male white pelican. Just call me Pelican," the bird said. "I live in the area during the summer. I'm a strong flier and swimmer feeding mostly on fish."

When Wong noticed that Pelican was favoring his right wing, he asked, "What happened to your wing?"

There was no hesitation. "I was flying to a lake north of here when I struck a power line and then a bullet pierced my wing."

"Why would anyone want to take a shot at you?" Ogopogo wondered. "Don't they know it's illegal to kill apelicans or to disturb their eggs or nests."

"Good question."

Then Wong said, "Your wing."

"What about my wing?"

"I can repair it," Wong said, and then taking a strip of fruit leather from his pocket, gave the bird a strip to swallow.

As soon as the Pelican swallowed the fruit leather, the pain disappeared instantly, and the bird could flap its wing again. It was while Pelican was flapping his wing that Wong turned to him and asked the inevitable question, "Would you like to come to St. John's, Newfoundland with us?"

Pelican leaped at the opportunity, "Why not? I have been to United States and visited with cousins throughout north and Central America, the coastlines of California, Florida, and Mexico and even in northern South America and often wondered what Newfoundland is like. I accept your offer."

After several hours of driving, darkness was coming on, and the lights of Winnipeg began to shine in the distance. One of the first buildings to come into view was an Orthodox Church and a short distance further the Winnipeg Cultural Centre where that night the Winnipeg Ballet was performing *Swan Lake*, which Wong, Ogopogo and Pelican attended and gave the performance an excellent review.

After the ballet the threesome went to the Perohy Restaurant, where the staff was as varied as the patrons. The waitresses were dressed in Ukrainian costumes. the bus boys were Black and the manager a Sikh who kept a copy of Pierre Burton's book, *National Dream* next to his telephone.

Among the customers present were other characters that prompted Ogopogo to say to Pelican, "We aren't out of place here."
One of the more interesting characters was a middle aged woman by the name of Petra Luckowitch, who was a lawyer, practicing her speech of acceptance should she win a federal by-election for the constituency of Winnipeg North, that was about to take place. "Thank you for electing me as your member of parliament," Ms Luckowitch repeated over and over, which prompted Wong to hand her a strip of fruit leather to protect her voice.
"Thank you, sir," Ms. Luckowitch said, and then engaged in a conversation with Wong, Ogopogo and Pelican discussing politics and the economic state of Canada.
"Planet Earth is in a terrible state," is how Ms Luckowitch summed up the Canadian and global situation.
Also at the Perohy House was a poet who was reciting a sonnet she had written, two artists debating paintings by Canadian, Janvier, a female photographer who thought she was a Karsh. There were other patrons too. An Indian Chief was discussing land claims with a White man and a farmer whose crop was infested with grasshoppers, but still he was happy because he had won a 649 lottery.

The fact that the prize was $60,000, the value of a new tractor, did not matter. What did was the farmer wanted everyone in the Perohy House to be happy.

"A round of beer to everyone!" the farmer called out to the barmaid, and she delivered.

While Wong, Ogopogo and Pelican were non-drinkers they did accept the kind gesture. As soon as Pelican had several sips of his beer he had a fainting spell and was carried seemingly unconscious to the lavatory by Wong and Ogopogo. It's still not clear whether it was another strip of fruit leather Pelican had ingested or the odder of a disinfectant that revived him. At any rate Wong, Ogopogo and Pelican slept in a motel that night and at sunrise, after breakfast, climbed into the station wagon and headed east towards Kenora, Ontario.

Near Kenora, Wong, Ogopogo and Pelican set their watches ahead an hour because they had reached the Eastern time zone. It was in Kenora, a mining and pulp and paper town, that they decided to book into the Lake Of The Woods Lodge and do some fishing.

After paddling a rowboat for five minutes the travelers didn't see fish jumping but a magnificent sunset and a regal-looking moose munching lily pad stems. The moose seemed only vaguely interested in the intruders who paddled within speaking distance and Wong said, "Mr. Moose, are you interested in joining us for a movie audition held in St. John's, Newfoundland?"

The moose eyed the boat momentarily, then swung his rack around and dipped his entire head under water to grab another lily pad.

And when the boat drifted still closer the animal had enough of his uninvited guests. He swung his head and rack towards shore and began half-swimming, half-wading through the neck deep water.

Realizing the moose wasn't interested in traveling to Newfoundland, Wong, Ogopogo and Pelican quit fishing and decided to see what downtown Kenora was like. They, like many hockey fans were surprised, when they arrived at a park and a plaque inside commemorated the: *Thistles Hockey Team of 1907 winning The Stanley Cup for Kenora.* They were told by park patrons that Kenora is the smallest community ever to boast a Stanley Cup victory.

Next day, Wong, Ogopogo and Whoop reached Thunder Bay and stopped in front of City Hall for additional travel information. As soon as the trio stepped inside City Hall Chambers, the Mayor was paying tribute to a crew of a Russian freighter, *Nasha Baba.*

The Russian government had purchased Canadian wheat that was stored at the Lakehead Terminal and the freighter was about to sail home.

"Better to be friends than enemies," the Mayor was heard saying as Wong, Ogopogo and Pelican sat silently in the back row. Turning to the Russian captain, the Mayor continued, "And now I want you to meet Rex Widespread and his accountant Bob Dean, who were instrumental in negotiating the wheat contract with your country."

As Widespread stood up to acknowledge the recognition he shook hands with the Mayor and then spotted Wong and Ogopogo sitting in the back of the chamber.

After the ceremony was over, Widespread walked up to Wong and said, "We meet again. Dr. Wong, have you changed your mind about an endorsement contract offer?"

"Out of the question," Wong snapped and Ogopogo shook his head.

"Money doesn't sleep and is loyal to no one but it sure helps to lead a life of luxury," Dean reminded Wong.

"Look," Wong finally said. Stop stalking us. Please don't bother us. We aren't interested in negotiating a contract, so get lost."

"Both of you are difficult to deal with and remind me of freaks from another planet," Widespread said and continued in an irritated voice, "I've never been so humiliated in my life and don't you ever speak to me that way again."

When Ogopogo made the uncomplimentary remark, Widespread turned to the Russian captain and said, "I find his sense of humor difficult to follow.

"Let's take Wong, Ogopogo and the big bird to your freighter. With a little torture I'm certain the two Kelownaites will come to their senses and sign an endorsement contract."

"Okay," the Russian captain said.

Turning to Dean, Widespread went on as he tossed him a handgun. "Make sure you have their photographs taken before the freighter leaves Thunder Bay in the morning."

"Yes, sir. I'll have a photographer take their pictures right away," Dean said and at gunpoint led Wong, Ogopogo and Pelican to the Russian freighter docked on Lake Superior.

"How about our station wagon?" Wong pleaded, but Widespread said he had more important things on his mind.

It was evening when *Nasha Baba* began sailing for Russia. Fifty miles from the Lakehead the freighter encountered gale-force winds on Lake Superior and the crew members began crying and screaming and then there was a huge explosion.

Wong, Ogopogo and Pelican grasped the first piece of wreckage they could find. And then when the explosion was over and the freighter sank, they found themselves huddled on a raft that the waves drifted at will. As for the Russian victims of the disaster, there was no sign of them. Hour after hour the three travelers watched the horizon but it wasn't until the following morning that Pelican cried out, "Look, there's land ahead."

As it turned out it was a tiny island, and when they reached it, Wong said, "To set foot on land again is like returning to life from a grave."

As soon as the three travelers dried and warmed themselves, their first impulse was to explore the tiny island, far from civilization.

A quick survey, however, was sufficient to raise their spirits. The island was not of barren rock like most of Northern Ontario. There were wild berries, large stands of forest and at one end a lighthouse. They could survive if necessary on the island, but Ogopogo and Wong were determined to reach Newfoundland. but lacked many things that they were accustomed too.

Among them, although Wong could communicate with Saint Holi in Heaven, was a high-teck communication means.

As Ogopogo, Wong and Pelican were sitting at a sandy beach, discussing their problem, they saw a rowboat approaching with two occupants inside paddling furiously.

As the boat approached closer and closer, the occupants were identified as Widespread and Dean, who had survived the Russian freighter explosion.

After rejecting an endorsement contract proposal for the umpteenth time, Wong said to the two advertising men, "Look. We haven't much to complain about.

The island is filled with wild berries, timber, fertile soil, and there are plenty of fish in the lake. We do however; lack one thing to make it easier for us to reach Newfoundland."

"What is that?" Widespread said.

"A cellular phone, so we can contact another ship that would take us through the Great Lakes."

"I know where there is one," Widespread said.

"A cellular phone or a ship?"

"A ship. It's near the other end of the island. Dean and I were there but when we saw you through a set of binoculars, we rowed here to see if you have changed your mind about signing an advertising contract."

"Our mind is set, no deal," Wong said.

"I'll go and explore the other ship," Ogopogo said, determined to find out its name and perhaps, if lucky, speak to the captain.

Ogopogo dove into the water and when he reached the ships bottom, he became disorientated. He could see no more than an arm's length in turgid darkness. His fluttering legs kicked by swirls of silt, made visibility even worse. When Ogopogo got orientated again, he swam to the bow of *Thistle 2* and said to the captain, "What are you doing here in the middle of Lake Superior?"

"The crew and I are searching for the wreck of the *Edmund Fitzgerald*," the captain replied and explained that the iron ore vessel with twenty nine crew members, sank on November 10, 1975 during a gale-force wind like the one Ogopogo, Wong and Pelican had experienced the day the Russian freighter *Nasha Baba* sank. The captain then said that the search was a failure to this point and that the ship was about to leave for Toronto.

Ogopogo spoke to the captain for several minutes and then asked if he, Wong and Pelican could climb on board and hitch a ride through the Great Lakes."

"You certainly may. And if you can vouch for Widespread and Dean tell them to come along too."

The captain said that *Thistle 2* had rescued two advertising executives. "And when they saw you stranded on the beach, they picked up a rowboat, plunked it into the water and headed towards your direction."

It was difficult for Ogopogo to vouch for Widespread and Dean, but taking a risk he said, "I'm certain they will be excellent passengers."

After two days of sailing, *Thistle 2* came to an unexpected sudden halt.

"The ship isn't moving because of the Welland Canal," the captain said and went on, "A section of the lock has been blown apart stranding vessels along the St. Lawrence Seaway. The last time a similar thing happened was in 1985."

Amid charges by the media that the twenty seven-mile long, canal was an, 'Operational Time Bomb,' Seaway authorities called the incident, 'Isolated and Unusual'.

While Widespread and Dean were developing a migraine headache coping with the delay, Wong and his companions realized that they had a deadline to meet and must find a way to proceed to Newfoundland.

"If we wait any longer, we could be stuck here for at least three months," Pelican agreed.

"I have a plan that will enable us to proceed," Ogopogo said.

Pelican and Wong stared at Ogopogo. Then Wong said, "What's your plan?"

Ogopogo explained his plan by saying, "As soon as it gets dark and the captain and crew are asleep we'll jump out of the cabin window, into the water and swim eastward."

"But how?" Pelican said. "I don't particularly enjoy swimming in or flying above polluted water."

"Listen carefully," Ogopogo said as Wong and Pelican huddled near him. "I'll slip away under the cover of darkness, and when the appropriate time comes, the two of you can drop on my back, and I'll begin swimming. It's as easy as that."

"But not before you eat another strip of fruit leather and become your normal size" Wong suggested.

When it was pitch dark and the first opportunity came, Ogopogo said to Wong and Pelican, "This is the moment to make our move. Follow me."

Ogopogo then opened the window and from the sill dove into the water, that caused a loud splash, but not loud enough to awake anyone on the ship. Wong jumped next and landed on Ogopogo's shoulder. Pelican because of his wingspan experienced difficulty at first but once he got balanced, his trajectory was on target and landed behind Wong. Having their legs and wings on each side of Ogopogo, Pelican said, and "Come on horsey. We better get out of here as quickly as we can."

While the escape was taking place, Widespread and Dean along with the ship's crew were sleeping. By the time they woke up, Wong, Ogopogo and Pelican were in Niagara Falls interviewed by a radio talk show host."

"Tell us about your journey to Newfoundland," the host said and when Wong, Ogopogo and Pelican did, they took phone calls from listeners pertaining to the movie *From Sea To Sea.*

The radio station where the talk-show host was conducting the interview, was located underneath the Rainbow Bridge. As the interview moved along a transport truck crossed the bridge and the vibration made a loose ceiling fall striking Pelican on the wing.

"Oh my goodness!" the host apologized when he noticed was scratching his wing. "Are you okay?"

"I'm fine," Pelican replied and began laughing.

The host shut of the microphone switch and said, "What's so funny?"

"I'm laughing because in preening my feathers, I tickled myself under the wing," Pelican replied. and allayed any fear the talk-show interviewer had, that the big bird was seriously injured.

When the program was over, the host asked Wong how he and his friends intended to reach Toronto.

"Good question," Wong said, "Looks like we'll have to hitchhike."

"I'm near the end of my shift and will drive you to Toronto, if you wish," the host said.

"But your radio time is important, don't you think? Wong said.

"No problem. My parents live in Toronto and are celebrating their golden wedding anniversary today. I'd be delighted if you accompany me."

Wong, Ogopogo and Pelican accepted the offer, and when they reached the outskirts of Toronto, noticed billboard signs along highway 401.

Most of the signs had photographs of either Wong or Ogopogo endorsing various products, ranging from peanut butter to an insurance company.

"It's a dirty trick by Widespread and Dean," Wong said as he watched the signs go by. "We didn't give Best Advertising permission to endorse these products."

When the talk-show host asked the trio where they wanted to be dropped off Ogopogo was quick to reply, "At the CN Tower. We'd like to have dinner there and have a view from the top."

While enjoying their dinner at the top of the CN Tower, a woman dressed in a gray woolen suit, passed by their table. Upon seeing Ogopogo, she backtracked several steps and said, "Excuse me but haven't we met somewhere before?"

"We have. In Winnipeg. Aren't you Petra Luckowich?

"I am and your friends are Mr. Wong and Pelican."

"You have a good memory," Wong said and then asked, "How did you make out in the Winnipeg by-election?"

"I won with a majority of 623 votes," and then during a chit chat said, "Incidentally, I have fallen in love with Famous Okanagan Fruit Leather and use it regularly during my busy schedule. Fruit leather is a terrific meal replacement."

"Thank you. Are you alone?" Wong then asked.

"I am."

"Then why don't you come and sit at our table?"

"Thank you for the invitation. I'll do that."

As soon as Ms Luckowitch changed tables Wong said, "Tell us, why are you in Toronto?"

"I'm here to discuss with the Ontario Minister of Culture, a movie our government is funding. The movie is being produced by Film Canada."

"What is the movie called?"

"I'm not certain if it has a title yet but I know it deals with the 500th anniversary since explorer John Cabot first landed in Canada."

"It's titled *From Sea to Sea*," Wong said.

"And what is the nature of your business in Central Canada?" Ms Luckowitch asked.

"We are on our way to St. John's, Newfoundland to audition for the movie that you just spoken about."

"Great. I wish you luck with the auditions," Ms. Luckowitch said and then changed the subject by asking Wong, "Have you ever been to Ottawa?"

"We haven't," Ogopogo said.

"Then be my guests. I'm driving alone and as soon as we are through eating, we can be on our way."

"We appreciate your kindness," Wong said and as soon as they had finished their dinner, climbed into Ms. Luckowitch's car, and were heading towards Ottawa where after several miles of driving Ms. Luckowitch asked Ogopogo, "Do you know your Member of Parliament?"

"I wrote him a letter about the City dumping raw sewage into Okanagan Lake, but for some reason he hasn't replied."

"I hope I'm not as delinquent but on the other hand, one must remember MP's have a lot of constituents to look after, and at time must travel the country. Have you ever watched *Question Period* on television?"

When Wong and Ogopogo said not regularly, because they found the program boring, Ms. Luckowitch's comment was, "You won't be tomorrow, when the opposition parties will field questions about the movie you are auditioning for."

When they reached Ottawa, Ms. Luckowitch registered her guests, at the Château Laurier Hotel where they slept. The following morning they had breakfast together and with Ms. Luckowitch as a guide, rode on the Rideau Canal, toured the parliament buildings and later, while the trio sat in the House of Commons gallery, Ms Luckowitch joined her MP colleagues for *Question Period*.

As the Prime Minister rose to speak there was booing from the Opposition members. When he introduced the Minister of Culture, the booing turned too dead-silence as the Minster said, "Mr. Speaker. On the advice of Rex Widespread our advisor on culture and because of Canada's huge deficit, it is with profound regret that I announce the production of the movie *From Sea to Sea* has been cancelled."

Opposition members could not believe what they had heard and became boisterous. Wong, Ogopogo and Pelican could not believe what they had heard either, and for several seconds lumps formed in their throats and tears began filling their eyes.

"Let's go back to Kelowna," Ogopogo suggested.

"Let's go on a hunger strike to gain public support." Pelican suggested.

"Calm down both of you," is what Wong said, and while looking across the House of Commons to where Ms Luckowitch was sitting, he could tell the new MP for Winnipeg North was as upset as he was.

The disapproval was confirmed when Ms Luckowitch stood up and said, "Mr. Speaker. I do not wish to whip up a storm but in my opinion scrapping the movie *From Sea to Sea*, even though it will cost tem million, is wrong on the part of our government. Mr. Speaker. In the end the movie will benefit Canada tenfold and unite many ethnic cultures into a single force. Canada is a young country and down the road of history. our children and even their children, will know what it took to make Canada what is today, a great nation."

The leaders of opposition parties said something similar, and when she stopped speaking, several members even suggested that Ms. Luckowitch switch parties.

"Let's go and plead our case in the Public Square on Parliament Hill," Wong, determined to proceed with the project, suggested to Ogopogo and Pelican as soon as *Question Period* was over.

When they arrived at the Public Square and stood on a soapbox. Wong, Ogopogo and Pelican pleaded their case why the movie should be made and asked the audience for donations in hopes of embarrassing the government.

"A movie depicting five-hundred years of Canadian history," Wong repeated over and over as the crowd in front of the soapbox got larger and larger.

"A movie that will include Canada's explorers, fur traders, homesteaders, financiers,

Athletes, and the environment," Ogopogo took over.

"And how about bootleggers?" a stray voice from the crowd shouted.

"Them too" Wong answered and went on, "A movie that will depict how Canada polluted its lakes, rivers and air which destroyed fish, birds and animals."

Ogopogo took over, "*From Sea To Sea* is going to be a movie which will show our heritage and achievement in science, arts, technology and sports."

"And how we repatriated our constitution from Britain and prevented the province of Quebec from separating from the rest of Canada," Wong continued when he was interrupted by another stray voice, louder than the first.

"And how during World War 1, 8500 Ukrainians were put into Canadian twenty four concentration camps, because as immigrants they were registered as Austrians, part of the Austro-Hungarian Empire, which was at war with the British Empire."

"That too will be in the movie," Wong answered, "And so will the mistreatment of my ancestors while building the Canadian Pacific railway through British Columbia and During World War 11 how Japanese Canadians lost their property because the Canadian government at the time was afraid they would help Japan in conquering Canada."

Still another stray voice came from the crowd. "And how the White man took away land which belonged to the Indians?"

"I'm certain that part will be in the movie too," Wong said and then there was a voice louder than the rest. It was a woman's voice. "And how women are paid less for comparable work done than her male counterpart."

"Women issues will be covered too," Wong said when there was a second female voice that said, "My name is

Petra Luckowitch the new MP for Winnipeg North. I'm
prepared to give up ten percent of my salary so that we
continue making the movie *From Sea to Sea.*"

By the time Wong, Ogopogo and Pelican left Ottawa
they had one hundred and forty thousand dollars in cash,
and another three hundred in pledges and appointed Ms
Luckowitch as trustee and chairperson of the Save the
Movie *From Sea to Sea* Committee.
Ms. Luckowitch was appreciative of her appointment,
believing it would gain her stature that she drove Wong,
Ogopogo and Whoop from Ottawa to Montreal so that
they could continue their journey. Her parting words in
Montreal were, "Best of luck. I will see you in Halifax."

"You must not take time off from your parliamentary
duties on account of us." Wong said.
"That's okay." Ms. Luckowitch replied. "I've been invited
to speak at the Halifax Chamber of Commerce about the
same time that you should arrive there."

It wasn't until Wong, Ogopogo and Pelican arrived in
Montreal, and were in a popular lounge that they had
another encounter with Widespread and Dean. This
occurred while the trio was at the Le Caustic nightclub
after the regular entertainer didn't show up for work,
because of an appointment with a dentist.
Wong played the piano, Ogopogo a guitar and Pelican
the flute. The type of tunes they sang and played dealt
with the rivalry between the Montreal Canadiens and

the Toronto Maple Leafs and had patrons in stitches with laughter.

It was during one of the outbursts that Widespread and Dean entered the club and like Jack Horner, sat at a corner table. After consuming several cocktails Widespread recognized the trio and said to Dean in a whisper, "Let's not make a scene but when the opportunity comes we will kidnap Wong."

"Fine," Dean whispered back. "As soon as they are through performing I'll have a kidnap plan in place."

Widespread and Dean consumed several more cocktails and walked out of the door.

By the time they returned the previous entertainer was playing the piano and Wong, Ogopogo and Pelican were nowhere in sight. They had made prior arrangements to rent a hot air balloon that would take them from Montreal to Quebec City.

The balloon was halfway between Montreal and Quebec City, when Wong was checking the tanks of propane, which sent the hot air into the canopy above. The sounds of the ground fell away until there was no noise but the sound of breathing. The three travelers had lost their sense of earthliness and felt they were part of space.

"This is the nearest I've been to Heaven," Pelican said during a silent spell and the balloon proceeding eastward.

"Beautiful, isn't it? Ogopogo went on describing the scenery below.

It was during the peaceful flight, that Wong and Ogopogo agreed, that should Widespread and Dean approach them another time, they would sign an endorsement contract with Best Advertising Agency because as Wong phrased it succinctly, "Without our endorsements and the lagging Canadian economy there will be no *From Sea to Sea* movie. The challenge to gather ten million dollars at this time is, too great."

"Although it's against our principle, I agree," Ogopogo said.

Suddenly there was a sound of a shot fired from below. In a split second the propane tank burst into flames and the balloon drifted downward.

"Look! There's a car with two men by its side beneath us," Ogopogo said while pointing below.

Wong took out his binoculars, adjusted them and said, "The men are Widespread and Bob Dean."

Fortunately, the balloon landed silently near a freight train that with luck was parked along a side railway. The engineer watched what was happening and seeing Ogopogo and Wong near his proximity said, "Hey, we have met before, haven't we?"

"We have, near Revelstoke, B. C.," Ogopogo said as soon as he recognized the engineer as Gaston Hamel.

"I remember, you are on your way to Newfoundland."

"Were," Ogopogo said.

"What do you mean, were?"

"As you can see we have no means of transportation to get there."

"One good term deserves one in return," Hamel said. "The three of you may ride in my train cabin."

Minutes later, the freight train was heading at full speed towards Quebec City. When the train arrived in the capital of the province of Quebec, it was still morning and birds were singing as though they were in awe with its beauty.

When Hamel got off his shift, he introduced the three Westerners to the city's official host, Bon Homme, a talking snowman, six feet tall and wearing a blue scarf and hat.

As soon as Hamel made his exit Wong asked Bon Homme that since he was made out of snow and the temperature was rising, was there danger he would melt away by the heat of summer.

"I have power to withstand heat up to 90 degrees Fahrenheit," Bon Homme, who could speak English, said quite succinctly.

"You seem to have the same magical power that the food replacement Famous Okanagan Fruit Leather has," Wong said and went on, "Since signs in the province of Quebec are in French only, why don't you show us around so that we experience some Quebec culture and don't get lost?"

"Glad too," Bon Homme replied and while strolling near the Chateau Frontinac Hotel said, "This is the city of Samuel Champlaine and Jacques Cartier. Quebec City is a city that loves to party and eat. Why don't you join me at one of our fine restaurants for breakfast?"

"An excellent idea," Ogopogo said, and while he Wong, Pelican and Bon Home were enjoying their meal, through a restaurant window, they could see ships plying the St. Lawrence River.

As they were enjoying their breakfast, Bonne Homme told his guests several things about Quebec's history, culture and the Snow Festival held each February. In turn, Wong told his guest about the Kelowna and the Okanagan Valley.

After they were through eating, Wong yawned, but still had enough energy left, to ask Bon Homme, "Why don't you come with us to St. John's, Newfoundland and audition for a part in the movie *From Sea to Sea*?"

"But I thought there isn't going to be a movie. I'm certain I saw on televisions Question Period, that the Minister of Culture canceled the project. This was confirmed by the Prime Minister in the media." "There will be a movie," Wong insisted, even it means through corporate sponsorship. The next time Widespread and Dean approach us we'll bend, and sign an endorsement agreement that will provide the necessary funding."

"And if you decide to come along, you'll be able to see other parts of Canada and promote your annual snow festival," Ogopogo suggested.

Bon Homme believed in promoting his city, and resolutely said, "That I would like very much. I rode in the Calgary Stampede once and that drew many Westerners to our city. There is a problem however."

"What's the problem?" Ogopogo asked.

"My power not to melt to 90 degrees extends only to city limits. If I venture any further the risk is that I may melt and disappear from Planet Earth."

"I'll take care of that," Wong said recalling he had a similar situation when Alice Nichol, wasn't feeling well. Surprised, Bon Homme said, "You will, how?"

"Famous Okanagan Fruit Leather that I always carry with me has power to extend you melting limit as high as the thermometer hits to one hundred and ten degrees," Wong said and handed Bon Homme a strip to enjoy. "Here, try this?"

"And what if the temperature surpasses one hundred and ten degrees? What then?" Bon Homme asked.

"Then you can use another a strip of fruit leather which will extend you melting point to one hundred and twenty."

As soon as Bon Homme swallowed his strip he became ecstatic, "Whoopee! I'll immediately inform the Mayor of my temporary absence."

And when the Mayor granted Bon Homme approval, the snowman packed his personal belongings, grabbed Wong by the hand, nearly knocking him over and said, "Let's get going, the next flight for Halifax leaves at one-thirty."

Bon Homme called a taxi and the foursome was on their way to the airport. The taxi was speeding when it came to a stretch of highway that was flooded and a beaver standing on its hind legs crying.

"Poor little Beaver," Bon Homme said. "A construction company building a subdivision has destroyed his home."

Bon Homme asked the driver to stop, and seeing the plight the beaver was in, Wong asked, "Why don't you escape your misery and come along with us to Newfoundland?

After some thought, the furry animal with a tail shaped like a paddle, replied, "Ever since the Hudson Bay Company ran the country beavers have been prime catch because of our fur. As time progressed however, the trader disappeared and now our dams are ruined by real estate speculators."

"That's what the movie we are auditioning for is about. I'm certain if you come with us the director will have an acting part for you." Wong said.

"He'll have to because no other animal has influenced a nation's history to the extent that beaver has. Canadians now celebrate the beaver as a national symbol on stamps, coins and emblems; in addition, literally hundreds of Canadian lakes, towns, rivers and hill ranges. bear its name."

"You've convinced me," the Beaver replied. The tears now turned into a smile.

The quartet had become a quintet, and arrived at the airport just as a jet was about to taxi for take off. They boarded the jet, and several hours later arrived in Halifax amid a celebration.

"Why is Halifax celebrating?" Beaver asked Wong as they walked through the terminal building, and then saw a parade on its way from downtown to Point Pleasant Park that hand a panoramic view of the harbor and Atlantic Ocean.

"It's July 1, Canada's birthday! Come let's join the parade," Wong said.

In this particular parade, there were various floats, Mounties dressed in scarlet tunics, Highland dancers, marching bands and more bagpipes than usual.

When the parade ended Wong, Ogopogo and their friends found themselves in a park crowded with celebrants, and near a band shell, where a band just stopped playing. After Wong and Ogopogo approached the bandmaster, he said to them that his band had been playing since morning and that it was a time for a break. The bandmaster was patting his German shepherd dog as he spoke.

"Do you mind if my friends and I take over until you return from your break?" Wong asked the bandmaster to which he replied, "Sir, that's an excellent idea."

After arrangements were made the bandmaster looked at his prized dog and said, "Come King, Let's go for a swim and then relax on an air mattress."

Within minutes, Wong, Ogopogo, Pelican, Bon Homme and Beaver, were performing in the bandshell before a large crowd. It isn't certain if the size of the crowd was due to the type of music the band was playing or the members' apparel. At any rate fifteen minutes into the concert Widespread snuck behind the drapes of the stage, grabbed Wong from the rear, placing his hand over Wong's mouth to mute any sound he would make.

Widespread used brutal force and before Wong could say 'Happy Birthday Canada,' Wong was blindfolded and told, "You'll sign the endorsement contract or else it's your life." Wong made a gesture that he and Ogopogo were prepared to sign an agreement because they needed funding so that the movie *From Sea to Sea* would be produced.

Widespread, however, interpreted the gesture as an act of defiance so he, while other members of the band continued performing, said, "Wong, don't make a scene or a sound or else it will get you into trouble."

To Dean Widespread said, "Let's take Wong to a more private part of the park."

"You do that while I go pick up a copy of the contract which is in our car. I'll be back shortly."

"Better hurry."

Before making his exit, Dean pointed to the part of the park where large pine trees grew and a cobblestone path traversed. "That's where I'll meet you."

As soon as Widespread and Wong were alone in a forested part of the park Widespread said to Wong, "I insist that you and Ogopogo sign the endorsement contract, because if you don't, Dean and I will harm you."

"That won't be necessary," Wong said as Ogopogo and I have decided to sign, but on four conditions."

"What kind of conditions?"

"That we receive five million, in advance."

"And the second?"

"That our contract expires after one year."

"Third?"

"That the Best Advertising Agency deposit five-million dollars in escrow at a bank or credit union."

"Thus far, no problem. And the fourth, condition?"

"That the contract is subject to approval by our lawyer."

"We understand each other clearly," Widespread said, and shook Wong's hand agreeing to the contract in principle.

For the next several minutes Widespread and Wong stood in silence waiting for Dean to return. Their silence was broken, when Petra Luckowitch, the MP for Winnipeg North, was walking along a path and noticing Wong said. "Dr. Wong, are all right?"

"I'm fine," Wong replied but Ms Luckowitch fearing something was the matter, came closer and seeing a bruise on Wong's face said, "Are you sure?"

"Believe me I'm okay," Wong said, as Ms Luckowitch was about to touch the bruise.

"As a matter of fact I'm very happy, because Widespread, Ogopogo and I have just agreed to an endorsement contract that will provide enough funding to pay one half of the cost of producing *From Sea To Sea*. First however, before there are any signatures on paper we'll need legal advice."

The first question Ms Luckowitch asked was, "Are there any conditions?'

"Four." Wong said, and after perusing the conditions, Ms. Luckowitch said, "They appear fine, to me."

Widespread and Wong after saying they understood each other. and there was just the formality of putting the information on paper, and Ogopogo witnessing the document form being signed. Dean was to deliver the form but hadn't to this point.

After Dean failed to show up for another fifteen minutes, Widespread, Wong and Ms Luckowitch began searching for him. They first returned to the band shell but Ogopogo, Pelican, Bon Homme and Beaver were nowhere in sight.

"Good heavens! Where is Bob Dean?" Widespread repeated over and over. "Has something gone wrong with my accountant?"

The search lasted for another one-half hour before Widespread called the emergency ward at the Victoria General Hospital, the Public Information booth, Lost and Found and police. As the search continued Widespread, Wong and Ms Luckowitch were bewildered by what may have happened to Dean.

The first clue came with the trio reached Point Pleasant Beach and noticed a crowd had gathered with many gesticulating towards the Atlantic Ocean.

"What happened?" Widespread asked Bon Homme who was standing on the sandy shore.

Bon Homme's answer was, "A man was seen chasing a dog towards another man who was floating on an air mattress. The first man jumped into the water trying to retrieve an envelope, which the dog was carrying. Suddenly the man went under."

At this point the temperature reached 100F degrees and Bon Homme became ill. Seeing that he was about to melt, Bon Homme said to Wong, "Quick. I need a strip of fruit leather to maintain my equilibrium."

Confirming that the temperature had reached 100 degrees Wong dug into his pocked but the fruit leather he had with him earlier was missing.

"I must have left the fruit leather at the spot Widespread and I agreed to a contract. I'll run and try to find it," Wong said.

"Relax both of you," Ms. Luckowitch whispered, "I have some."

Fortunately Ms. Luckowitch made it a habit to carry various flavouered fruit leather strips with her. "Here," she said and placed one into Bon Homme's mouth.

Within five seconds Bon Homme recovered and Widespread said to him, "Have you seen my accountant, Bob Dean?"

Bon Homme pointed towards Pelican who was flying in circles above Ogopgo and Beaver.

Seeing Pelican, Widespread fixed his eyes on the bird, and then seeing Ogopogo and Beaver fighting waves, took out his binoculars, adjusted them, and let out a piercing scream, "That's my accountant, Bob Dean that they are rescuing. Dean can't swim!"

Ogopogo and Beaver were bobbing up and down holding on Dean until they reached shore, where Bon Homme gave Dean resuscitation and called 911 for an ambulance for the paramedics to check him over. Thanks to Bon Homme, Dean began breathing, his pulse OK and his heart beating. His eyes opened and minutes later he was able to speak.

When Widespread asked Dean what happened is explanation was, "As I went to the car to pick up the contract form I accidentally dropped the envelope. A German shepherd that belongs to the bandmaster picked up the envelope and swam towards his master who was relaxing on an air mattress some distance from shore.

"I ran after the dog in order to retrieve the envelope but it was unintelligent of me to plunge into the water so deep because I cannot swim."

By the time the ambulance arrived, Dean, Pelican, Bon Homme, Beaver and Ms Luckowitch witnessed the signing of a five million endorsement contract. As the ambulance sped away it was a happy moment. Bob Dean was still alive and Wong had one-half of funding necessary to produce the movie *From Sea to Sea*. It was even a happier moment when the ambulance was out of sight and Widespread walked up to Wong and Ogopogo; and said to them, "Please change the five-million figure to ten million."

Ogopogo was the first to cry out, "Ten million dollars! Why the extra money?"

Widespread's answer was, "The additional five million is for saving Dean's life. As I said earlier, an advertising agency without a first-rate accountant isn't worth a penny."

Widespread, Dean, Wong and Ogopogo became the best of friends and Ogopogo and Wong even visited Dean at the Victoria General Hospital, where the doctor attending Dean said, "Mr. Dean will be out of the hospital tomorrow."

In their hotel room that night, Wong said to the rest of the potential actors, "At last we have the funding necessary to make the movie *From Sea to Sea*. It's onward to St. John's, Newfoundland, first thing in the morning."

When morning came, Widespread and Dean had breakfast with Wong and Ogopogo. This done, Widespread, drove the holders of a movie contract to North Sydney Nova

Scotia, where the potential actors took a ferryboat bound
for St. John's

While on board the ferry Bon Homme led his friends and
other passengers, in singing *Alouette* and then Wong led
everyone in singing *Jack Was Every Inch a Sailor*.

I was an extremely foggy day, when Wong and Ogopogo
reached St. John's. Because of the fog they had difficulty
locating the Film Canada office and studios. Another
problem they faced was that almost everyone spoke with
an accent that was difficult to understand, particularly
when it came to giving directions.

It wasn't until Wong heard a strong distinctive clear
honking call, and met a Canada goose, strutting along
a sidewalk, that they got proper directions. Initially the
goose appeared to be a formidable adversary, and his
wings were flapping and capable of delivering a blow
of surprising force, sufficient to rout predators, not to
mention humans. Following formal introductions the
goose said, "You may call me Goosy Gander."

When Wong asked Goosy why he was in a state of turmoil
and such hurry, he replied, "Early today St. John's City
Council passed an ordinance that Canada geese living in
the city had worn out their welcome."

"But why?" Ogopogo asked.

"Because we urban geese peck up lawns and golf courses,
and in the process cover them with blobs of doo-doo."

Then Goosy said that St. John's officially tried scaring
the geese by chasing them in golf carts, and by blasting a
starter's guns and even the cannon, on Signal Hill.

"The Mayor even said City Council was going to recommend to local restaurants to include cooked geese on their menu."

Goosy also said that, while the *Coalition To Prevent Destruction Of Urban Canada Geese,* came to the birds' defense, the Mayor's exasperation was echoed by many who lived in St. John's, including the Health Department.

As Goosy, Wong and the gang, were talking about the hazardous life an urban goose lives, there was a loud noise at Signal Hill, as if a cannon had exploded and Canada geese that had become a permanent fixture in St. John's, were seen flying in the sky.

"Pardon me for cutting our conversation short, but I must fly with them," Goosy said, while looking towards the sky. But, Wong cut the Goosy short, and said to the bird, "Why don't you come with us?"

"Where?"

"To the Film Canada office and studio, where we will be auditioning for a movie. Canada geese like beavers, have been subjects of painters, sculptures and artists for centuries. I'm certain the director of the movie, Jean Croteau, will have a part for you."

Goosy looked towards the sky one more time. The flock frightened away by the cannon blast, had already formed a V formation and almost out of sight.

"Okay, I'm delighted to join your group and lead you the Film Canada studio. Follow me," he said.

The Film Canada studios were situated on the second floor of a five-story brick building.

"We want to speak to Jean Croteau, the movie director," Wong said to the receptionist, as soon as he was inside the lobby of the Canada Film office.

"Have you an appointment?" the receptionist said.

"We have, so long it's before July 8th."

"But Monsieur Croteau is unable to see you."

"Why?"

"Because he's packing."

"Is he in a fowl mood? Whoop asked.

"You can say that," the receptionist said, when a voice from the back of the room hollered, "Who is it?"

"It's me, Lo Wong, from Kelowna, British Columbia."

Seconds later, Monsieur Croteau was beside the receptionist and seeing Wong said, "You have come a long distance. Please, come into my office, all of you."

As soon as the group was seated in Croteau's office Croteau turned to Wong and said, "I haven't forgot you and Ogopogo. I assume all of you are here to audition for the movie *From Sea to Sea*. Unfortunately production has been cancelled. I'm sorry to disappoint everyone."

Playing the role of a devil's advocate Wong said, "Who did the cancellation?"

"The federal minister of Culture. I heard the news from the horse's mouth," Croteau said and then corrected himself. "I saw the Minister make the announcement on the program *Question Period*."

Croteau handed Wong a letter from the Minister, which he had received and when finished reading, took the letter and read the last paragraph out loud. ". . . . And I repeat. Production of the movie *From Sea to Sea* has been canceled for lack of funding. Jobs, and not movies, is the federal government's priority at a time when Canada has a huge deficit."

Wong's and Croteau's eyes met. "Politics have stymied plans to make the movie, but don't despair. Some climb mountains. Some swim the sea. We are here, however, to continue with the movie. I understand the script has already been written," Wong said.

"If there's no funding there's no movie," Croteau insisted. "That's why I'm packing and will be leaving this studio for one in Hollywood."

Croteau's sad face turned into a smiling one, when Wong pulled out a copy of the ten million endorsement contract he and Ogopogo signed with Best Advertising Agency. Pointing to the ten million number Wong went on, "That should cover the cost of production. Don't you think?"

Croteau read the contract, including the fine print, and then said, "It certainly will."

As Croteau said those words the telephone rang and he picked up the receiver after the third ring. After speaking to a long distance operator, Croteau handed the phone to Wong, "It's for you."

On the other end was Ms Luckowitch from Winnipeg who said, "*Save the Movie from Sea to Sea* Committee has collected over one-million dollars in cash and pledges."

When Wong told Croteau the news Croteau's reaction was, "Unbelievable! At last we have all the necessary funding!"

"We do," Ogopogo confirmed. "Let the auditions begin."

Croteau took his guests to the studio and said, "Before we hold auditions the script will have to be changed slightly, but rest assured, each of you will have a role to play."

"And will the movie premier take place in Kelowna?" Ogopogo asked.

Croteau assured Ogopogo that it would."

Nearly a year later, on June 23, 1997, the premier of *From Sea to Sea* took place at a theatre in Kelowna. Special guests included Widespread and Dean, Ham, Brenda and Eddie. Also attending were, Alice Nichol, Pelican, Bon Homme, Beaver and Wong.

Also present were, Ogopogo, the Mayor of Kelowna and its Chief of Police. There were other guests to numerous to mention.

The following day, June 24, *From Sea To Sea* played to packed theatres across Canada. As soon as the movie was over, Canadians were rejoicing and greeting each other with the Italian word "Ciao" as they became Italians at least for an evening. There were fireworks, parades, and flotillas, dancing and singing with plenty of spaghetti, pizza and delectable food served from the Atlantic to the Pacific oceans.

At Bonavista, Newfoundland, where it all began, the celebration was especially exciting because not only did the residents of the coastal community have an opportunity seeing *From Sea To Sea,* but the unveiling of John Cabot's statue, a full scale non-sailing model of the *Matthew,* and an interpretation centre to house it.